A FRIEND LIKE YOU

The Bishop Smoky Mountain Thrillers
Book 8

LAUREN STREET

Copyright © 2024 by Sterling & Stone

All rights reserved.

No part of this book may be reproduced in any form or by any electronic or mechanical means, including information storage and retrieval systems, without written permission from the author, except for the use of brief quotations in a book review.

The authors greatly appreciate you taking the time to read our work. Please consider leaving a review wherever you bought the book, or telling your friends about it, to help us spread the word.

Thank you for supporting our work.

Chapter One

IT WASN'T REAL. It could not possibly be real. It was too perfect. No human female had ever actually grown an ass that round and firm.

Rileigh let out a sigh as she studied the backside of the new waitress named Cookie and decided that pretty much everything about the young woman was too perfect — flawless skin, china-doll face, bright blue eyes, pouty lips, a single dimple in her right cheek, and massive jugs that were in danger of leaping to freedom out the front of her blouse.

One button unbuttoned — acceptable. Two buttons — showy. Three — definitely on the prowl.

You're jealous.

It was that maddening voice from the essential Rileigh, the voice she hated because it always told her the truth.

You don't like the way she's flirting with Mitch.

Well, of course, she didn't. This was *her* date, the *big* date. The last thing Rileigh wanted was to sit there while some cute, tight-assed twenty-year-old put the moves on Mitch.

"Do you want fries with that burger, sugar?" the young woman asked Mitch in her affected squeaky voice, the same one that belonged to half the women under age forty in the country.

"Do you have crinkle fries?" he asked.

Cookie leaned over, almost jamming Mitch's nose into her cleavage, "Honey, if you want your fries crinkled. I'll go crinkle 'em myself."

She favored Mitch with a dazzling smile, all bright white teeth, then flitted away, shaking that too-perfect ass in a motion like a battleship on a rolling sea.

"If you want crinkle fries, I'll go crinkle them myself," Rileigh mocked, and Mitch grinned.

"Yeah, she's a little over the top."

"Over the top? Don't you mean *on* the top? She is a wardrobe malfunction looking for a place to happen. Any second now, one or the other of those monstrous things is gonna take a header out of that shirt and go plop into somebody's milkshake."

Mitch burst out laughing so loud that people at other tables turned to look. He coughed and sputtered, trying to control himself.

"You get—" he gasped for air "—a full ten points for that one."

Rileigh chuckled along with him. This total dumpster fire of a *big date* had gone so ludicrously off the rails that now everything was funny.

"Goodness gracious, great balls of fire."

Jerry Lee Lewis's voice blasted out through speakers mounted near the ceiling all around the dining area, delivering a decibel level of sound only slightly less than the takeoff of a 747. Obviously, the jukebox had been repaired, and somebody had popped a quarter into it.

Rileigh didn't like going to restaurants with TV screens

mounted everywhere because she understood that the human eye is drawn to movement. It's in the DNA. The caveman who saw the wooly mammoth before it stepped on him lived to reproduce. So even when you had no interest in the basketball/football/hockey/tetherball/ping-pong/pickleball game on any one of fifteen different screens, your eye would be drawn there anyway. But this throwback diner called Red Eye Gravy, with stools at the bar, a soda fountain, and tables with checkerboard plastic tablecloths, served up a wall of sound as distracting as any TV set.

"Maybe we should have kept our reservation at Bahama Mama's," Mitch said — loud because you had to shout to be heard over the din of music and rowdy humanity. It was, after all, Saturday night. Party time! "They've probably got the fire under control by now."

"Hmm," Rileigh said, weighing invisible objects in the air in front of her.

She lifted her left hand, palm up. "Noisy, crowded, flirty waitress ..."

Then she lifted her right hand. "Third-degree burns ..." She weighed them up and down. "You're right. We should have gone with flames and smoke."

"Hey, this place was–" he began, then each pointed a finger at the other and said in unison, "*Your idea.*"

But neither one of them had suggested it. Mama had.

This disaster date hadn't started out a disaster. It started out pretty good, as a matter of fact. Rileigh had actually purchased a new dress. She couldn't remember the last time she'd bought something new to wear. Certainly nothing form-fitting. Sexy, maybe? It was a sparkling jade green, the color so rich and deep the folds looked black. Wearing green brought out the green in what her driver's license said were hazel eyes, and this particular shade of green made them look like twin emeralds. The dress fit her like — in Mama's words — "like you was melted and poured into it."

Rileigh had taken a good long look at herself as she was getting ready and decided she needed to put on just a little weight. Not a whole lot, but some. She was still too thin. But the face and the body that looked back at her from her full-length mirror in her bedroom was acceptable on most counts. She'd had her chestnut hair cut into a style with lots of layers that reminded her of that gymnast from years ago, Mary Lou Retton. All of Jillian's friends had gotten a Mary Lou Retton haircut after they saw her perform in the Olympics. Rileigh had seen videos of the gymnast swinging her head back and forth, spinning in circles, and her hair flowing away from her face, then instantly falling back into place. Rileigh's did not do that because it wasn't straight. It was curly. So mostly she had a mass of chestnut curls that bounced around on her head in what she hoped was "charming" wild abandon.

Rileigh had to admit she had gotten dressed very early. Kept second-guessing her choice of clothing, but the dress was a have-to because she didn't really have anything else that was appropriate for Bahama Mama's, where she and Mitch were to have a luxurious dinner tonight in Gatlinburg.

The way she came down the stairs just as Mitch came in the door looked like something out of an old forties romance movie. He stood there looking up at her as she descended, concentrating really hard so she wouldn't trip in her new shoes with heels that provided the couple of inches she needed for the top of her head to be higher than his shoulders.

Mitch did look good. He wore a simple sports coat and tie. It wasn't the first time she'd seen him out of uniform. He came over often in jeans and t-shirts. But she had never seen him in a coat and tie. That handsome face set atop that to-die-for hunk of a body was indeed impressive.

Mama thought so. She took one look at him and whistled. A big loud wolf whistle, a sound Rileigh didn't even know Mama could make.

"Why, don't you look plum good enough to eat?" Mama said.

Jillian emerged from the kitchen, wiping her hands on a towel. She looked Mitch from head to toe and back to head. "Mmm, mmm, mmm. You are looking fine."

Up to that point, the date was going daydream-smooth.

But the fairytale was short-lived. They hadn't even got off the porch when things went south. Mitch's phone rang. He looked at caller ID and rolled his eyes. It was the dispatcher. He was not on duty tonight. She wasn't supposed to call him. Let somebody else deal with whatever mayhem had occurred. But he answered, and Sylvia informed him that she thought he'd like to know that the restaurant where he and Rileigh were headed for dinner was on fire.

They'd both stopped in their tracks.

"On fire?"

"I heard when they called Pete and asked for assistance." Pete Brady was the Yarmouth County Fire Chief. If they were calling neighboring counties for assistance, it was more than a little grease fire in the kitchen.

Of course, Mama had the perfect solution. "Why, you can go to Red Eye Gravy. Mildred was telling me the other day that John Clancy just got finished renovating the place. It's almost twice as big as it used to be and all new on the inside. She said she had the best bacon cheeseburger she ever had in her whole life at that place. And a vanilla milkshake."

A *diner*?

But it was a Saturday night in early July, and all the nice restaurants would be packed with tourists. Without a reservation, they'd have to wait at least an hour, maybe longer. Rileigh was just about starving to death. And the thought of a bacon cheeseburger made her mouth water. Nobody went to Red Eye Gravy but locals, and though it'd be loud and rowdy on a Saturday night, they'd be able to get a table.

So now they sat in a corner table by the windows, beneath the picture of the 2013 Black Bears basketball team that won the regional championship, which hung next to the 2007 Black Bears baseball team, who hadn't won anything at all. They were just a bunch of boys grinning into the camera.

The song on the jukebox changed. Suddenly, Johnny Cash was crooning, "I fell into a burning ring of fire."

"Okay, that's two songs about fire, back to back," Mitch said. "Even the music's rubbing it in."

The place was jammed with an eclectic assortment of young people on dates, a few teenagers, and some other older people with children.

Plus Rileigh and Mitch, who were the object of everyone's surreptitious observation, given that they were significantly overdressed for a greasy spoon diner. The rumble of voices was pleasant. But add in Johnny Cash crooning, and the possibility for any meaningful conversation was pretty slim. Since Mitch was smiling, relaxed, and enjoying himself, Rileigh decided it was all good.

Big John Clancy stepped up to their table. "You doin' a'right, Sheriff?"

"Fine,' n you?"

"Can't complain."

Mitch had the "official" call-and-response greeting in the mountains down now and delivered his lines flawlessly. He might be a city boy from Nashville, but he was learning.

Big John Clancy was everything that name implied. He reminded Rileigh of Bluto, the brute in Popeye cartoons. His upper arms were bigger than Rileigh's thighs and way more muscled. He did not have a single hair on his shiny bald head, a thick black beard, and an earring in his left ear — he even had an anchor tattoo on his upper forearm. Big John cruised around among the tables, made a circuit every half-hour or so, just to make sure nobody had forgotten he was there. He kept the peace in this rowdy watering hole with the baseball bat he displayed in a rack behind the bar. Easy to get to. And everyone in the county knew he could wield it in a swing that'd send a baseball sailing over the centerfield fence. If a baseball was what he hit with it.

"If we'd made it to Bahama Mama's, I was planning on having lobster tails," Mitch said.

"I was drooling for a big chunk of red meat."

"I never knew you were such a carnivore. The cheeseburger may not be prime rib, but it's meat."

Cookie, the new waitress, sashayed past, swinging that perfect ass. And Rileigh watched Mitch's eyes go to it, drawn to it like a moth to the flame.

"You think it's real?"

"What's real?"

"That ass."

"You mean there's such a thing as a phony ass?"

"If you can get breast implants, you can get butt implants. And that one is just too round and perfect. I call bullshit."

The music changed to Dolly Parton singing one of Rileigh's favorite country songs.

"Jillian says there was some discussion before I was born about naming me Jolene."

"Would you prefer that to Rileigh?"

"Of course, I would. Nobody likes their own name."

"I do. I like Mitch. Has a nice solid sound to it."

"Speaking of Jillian. You know we've been going to that firing range in Gatlinburg?"

"Uh-huh."

"She's good. You know how beginners are. They hold the gun like a loaf of bread. And the first time they fire it, and it kicks, they usually drop it."

"What kind of gun does she have?"

"A Ruger 38-caliber revolver."

"That baby's got some kick."

"But she does fine. She doesn't tense as she anticipates the kick or unconsciously points the barrel down off her aim a little to compensate for it. She's a good shot."

The song on the jukebox changed again. Jimmy Dean rumbled out, *Big Bad John*. Soon, half the people in the diner were singing along as John stood behind the bar, grinning.

In fact, most everyone was looking his way and probably didn't see what Rileigh saw, which was Della Faye Morris heading into the hallway at the left end of the bar that had three doors opening off of it: the men's room, the women's room, and the storage room. That was not a surprising thing for Della to do, except that Rileigh had noticed her flirting with Kai Tadaka, and he was *not* the date she'd come with. Della Faye was a couple of sheets to the wind, and Kai had just disappeared down that hallway a minute or two before. Rileigh picked up on a tiny body language cue from Della Faye — the way she'd shot a look back over her shoulder — that implied whatever she was about to do, she didn't want to get caught at it.

If Della Faye Morris wanted to hook up with somebody for a little extracurricular bump-and-tickle, that was her business. Thankfully, if her date caught her at it and the inevitable fight broke out, Mitch wouldn't have to deal with it. Big John would take his baseball bat and crack some skulls.

Rileigh tuned back into the music when it changed — "There is a house in New Orleans they call the Rising Sun" — and she began to speculate what the song might be about. "They say the Rising Sun was a real place, a jail back in the 1890s."

"A jail?" Mitch replied. "I thought it was a house of prostitution."

They talked about the song, how this recording by The Animals was the first folk rock song—

A sudden scream sliced through the air like a knife, high and horrified, so loud that it instantly silenced the crowd. Then Della Fay Morris came running out of the hallway leading to the bathrooms — almost naked from the waist up, her blouse and bra dangling off one shoulder. Screaming. Shrieking. Kai Tadaka was a step behind her, shirtless, struggling to fasten his pants.

"There's a body. Somebody dead," he cried. "And their face is ... *gone.*"

Chapter Two

DELLA FAYE'S exit from the hallway leading to the bathrooms in the diner, shrieking and naked from the waist up, got the attention of pretty much everyone in the building. There was a moment of shocked silence, and then everyone moved as one, leaping to their feet and dashing to the hallway to see what Della was so freaked out about. Mitch shot a look at Rileigh as the two of them rose and hurried along, pushing their way through the crowd that had formed in front of the hallway.

Rileigh could see a commotion in the hallway before they got to it. The door was open to the storage room on the left side of the hallway. The men's and women's bathrooms opened off the right side of the hall. As she watched, people who got to the doorway first looked in, then recoiled in horror and instantly turned around, pushing and shoving upstream against the current of the crowd. One man turned and stepped across the hallway into the men's room, where you could hear him heaving violently.

Mitch called out, "This is the sheriff. Let me through."

The crowd in front of the hallway entrance parted like the Red Sea. But the group in the hallway was in such chaos that no one was listening. To make his way through them, Mitch had to move from one person to the next, taking them by the shoulders or arms and physically pushing them back out of the way.

The reactions of the people in front of them should have prepared Rileigh for what she was likely to see. People didn't often get that special kind of shocked look on their faces, and usually, it was in response to death. Rileigh had seen a lot of it, so she was seldom as shocked as most people.

But when she and Mitch finally stood at the head of the crowd with all the looky-loos behind them, and she got a good look into the room, bile crept up her throat. She swallowed to force it back down.

This storage closet was where Big John kept cleaning supplies, toilet paper for the bathrooms, paper towels for the dispensers, mops, brooms, and dust pans. It was about fifteen feet wide and deep, with shelves on all the walls, a drain in the floor, and a deep commercial-style sink in the corner. There was also a rather convenient piece of empty real estate in the middle of the room. Apparently, it was a geographical location that most of the young people in the crowd knew about ... the place where you went to engage in some horizontal time when you couldn't wait to make out in the car.

A body lay on its back in the middle of that area, a pattern of dried blood that spread all the way to the blood-splattered walls. It looked like a slaughterhouse.

The dead man was crusted with dried blood, scabbing over his black-and-gold plaid shirt, jeans, and cowboy boots. He had receding blonde hair, but other than that, there wasn't much to describe because the man had no face.

Rileigh stepped into the room and couldn't stifle her gasp. Mitch had been one step ahead of her. He stood beside the cowboy boots, looking down on the corpse.

"How in the ... what...?"

Rileigh couldn't even find words to put around the questions whirling through her mind as she tried to make some sense of what she was seeing. And what she was seeing was a head with no face on the front of it. Someone had removed the skin of the face. But why?

Rileigh didn't give voice to any of her questions because she suspected Mitch didn't have any better answers than she did.

Mitch looked up at her.

"Would you mind calling this in? And call Gus."

Rileigh stepped out into the hallway, where the crowd was hushed now. Whispered conversations traveled from the people in the hall to the crowd farther out, spreading like the prickling red flames of a grass fire.

Rileigh took out her phone and called the dispatcher at the sheriff's department. Then she called Gus.

"A body at the Red Eye Gravy Diner?" Gus asked. "Is the food there that bad?"

"You need to get here fast, Gus. This is really ugly."

Rileigh returned her phone to her pocket, then pushed her way back to the storage room door. Inside, Mitch had squatted on his haunches beside the body with one hand under it, feeling around in the victim's back pocket for a wallet. He found it and pulled it out, then reached up to the shelf above him for some paper towels to wipe the blood off his hands. He opened the wallet and looked at the driver's license in the little plastic window. It identified the man as Joseph Allen Hatfield, DOB 5/6/98, 379 New Market Road, Black Bear Forge, Tennessee.

Rileigh wasn't the only one who heard the name. It flew from one person to the other in the crowd behind her.

"That's Jody!"

"Jody Hatfield?"

"Is Jody Hatfield dead?"

"That dead body in there? That's *Jody?*"

Mitch stood and placed the wallet on the shelf next to the toilet paper rolls. He tore off another small piece of a paper towel from a roll of them and used it to wipe off the blood he'd missed on the side of his hand.

"Do you know this guy?" Mitch asked her.

Rileigh nodded her head, unable to drag her eyes from the heinous sight of the faceless body lying on the floor. "If that's Jody Hatfield, this could get ugly."

"How so?"

"Jody is the head of a street gang. The Hatfields."

"As in the Hatfields and the McCoys?"

"The Hatfields and McCoys' gangs were founded by guys who used to play football together in the Forge. You know, the kind of guy I'm talking about, the kind who gets out of high school but never really leaves. The ones who can't stop rehashing their memories and exaggerating their accomplishments in their school glory days."

"Their lives peaked, and nothing after that ever measures up. Yeah, I know the type."

"Both gangs' names come from the score of the 2016 Tennessee State 1A football championship game where the Bears of Black Bear Forge beat Knox County thirty-five to nothing."

"The gangs are named after the score?"

"The Hatfield gang's name is Smoked' Em. The McCoys gang is 35/Zip."

"So, where'd the Hatfields and McCoys—"

"That's just what the locals call them. You know how it is with nicknames — you don't get to pick them, and they tend to stick. And since the head of one gang is Jody Hatfield…" She paused. "*Was* Jody Hatfield."

Mitch nodded understanding. "Now, they're the Hatfields and McCoys."

"Whether they like it or not… and they *don't*."

"I'd think high school teammates would all join one gang?"

"Jody was the quarterback, the guy throwing the passes to Clive McCutcheon, the running back that scored all those touchdowns. But Jody teamed up with the team's center, last name's Bramley. I can't remember what his first name is. But McCutcheon formed his own gang. I think all three of them were buddies in high school. At least that's what I remember."

"So, street gangs, does that mean…?" Mitch let the question dangle.

"That means petty shit. I'm not sure they ever got into any serious crime. If they did, they didn't get caught. I think they pulled some burglaries, maybe breaking into cars. I'm sure they sold some drugs. But we're not talking the Crips and the Bloods here."

She paused.

"Mostly, they fought with each other."

"You think it got this bad?"

Rileigh shrugged. "But I'd say there's safe money to be made that as soon as word gets out about what happened to Jody, there's going to be a lot of blame thrown at the McCoys."

A Friend Like You

The sounds of sirens filled the air. Rileigh felt that instant rush of relief she always felt when she heard sirens. Maybe sirens made other people uneasy, made them wonder what bad thing had happened. To Rileigh, sirens always meant the cavalry was coming.

Chapter Three

BY THE TIME Gus Hazelton arrived, deputies had done what they could to secure the crime scene and put up black and yellow "don't cross this line" tape across that whole end of the diner. There was still a big crowd just standing around. People weren't going back to their tables and eating their burgers, not after that. But they were also reluctant to go home until they knew something. So they stood around, talking quietly. The music was now the only loud noise in the diner. Rileigh could hear Della Faye crying as Dolly Parton sang about growing up in Butcher Hollow, the daughter of a coal miner.

Rileigh looked up as Gus came in the front, crossed to the police tape, and ducked under it. He stopped when he saw Mitch and Rileigh, slid a look up and down them, head to toe, and briefly revealed the "Madonna gap" between his two front teeth. "Hey, I'd have dressed up if you'd told me it was a black-tie murder."

They followed Gus as he carried his bag down the hallway and into the storage room, leaving Rileigh to stand on one side of the door and Mitch on the other.

Gus surveyed the scene and whistled softly. "Holy shit."

"Yeah, that about covers it," Mitch said.

"What happened to that guy?" Rileigh couldn't stop the question.

"Won't know for certain until I do an autopsy." Gus craned his neck so that he could get a better look at the murder victim's head.

"It would appear that somebody sliced through the skin all the way to the bone right below his hairline and then pulled the skin down."

Rileigh shook her head in disgust. "Just *pulled it down*?"

"It's sort of a reverse scalping. It's really a lot easier to do than it sounds. You just have to get your fingers under the tissue so that you can—"

"Spare me the details," Rileigh said.

"Have you ever seen anything like this?" Mitch asked him.

"Nope. Can't say that I have. I've seen victims where somebody tried to remove the face, but this wasn't the method of removal."

"How'd he die?" Rileigh asked.

"Won't know for sure until I'm finished, but I can hazard a guess." He pointed to the bloody shirt and the pool on the floor. "Ripping off a face, however traumatic and painful it might be, wouldn't bleed like that. I'll find another wound."

"If he's this bloody, so was the killer," Mitch said.

"He was when he committed the murder, but maybe he didn't stay that way." Gus pointed to the industrial sink in the corner of the room, with streaks of what could have been blood down its sides. "Maybe he made himself presentable before he left."

Gus leaned over and touched the dried blood on the

floor. "He was killed here in this room, probably last night."

Mitch turned and caught Big John's eye. He was standing quietly, absentmindedly slapping the baseball bat he'd snatched off its rack in his hands.

"Was Jody Hatfield here last night?"

"Yeah, late. Not long before we closed."

"Was he with anybody?"

Big John grunted a laugh. "Jody? He was with everybody."

"Ok, anybody in particular that you noticed? Did he get into an argument with somebody, maybe?"

Big John shook his head. "Not that I saw. But you'd have to ask Cookie or Beth Ann. Maybe they saw something. They were waiting tables and working behind the bar last night. I ain't out front all the time."

Rileigh recalled that when they'd first come into the loud, rowdy diner, which seemed like a lifetime ago, no music was playing. She had glanced to the right at the jukebox, not some cheap knock-off but the real deal that actually played vinyl records, and saw it had been scooted away from the wall beside the hallway leading to the bathrooms. A man in a blue jumpsuit had been on his knees beside it, screwing the back panel back on.

"What time did they start working on that jukebox today?" she asked John.

"They got here right as I was opening up. It took them the whole day to figure out what was wrong with it."

Rileigh turned back to Mitch and Gus. "That jukebox was pulled away from the wall when we came in, and it blocked this hallway. If they've been working on it since this morning, the hallway's been blocked all day. That's why nobody found the body sooner."

As if responding to Rileigh's mention, the machine

sprang to life. "You're just too good to be true. Can't take my eyes off of you."

Who'd want to hear Frankie Valli at a time like this?

But she supposed several people had put their money into the machine and selected their playlist. The jukebox would play their selections one after another until the quarters ran out.

Rileigh stepped back and leaned against the wall, conscious now of how bad her feet hurt. She didn't often wear anything but running shoes. These were beautiful low-heeled pumps, a shiny green that went perfectly with her dress, but they were as uncomfortable as shoving her feet into orange juice cans.

This evening had certainly gone off the rails big time. And she had been looking forward to *the date*. It had become a big deal, but also a joke between them, because it had been postponed and postponed. They made light of it to ease the awkwardness. But Rileigh had been daydreaming about tonight for a long time.

In her mind's eye, she'd seen herself and Mitch ushered to a table in a dark restaurant with candles on the tables, white tablecloths, and black cloth napkins as big as baby blankets. She'd imagined the two of them looking at each other and laughing as the waiter brought them wine, Mitch doing the tasting. Rileigh didn't like wine any more than she liked beer or any other alcoholic drink. She certainly was not a connoisseur. She didn't think Mitch was either, but he at least knew the difference between white wine and red wine. That was more than she could say.

She had envisioned a dance floor, too. A small one, because this wasn't a nightclub, just a very posh restaurant. And there would be one of those shining balls in the ceiling that cast colored lights out from it as it spun slowly.

She'd only been in Bahama Mama's once, but she thought they'd had their own band.

Mitch would ask her to dance. She would follow him onto the dance floor. He would take her hand, pull her into his arms, and pilot her smoothly around as she lay her head on his chest.

That was the fantasy version of Part One of the big date. It never changed. But there were several variations of Part Two — what happened *after* dinner. In one variation, they left the restaurant hand in hand. He went to her side of the car and opened the door. They laughed about that — the silly tradition. But Rileigh enjoyed it, nonetheless.

Mitch invited her to his house to have a drink — a soft drink.

Rileigh accepted the invitation

And...

Rileigh had not allowed her imaginings to go any further than right there. For all manner of reasons. Among them, how awkward it would feel to go to work beside Mitch on some case and recall the silly fantasies she'd had about him the night before.

If things progressed as they might beyond the first drink in Mitch's living room, there wouldn't be a lot of mystery for Mitch. It's not like he'd never seen Rileigh naked. In fact, he'd been the man who'd stripped her clothes off. Not during an amorous moment, but when he'd found her body lying on the bank of the Pigeon River, chilled to the bone by hypothermia. He had stripped her bare and wrapped her in his own shirt to warm her up before the ambulance crew arrived.

Jillian and Mama had peppered her with questions about the big date when they found out she'd finally said yes. They'd stopped when they realized it wasn't a subject Rileigh really wanted to discuss. But she knew that when she got home from the big date, there would be questions then. Or maybe, if she didn't come home until breakfast time the next day, Mama and Jillian would just pretend it wasn't happening.

Too bad the big date ended up sidetracked to Red Eye Gravy. But before Della Faye came running out of that hallway, they'd been having a good time. Not the same time they'd have had if they'd been at Bahama Mama's, but it was fun just being together, laughing, not having any official responsibilities, no case to discuss, no evidence to talk about.

Then, the half-naked woman came running out of the hallway, and the evening went south pretty fast after that.

Rileigh leaned against the wall while Gus and Mitch talked. She spotted Cookie in the crowd, the drop-dead gorgeous waitress that every man in the place was salivating over. Cookie was standing very still, clutching the arm of Roger Abernathy, who worked for the post office, a man Rileigh was sure the waitress had not met until this evening. But she was clinging to him like a drowning person clung to a floating log. A strand of platinum blonde hair had escaped her messy bun and fallen across her face. She really did look like a Barbie doll, now that Rileigh thought about it. But that one little strand of hair helped Rileigh see her as a real person. All of the women were staring with wide eyes toward the storage room door. But Cookie's face was blank. Not wide-eyed with shock. Not upset. Just blank. Like she'd clicked the switch somewhere inside to turn off the awful, and now she was on dial tone.

An ambulance crew pushed their way through the crowd, lifted the police tape, and shoved a gurney beneath it, heading toward the hallway.

They shoved the gurney past where Rileigh stood in

the opening of the hallway, down toward where Mitch and Gus were in the storage room with the body.

Suddenly, there was a commotion in the crowd. Someone had come in the front door and was shoving their way through the crowd, knocking people out of his path like he'd probably knocked away tackles in his football days.

Travis Bramley. That was his name. He'd been the center on that team, blocking while Jody Hatfield retreated into "the pocket" and launched passes to Clive McCutcheon.

She turned toward the hallway and called out to Mitch, "That's Travis Bramley bearing down on us like a rhino," she said. "He's Jody's best friend and the second in command of the Hatfields."

"We're about to watch a drip of water hit hot grease," Mitch said, standing up from where he had squatted on the floor beside the body.

Bramley got to the yellow and black "don't cross this line" police tape. As he lifted it over his head, Deputy Crawford stepped into his path, but he shoved Crawford aside and barreled straight for the hallway. Obviously, somebody had told him where Jody's body had been found, and he would have run through a brick wall and parked cars to get to it. Crawford grabbed his arm to restrain him, but one look from Mitch, and he let go. Bramley thundered past Rileigh down the hallway, and she followed as he literally grabbed an EMT and shoved him up against a wall so that he could get past the gurney to the room where Jody's body lay on the floor.

Chapter Four

TRAVIS BRAMLEY MADE some kind of sound. A cry, a groan, a grunt. The sound a large animal in pain might make.

"That ain't Jody. That can't be *Jody.*"

Mitch stepped forward to block him from entering the room and said, "I checked the identification in the wallet in his pocket. His driver's license identified him as Joseph Allen Hatfield. Date of birth, 5/6/98."

The man leaned his head back, squeezed his eyes shut, and yelled. No words in it, nothing articulate. Then he began to bang his fists against the wall. *Bam, bam, bam.* He was a big black man with vitiligo that had splotched his face and arms with white spots. Built like a refrigerator, square and thick, he'd cut a dashing figure back in the day — strong, heavily muscled, and handsome. But a sedentary lifestyle as a part-time plumber's assistant, coupled with the consumption of beer by the six-pack, had changed that physique. Now, he could be called hefty or beefy or broad, but technically he was obese. Maybe he and his teammates had been juicing when he was in school, though that seemed to be reserved for college and professional athletes. If he had taken drugs to bulk up, he was now suffering the consequences.

Bam!

Bam!

He slammed his fist into the wall, shaking his head in mute denial another time or two, then he got hold of himself and stopped hitting the wall, though both his hands were still clenched into fists.

"What the hell happened here?" he demanded, his voice sounding tear-clotted.

"We don't know. That's what we're going to try to find out."

"What the hell happened to—" Bramley reached out and shoved Mitch aside, took a step into the room, but no farther, staring, gawking down at the faceless body lying in a puddle of blood. "Dear God in heaven, what the hell happened to his face?"

There was no answer to that question that would have appeased Travis Bramley. Neither Mitch nor Gus made any effort to explain.

Mitch gently took the man's arm and tried to steer him back out of the room.

"I'm sorry for your loss, Mr. Bramley, but—"

Bramley yanked his arm out of Mitch's grip and took another step forward toward the body, almost into the puddle of blood, at which point Gus stood up. He had been kneeling beside the body, and now he moved to protect the evidence.

"I'm sorry, Mr. Bramley, but this is a crime scene and you—"

"Leave me the hell alone."

Gus was instantly in his face.

"You want us to find out who did this to your friend?" He demanded harshly. "Do you?"

Bramley froze.

"We can't do that if you stomp around in here and destroy all the evidence!"

That stopped him when nothing else had. Bramley didn't try to move any farther into the room. He just sank down onto one knee and reached out as if to take Jody's hand.

"Please don't touch the body," Gus said.

Most of the fight had gone out of Bramley by now. He was moving into shock and horror and didn't seem to be aware that tears were streaming down his cheeks into his bushy beard.

"His ring's gone," he said, indicating the hand on the body he had been reaching out to take. "What happened to his ring?"

"What ring?" Mitch asked.

"He had a ring. We all got rings, all of us in Smoked' Em." He held up his beefy right hand — still black, though the vitiligo had turned his left hand almost completely white — and on the third finger was a wide gold band similar to a wedding band. There were words engraved on the metal, which Rileigh assumed were the words "Smoked' Em." There also were two stones of some kind, maybe diamonds, at each end of the words.

"You're saying that Mr. Hatfield had a ring just like the one you're showing me?"

"Not *just like*. His was different. His was the first one. He went to some jeweler in Gatlinburg, some guy who makes jewelry for rich tourists, and he described the ring he wanted. He said he wanted it to … wanted it to …"

He couldn't finish the sentence, so he closed his mouth,

swallowed a couple of times, and tried again. "He wanted us all to have a ring, but his ring was bigger than anybody else's. It had a big red stone on both ends of the words. Rubies."

Bramley cleared his throat.

"He took a long time picking it out. I went with him the second time when he went to look at what they'd come up with." He barked out something like a chuckle. "Jody took one look at it and told them tight-ass jewelers to shove it where the sun don't shine. What they'd made was all fancy and frilly and looked like something for a girl. He threw it down on the top of the glass case so hard I was surprised it didn't crack the glass. Said that wasn't what he wanted and reached into his pocket where he had a crumpled-up drawing of what he wanted the ring to be."

The memory faded, and so did the spark in Bramley's eyes.

"He went back sometime later to pick it up. I don't know if it matched his drawing. I just know when he showed it to all of us, he was proud of it. He said anybody who had that ring on his finger was yelling at the world, 'We Won!' Said he wanted all of us to get rings just like it and gave us the name of that jeweler."

"Everybody in your gang has one?" Mitch asked.

"Oh, they ain't all got rings yet. I do. So does Duane and Marty. Pete and Lucas ain't got theirs yet. Neither do Joe Dan and Ray. I think Jake and Kenny, Leo and Zach ordered them but ain't gone by to pay for 'em yet."

The fight had drained out of Travis Bramley now. The rage gone, replaced by grief and sorrow. He was struggling to hold it together and not cry.

"What happened to him?" He asked, his eyes looking from Gus to Mitch, then back to Gus. "How could his face be gone like that? Did somebody cut it off him?"

Gus answered as simply as he could. "I haven't

performed an autopsy yet, so I'm not sure of the specifics, but yes, somebody removed his face from his skull."

"Tore it off him, you mean," Bramley roared, getting to his feet. He stood very still and then spoke softly, as if to himself. "...because he was a pretty boy."

He turned abruptly and bumped into Mitch, shoving him to the side as he started out of the room. "I'm gonna get them sons of bitches." Pushing the empty gurney and the EMTs out of his way down the hallway, he turned back and fixed his eyes on Mitch. "You write it down, Sheriff. I don't care which one of 'em done the actual killing. I'm gonna get 'em all."

This time, when Bramley approached the police tape, he didn't bother to lift it up and duck under it. He just crashed through it like a sprinter through the tape at the finish line of a race, plowed through the crowd, and slammed out the front door. There was absolute silence for a heartbeat or two after he left before the crowd of people flowed back together to fill the gap in their ranks and began talking again.

Rileigh went down the hallway to stand with Mitch and Gus in the area beyond the storage room door so the EMTs could get into the room and remove the body.

"You know what that 'pretty boy' stuff is all about?" Gus asked. Both Mitch and Rileigh shook their heads. "You think he meant it, the threat?"

Mitch looked at Rileigh. "Is he that kind of guy? Is he violent?"

"Violent? Yeah. Like most guys his age around here, provoke him, and he'll beat the crap out of you."

"I'm not talking about a fistfight. Is he capable of murder?"

Rileigh shrugged. "Anybody's capable of murder if they're upset enough."

Chapter Five

RILEIGH STOOD by as the EMTs loaded the body into a black body bag, zipped it tight, and placed it on the rolling gurney to take it to the ambulance waiting outside. Gus left to set up for the autopsy.

Rileigh relaxed a little as Mitch turned to Deputy Crawford and told him to stay where he was, in front of the police tape, to prevent access to the crime scene.

Then he looked at Rileigh, and she knew what was coming. He was about to ask her if she would accompany him to the Hatfields' home to tell them that their son had just been murdered. Mitch was good at that kind of thing. He had a kind, deft touch, and a gentle voice. He delivered the news in short, simple sentences without elaboration while she watched the loved ones of victims receive that news. And with every sentence, they looked like he'd punched them in the gut.

Mitch didn't *need* her to come along with him, but he wanted her to. Bottom line, it was hard to go to some family you didn't know and tell them the worst news of their life. Rileigh was glad that he wanted her company to do it.

"If you want some company to go notify the Hatfields, I volunteer."

The smile of appreciation on his face lit up her whole world.

The Hatfields lived on the north side of Turkey Run Mountain off Bleaker Mill Road. It took a long time to wind among the connecting, narrow, steep roads to get there.

Neither of them was in uniform, and Rileigh didn't know if that was better or worse. When someone looks out their front window and sees two police officers coming up the sidewalk, they have to know it's not good news they come to deliver. So maybe not being in uniform spared the family at least a few moments of apprehension.

But it also didn't feel very official. In fact, it seemed kinda awkward to be all dressed up in a green satin dress with matching shoes to go tell a family that their son was dead.

"Did I tell you that you look really nice tonight?" Mitch asked without taking his eyes off the road.

"You did indeed, sir. Thank you."

"You look beautiful," he said. Turned his head toward her and looked directly into her eyes, then turned his face back toward the road. "I'm sorry that our date went to hell in a handbasket, but can I take a rain check?"

Rileigh thought he had a perfect profile, something that belonged on a statue in Greece, one of those armless things that had been carved by the masters centuries ago. His jaw was square and firm, his nose straight. With high cheekbones that any girl would have died for. She didn't let her mind linger on the full lips that she would now, after all these months, admit to herself she had imagined on hers.

"Rain check? Sure. But let's go somewhere beside Bahama Mama's."

"I'm all over that. Somewhere in Nashville?"

"That sounds good."

There was silence before Mitch said, "About that ring."

"Yeah, that was interesting. Why would somebody take it?"

"A souvenir?"

"Or a trophy. The motive for the murder certainly wasn't robbery. That ring symbolized something to Jody, and maybe it symbolized something to the murderer."

"You're implying that maybe he was killed by somebody in the McCoys."

"Not implying anything, just speculating."

"Do you think Bramley is going to make good on this threat?"

"I hate to say it, but I suspect he's going to try."

They rode along in silence after that until they got to New Market Road and pulled up at a mailbox that someone had used for target practice. The numbers 379 on the side were almost indiscernible.

The house was a double-wide trailer that had obviously been there for years. The siding was coming off on one side, as was the skirt that ran from the trailer to the ground to hide the wheels.

There was no lawn to speak of. Scraggly grass. If you wanted a lawn in the mountains, it was a thing you had to pursue. Grass didn't grow naturally in all the shade the mountains provided. People in Gatlinburg and the richer families in Black Bear Forge in Yarmouth County had lawn services bring them their lawn rolled up on the back of the truck so they could roll it out like a carpet in their yards. But these people had no roll-up lawn.

There were already several cars in the driveway, so

Rileigh knew it wasn't likely the family would be surprised by what they had come to say. The way news traveled in this county, they had probably found out as soon as Travis Bramley had. But it was Mitch's job to carry the official news of the death to the victim's family.

Mitch pulled his car into the driveway behind a beat-up red pickup, and as soon as they got out of the car, it was clear that the Hatfield family had indeed learned of Jody's death. She could hear crying inside, wailing almost.

When they stepped up onto the porch, Mitch drew back his fist to knock, but the door opened before he had a chance.

"You come to tell us he's dead, didn't you?" said a young man about Jody's age — skinny and tall with red hair and freckles, so he probably was a friend, not a family member. Rileigh glanced at the third finger of his right hand and saw a ring like the one that Travis Bramley had shown them. Like the one that should have been on Jody's body but wasn't.

"May we come in?" Mitch asked. The man stepped aside and made a sweeping gesture.

The inside of the house was dim. The shades had been drawn, and there were only a couple of lamps. The ceilings in trailer houses were always so low that Rileigh felt like hunkering down. She couldn't imagine what it must be like for tall men like Mitch.

"May I speak to Mr. and Mrs. Hatfield, please?" he asked the group of people gathered there, who had fallen silent when he and Rileigh had entered the room.

"Ma Hatfield's in the back bedroom, and she don't need no company," said a woman who pulled herself up out of a recliner with difficulty. She probably weighed three hundred pounds, and she had no front teeth. "But daddy's up here in the other bedroom. You can talk to him."

She gestured toward a door that opened off of the living room, where a small crowd was gathered.

The door to the bedroom was open. Inside, a man sat in a wheelchair with plastic tubing in his nose running to an oxygen tank. His face was gray and washed out.

Black lung.

Rileigh stepped into the doorway behind Mitch, but with the wheelchair and the bed and two other men and Mitch, there was no room for her inside.

"You come to tell me about my boy, didn't you?" The man looked up. His cheeks were so wrinkled that the tears sliding down his face went toward his chin like rivulets of spring water trickling down to a creek.

"Yes, sir. I have come to inform you that your son, Joseph Allen Hatfield, is dead."

"What the hell happened to him?" The old man spit the words out like they tasted bad in his mouth. "They told me he didn't have no face. What the hell does that mean—no face?"

"When Dr. Gus Hazelton has completed his autopsy, the body will be released to a funeral home and you can—"

"I can go look at it and see that he ain't got no face. I'm asking you now, what does it mean, no face?"

"It means somebody pulled the skin off it," said a young man on the other side of the bed. He looked like he could be a close relative of Jody's. He was about the right size and had curly blond hair, but since the body had no facial features for comparison, there was no family resemblance she could recognize.

"We done called his brothers." Jody's father took another gasp of air and continued. "Buster works on an oil rig in the Gulf of Mexico off Louisiana. And Carl is a soldier. He's stationed in Germany."

"I'm sorry for your loss," Mitch told the old man.

"Oh, there's going to be lots of people sorry for my loss." The old man gasped in another breath. "Lots of people." Another gasp. "Somebody's gonna pay for what they done to my boy, gonna pay in blood."

"Mr. Hatfield, I know that you're upset, but—"

"There ain't no buts, and I ain't going to get no less upset—" Either he ran out of air, or he was stifling a sob, but he choked and coughed and couldn't seem to stop coughing. On and on it went. He grabbed a tissue out of a box and put it over his mouth. When he pulled it away, Rileigh could see blood in it.

"Buster and Carl, they gonna get here as fast as they can. And then they're gonna to go find who done this and make them pay."

"Please understand, Mr. Hatfield, that further violence will—"

Hatfield barked out some sound that could have been a laugh. "Don't give me horseshit about 'further violence.' We're gonna kill some people. I'm here telling you right now, we're gonna kill some people. They're gonna pay for what they done to my boy. Somebody's gonna pay!"

Chapter Six

WHEN RILEIGH and Mitch finally rolled up into her mother's driveway, bounced over the lump at the top, and came to a stop in front of the house, there were no lights on inside. Rileigh didn't even look at her watch. She didn't want to know what time it was. Mitch stopped, turned off the lights and the engine, and turned to her.

"Look, I'm really sorry about how—"

"This wasn't your fault."

"No, but I'm still sorry that the date we were supposed to have didn't happen."

He reached over and took her hand, but that's all. Just took it and rubbed his thumb over the back of it. "I meant that about having a rain check on the big date."

"I'm looking forward to it."

Mitch let go of her hand and started to open his door.

"Whoa, whoa, whoa, whoa," Rileigh said. "You don't have to come around and open my door. That's date behavior."

"Yeah, this stopped being a date a long time ago, didn't it?"

She nodded her head sadly. He closed his car door. She opened hers and got out, walked through the gate in the fence, then up onto the porch. She turned back and waved at him. He flipped his headlights back on, started the engine, and drove away.

Rileigh opened the screen door carefully to keep the screeching cry from awakening Jillian and Mama. She eased it shut behind her, took off the shoes that were *killing* her feet, and started across the living room toward the stairs.

"How was your date?"

The words coming out of the darkness behind her startled Rileigh, and she jumped.

"You're as quiet as … as…"

"You're going to have to come up with some more 'as quiet as,'" Jillian said. "You've already used 'as quiet as a mouse in house shoes tiptoeing across a cotton ball' and 'so quiet I could sneak dawn past a rooster.' Got any new ones?"

"How about 'as quiet as the guests at a wedding reception **aren't** when they see a turd in the punch bowl.'"

Jillian made the sound of a quiz show buzzer — *BUZZ!* —and flipped on the light beside where she sat in the recliner.

"No points."

"Why did you wait up for me?"

"Actually, I just came downstairs to see what I could find to munch on in the kitchen."

Rileigh suddenly remembered how hungry she'd been. She had never even gotten the burger that she and Mitch had ordered, let alone eaten it.

"I'm for that," Rileigh said. "How about we raid the refrigerator?"

"You just went out to dinner."

"Well, not so much," Rileigh said.

She led the way into the kitchen, where Rileigh opened the refrigerator door and stood staring into the interior, then pulled out a package of ham-and-cheese loaf, a jar of mayonnaise and some sweet pickles, then set them on the table. When she went to the bread box to get out the bread, Jillian said, "Seriously, why are you hungry?"

"Because we didn't have dinner."

"Oh. I hoped … I really hoped. But as soon as Mama got the call—"

"So Mama knows about Jody Hatfield at the Red Eye Gravy."

"Yep."

Rileigh wasn't surprised.

"You must be exhausted. Sit. Let me make you a sandwich."

"Thanks, but no. I'm not used to being waited on. Don't you want something?"

"I'm hoping there are some of those powdered sugar donuts left in the cabinet." Jillian went to the cabinet to check while Rileigh started making her sandwich.

"So you two had to take over when the body was found, right?" Jillian asked.

"Yeah. We'd ordered but hadn't gotten our food. And afterward, well, it wasn't like you'd want to eat dinner after seeing that."

"Mama said that Millie told her something like his face was destroyed… or…"

"He didn't have a face," Rileigh said and was instantly sorry as soon as she said it because Jillian responded physically, closed up, and jerked back.

"What do you mean no face?"

"You don't need the visual."

Jillian stood for a moment, saying nothing. Then her

shoulders relaxed, and she said, "You're right. I have enough of those."

She turned back to her doughnut search.

"We had to go and tell Jody's parents."

"You told his parents?"

"Oh, they already knew. If Mama knew, they knew. But it's Mitch's job to deliver the official news of a death."

"My, what a wonderful 'big date' you had."

Rileigh pulled out the chair and sat down into it heavily, then picked up the sandwich and bit into it. Her ravenous hunger returned with a vengeance.

"So, what did you and Mama do tonight?" she asked between bites.

~

JILLIAN SAT on the edge of her bed, listening to the sounds of the silent house. Rileigh was finally asleep.

She had managed to keep up an inane conversation because she knew Rileigh needed to unwind after what she'd been through.

Why did she want to go out in the middle of the night to the scene of some awful crime? Or to deliver devastating news to a grieving family? It was just so out of character for the cute little girl who used to look up to Jillian. Who apparently had put a note into Jillian's suitcase the night before her wedding, begging, 'Please don't forget me.'

As if Jillian could forget Rileigh. The image of that little girl, that cute face, and those big hazel eyes. She had conjured it up a hundred dozen times in the years since she'd left, knowing that even if she escaped, she'd never see that face again, that Rileigh would have a grown woman's face, even though she was still frozen in Jillian's memory as a cute little girl.

Jillian had to come to terms with this. She could not get upset every time Rileigh responded to some police emergency. It was just so hard to reconcile the two images. It was beyond anything Jillian could imagine that her little sister wanted to be involved in such gruesome work.

Then there was *the box*, the one nobody talked about anymore, the one that had shown up in the mailbox in June addressed to Rileigh that had contained a *human finger bone*.

If anybody in the world was an expert at not thinking about unpleasant things, it was Jillian Bishop. She had turned it into an art form. It was a necessary part of survival in the world where she'd lived for almost three decades. So she couldn't claim to be *unable* to stop thinking about it. She *could* stop thinking about it if she chose to. But sometimes ... *often*, she didn't choose to.

Rileigh had finally demanded that the whole family shut up and stop talking about the box because it had been the only subject of conversation for at least a week after it arrived. Who would send human pinky bones to Rileigh? What reason could there be for the hideous gift? They had floated every possibility they could think of — and not one suggestion made any sense.

Mitch had done his best to track down the box, of course, but it was a simple box mailed from Chicago. Anybody could have sent it. There'd been no point in trying to lift fingerprints off of it, though he had tried to lift prints off the piece of folded paper in the box with a crudely drawn, sneering frowny face on one side and the number 5 on the other. But it had been wiped clean.

Gus had sent the bones themselves off for DNA analysis but found no match for them. As the coroner had pointed out, DNA was a great tool to use in the prosecution of a suspect, but you had to find the suspect first, and unless you got lucky and somebody's DNA happened to be "in the system," DNA didn't help with that part.

The twisted frowny face had obviously been intended to echo the years Mama and Rileigh had lived with the annual postcards that seemed to be from Jillian when Jillian had been a prisoner halfway across the world. Whoever sent that box knew about the previous postcards. But that was a very small group of people — none of whom would have sent Rileigh finger bones. And by the way, why finger *bones?* What message was *that* supposed to convey?

Finally, Mitch had put the whole thing in the evidence locker at the sheriff's department, and they'd all tried to stop thinking about it.

Jillian had mostly succeeded, except at times like now when she was already worried about Rileigh's safety. At such times, the image of the bone and everything the box implied stood up on center stage in her mind and demanded the spotlight. Somebody out there had a serious ax to grind with Rileigh Bishop, and every time Rileigh left the house, Jillian thought about that.

If she'd been here when Rileigh was in the military, if she'd been here when Rileigh was a police officer … you can get used to those things. Slowly, over time, they'd just sort of seep into your psyche like ink through a blotter. But it was so abrupt to come back and discover that her little sister was a soldier and a cop.

But she was.

Jillian ground her teeth. She *was.* Jillian's fearfulness was not normal. She understood that. Rileigh had not been in any danger tonight — but she had been at other times. Rileigh thought Jillian didn't know what had happened when Rileigh had gone out to that Holiness Church up in Juniper Hollow. Mama had picked the story up in bits and pieces from various sources. It drew a picture too horrible to countenance — that the crazy preacher was about to *sacrifice* Rileigh when Mitch shot him. Police work was dangerous. And if Rileigh kept doing it…

No, not *if* she kept doing it, *when* she kept doing it. She wasn't going to give it up. And in truth, it wasn't Jillian's right to ask her to. It was what she wanted to do with her life. Jillian was the issue. Her fear was the issue. But she couldn't even explain to Rileigh why she was so frightened. To do so, she'd have to tell stories she didn't want to tell.

The image of Starla's face formed in Jillian's mind unbidden. She shook her head to make it go away. But it wouldn't. Of course, it wouldn't. Starla had reminded her of Rileigh. She'd been so young when they brought her in. So terrified. So traumatized. Jillian had done everything she could to comfort her. To shield her and protect her. But there was no way to keep horrible from happening to any of the girls who were owned body and soul by the organization.

Jillian remembered the night Starla was brought back to their room in the hotel. Axel just shoved her down on her bed and told her to get cleaned up and get some sleep, they'd be leaving in the morning.

The other girls saw Starla's split lip and the bruises forming on her upper arms. Jillian knew the kind of pressure it took to make those finger bruises. But what was most disturbing about Starla was her blank stare. She didn't reach up to wipe the blood off of her chin. She just let it slide down from her lip and drip into her lap. Jillian sat down on the bed beside her and put her arm around Starla.

"It's okay, sweetheart. It's going to be okay."

Starla looked at her, uncomprehending. "It's going to be *okay?*"

"What I mean is, you can do this. You can—"

"Oh no, I can't." She looked full into Jillian's face then. "And I *won't*. I won't let them do this to me."

She got to her feet, brushing aside Jillian's embrace, went into the bathroom and closed the door. Two weeks later, she was dead. She leapt in front of a taxi in Khartoum. The other girls heard about it from Axel, who railed about how she had involved the law in their affairs. How the man she was with had only barely been able to escape without being connected to the crumpled body on the sticky hot asphalt.

Jillian never knew what had happened to Starla's body. She never knew what happened to the bodies of any of the girls who died. Or what happened to the girls who didn't die. Who just left. She tried not to become close to any of them after that but failed miserably. She couldn't help caring. But then she was sold to the Arab, and she never saw any of them again.

Starla was not Rileigh and Rileigh was not Starla. Jillian had so wanted to protect Starla, but she couldn't. Now, she wanted to protect Rileigh, and she couldn't do that either. She had to give up on that. She had to let Rileigh be who she was. And she had to support Rileigh's decisions, even if those decisions terrified her.

Jillian shook her head, aware of the urge to go into Rileigh's room and watch her sleep as she had occasionally when Rileigh was a little girl. But she didn't. She heaved a big sigh. Tried to square her shoulders and her psyche into being resolute. Then turned off the bedside lamp and went to sleep.

Chapter Seven

ORDINARILY, Mitch wouldn't have been in the office on Sunday, certainly not this early in the morning. But finding a body last night at the Red Eye Gravy Diner had set his life into overdrive. He would go by later today and talk to the coroner, Gus, to find out Jody Hatfield's cause of death. Unless Mitch could find out who killed him, arrest that person, and lock them up, there was likely to be more bloodshed between the "Hatfields and McCoys."

A 911 call was patched through to Mitch by the dispatcher, who said it was about a picture.

"Oh, Sheriff Webster, I'm so glad to talk to you. It's terrible. It's awful. I'm so upset."

Mitch almost didn't recognize the voice, which was high and squeaky. Affected, cutie-squeaky. Rileigh hated that affectation and on more than one occasion had commented on how ridiculous it was that so many girls had decided that was an attractive trait.

He recognized the speaker as Cookie, the new waitress at Red Eye Gravy.

"Could you slow down, please?" Mitch said, interrupting the squeaky stream of consciousness coming from the phone. "I'm having trouble understanding you. What is terrible and awful?"

"What somebody did to the pictures."

"The pictures."

"Oh, you know, all over the building there are pictures.... Well, somebody defaced the ones with Jody in them."

Why exactly the new young waitress had decided that a defaced picture was worthy of a 911 emergency call, he couldn't quite fathom. But the girl had appeared to be a couple of sandwiches shy of a picnic when he met her. She had cooed, "They call me Cookie. Everybody likes to nibble on a cookie."

"All right, Miss..."

"Ashlie Neal."

"All right, Miss Neal, I'll be by later on this morning. Please don't touch the photograph or let anyone else touch the photographs."

"Oh, that's because of fingerprints, right? You're looking for fingerprints." She paused. "Well, mine are going to be on it. I touched it. I'm sorry. I didn't think."

"Don't let anyone *else* touch it. I will see you shortly."

Mitch decided to invite Rileigh to take a look at the pictures with him. Oh, she always offered valuable insights, but he was self-aware enough to know that this time he just wanted her company. The whole night before had been gobbled up by finding the body of Jody Hatfield, and then dealing with Travis Bramley, and then with Jody's parents.

But that's not the way last night was supposed to play out. Last night was, drum roll, please, *the big date*. The big date that wasn't.

When he'd seen her coming down the stairs at her mother's house in that green dress, it literally took his breath away. It's funny how he had been around her almost every day for months, and he'd certainly recognized that she was pretty. But he hadn't realized how exceptionally beautiful she was until he saw her last night in that dress. The dress itself was stunning, and it clung to Rileigh's body, tight in all the right places. But it was the color ... that jade color ...

Mitch had looked into Rileigh Bishop's eyes a thousand times. They were hazel, a lovely shade of hazel. But last night, when she was wearing that dress, they were *green*, jade green, almost like a cat's. And that had almost magically transformed her face — not that it needed transforming — but the green eyes had changed Rileigh Bishop from a beautiful woman into a staggeringly beautiful woman.

What was supposed to happen last night was that he was going to take that staggeringly beautiful woman on his arm to dinner at a nice restaurant, and then ...

He tried not to let his mind linger on the "and then" part, but of course, he couldn't help thinking about it. Even after their plan to go to Bahama Mama's was derailed, forcing them to settle for the Red Eye Gravy Diner instead. His fantasies about "and then" didn't change. They didn't change until a woman, half-dressed, came screaming out of the hallway at the diner with a young man behind her, crying, "There's a body in there, and it ain't got no face."

At that moment, all possibility of "and then" went up in smoke, as surely as the black pall rising up from the scorched remains of Bahama Mama's.

Mitch called Rileigh, and the sound of her voice brought a smile to his face in a way that very few things in his life could do.

"Have you had breakfast?" he asked.

"No, I slept late. Coffee's all I've managed to get down. I think Mama's planning to —"

"Would you like to have breakfast with me at the Red Eye Gravy Diner?"

"Somehow, that doesn't sound like a spontaneous invitation. It sounds like—"

Mitch interrupted. "I got a call this morning that a picture on the wall in the diner had been defaced — the one of Jody Hatfield."

Rileigh pointed out the obvious irony in the word 'defaced.'

"I need to go take a look at it," Mitch continued. "Would you like to join me?"

"I'll meet you there."

Mitch got to the diner before Rileigh did and was sitting at the bar on a stool, drinking a cup of coffee and talking to Big John when she came in. He turned to look and was surprised to discover that somehow, the image of her face last night in all its perfection was still there when he looked at her. Maybe even more amazing were the green eyes. Her eye color had obviously not changed overnight, yet the jade green that the dress had brought out in them was still there, even though she was wearing jeans and a black tee shirt with a picture of a black bear and the slogan: "Forest fires prevent bears."

"I was just educating your city boyfriend here on the name of the diner," Big John said as she approached, "but I told him that before I could explain what red-eyed gravy is, he had to know what country ham is."

"Do you know what country ham is?" Rileigh asked.

Mitch did, or at least assumed he did, but he played dumb. "Nope, but I'm sure you're about to enlighten me."

"Actually, you've had country ham at Mama's. She's

made it several times, but nobody bothered to tell you what you were eating."

"I'd eat fried Volkswagen if your mama cooked it."

"Country ham is ham preserved by early settlers, so they'd have something to eat over the winter. But like a lot of things, making country ham became an art form. The flavor varies according to all kinda factors, and families took it as a matter of pride to have the best country ham around."

"We get our country ham from a wholesale supplier," Big John said, "but I remember the country ham my granny used to make. She would invite all the neighbors in the hollow to breakfast, and we'd have eggs and scratch biscuits, grits, fried corn with homemade peach preserves, and sorghum molasses, but the center of the meal was the country ham."

Rileigh took up the description at that point. "You start with a whole bone-in fresh ham, and you hand rub it with a mixture of salt, sugar, and curing agents. You do it a couple of times to make sure the ham has absorbed all the ingredients, and then you hang it up somewhere and just leave it hanging there."

"How long?"

"Mama says country ham's not worth eating if it hasn't been aging for at least ninety days," Rileigh said. "But even that varies from family to family."

"And you have to have country ham in order to make red-eye gravy," Rileigh said. "Red-eye gravy is …"

A voice from behind Big John spoke up then. "Red-eye gravy ain't something any fool could cook up, neither. Really good red-eye gravy is scarce as hen's teeth."

The voice came from Junie Thomas, the man in the kitchen. Junie was the acknowledged best short-order cook in east Tennessee, whose presence at the Red Eye Gravy diner had elevated the restaurant's cheeseburgers from ordinary to sublime. He was something of a local legend, had worked mostly in Gatlinburg in the touristy establishments, but Junie had a bad habit of vanishing in a puff of smoke without a moment's notice, leaving some restaurant scrambling to find a replacement. Nobody knew where he went or why, but he always showed up back in Yarmouth County a few weeks later and had no trouble finding employment when he did.

Big John gestured, "Come on out here, Junie, and tell this poor city boy how you whip up that magical red-eye gravy."

The man appeared moments later, pushing through the swinging doors from the kitchen into the area behind the bar. He was a short, squat black man with a perfect circle of white cottony hair beneath a perfectly bald dome. He was wiping his hands on a towel, talking as he approached.

"The point of red-eye gravy is to enjoy every speck of that glaze that's left in an iron skillet, salty and sticky and the color of rust, after you fry a slice of country ham."

He stopped then and cocked his head to the side.

"Now, I ain't sure if white folks make red eye gravy same as black folks, but my granny always said that red eye gravy was invented 'cause somebody wanted some gravy to put on their biscuits, and country ham don't make the same kind of grease as other things. I mean, you fry up bacon, and it leaves you a pan full of grease. All you got to do is add some flour and some milk, and you got white gravy. But it ain't the same with country ham. It don't leave no grease behind, just that glaze. Somewhere along the line, somebody figured out that if you just pour a little bit of liquid in the skillet with the glaze, it'd make gravy. And what kinda liquid is within arm's reach every morning? Coffee."

"I think my grandmother made red eye gravy the same way your grandmother did," Rileigh said, "just two ingredients — country ham and black coffee."

"While you don't need nothing to thicken it, they's folks that add flour or cornmeal, but that'll lump on you, and ain't nothing worse than lumps in gravy."

Cookie approached then from the other side of the diner. Mitch kept his eyes on her face, which, for any red-blooded male, was a difficult task. He noticed that she had a lone dimple in her right cheek. Then he thought of Rileigh's remark last night that one of those ... what had Rileigh called them... "monstrous things" was in danger of falling out of Cookie's blouse and into somebody's milkshake. He had to stifle a laugh.

"Oh, Sheriff, I'm so glad you came, I've been so upset." Out of the corner of his eye, Mitch saw Rileigh roll her eyes.

"Miss Neal called me this—"

"Miss Neal?" Rileigh asked.

"My name's Ashlie Neal, but everybody calls me Cookie because—"

Rileigh held up her hand. "I know everything I need to know about Cookie nibbling."

Mitch grabbed the conversation before it could go totally off the rails.

"Cookie called this morning to tell me one of the team pictures on your wall had been vandalized," he told Big John. "The one with Jody Hatfield in it."

"Come this way, I'll show you." Cookie headed toward the hallway that led to the bathrooms and the storage room, snatching something off a tray behind the counter as she passed it.

The whole diner was decorated with large pictures of various teams that had played various sports locally, dating back to the 1930s. Apparently, the picture of the 2016 state championship football team was in the hallway between the two bathrooms. Mitch and Rileigh followed Cookie, who swayed her way to the hallway and pointed at the picture.

"Look at that. Just look at that. Somebody marked out their faces, almost like they were trying to erase them." She paused, and when Mitch turned his back, she purred provocatively, "Sheriff ... would you like to nibble on a cookie?"

Mitch was jarred by the non sequitur, turned toward her ... and saw a cookie in her hand.

"Chocolate chip with walnuts," she said, enjoying the consternation she'd intended for the double meaning of her offer to cause.

"No thanks, I'll pass," Mitch said.

She held the cookie out to Rileigh.

"Actually, I *can't stand* cookies," Rileigh said icily. "They make me want to puke."

Mitch coughed to cover up a burp of laughter, but either the girl wasn't bright enough to understand she'd been insulted or just didn't care because she smiled brightly.

"Suit yourself," she said. When she popped the cookie into her mouth, chomping on it in loud abandon, Mitch noticed her tattoo. It went around her wrist like a bracelet, little pig figures chasing each other. Rileigh noticed it, too.

"What's that?" Rileigh asked.

The girl gave her a condescending look, like ... well, duh. "It's the three little pigs. I looooove nursery rhymes."

Why was Mitch not surprised?

He turned his gaze back to the photograph on the wall. It wasn't just Jody whose face was marked out. So were the faces of Clive McCutcheon and Travis Bramley.

"All three of them," Mitch mused. Someone had used a black magic marker, or maybe a Sharpie, to scratch across the faces of those three players, totally removing them from the picture.

"Somebody removed their faces ... like somebody removed Jody Hatfield's face," Rileigh said.

"Ouch!" Cookie cried, a sudden look of pain on her otherwise perfect features. Must have bitten her tongue. Rileigh appeared delighted to see the girl disappear into the women's restroom. Mitch managed not to grin, just stood with Rileigh as she kept staring at the photographs.

"So only the quarterback, the running back, and the center on this football team have been erased," Rileigh said, shaking her head. "I wonder what that could mean."

"I don't think there's any sense in hauling Gus down here to check for fingerprints," Mitch said. There was no glass in front of the pictures in most of the frames, and untold dozens of people had passed by this one on their way to the bathrooms.

Mitch turned to Rileigh. "Let's eat."

They left the hallway and went to sit at a table by the window, the same table they'd had last night. But they could talk now, without the loud music and the hum of rowdy voices around them. There were only about half a dozen customers here early on a Sunday morning.

Mitch tried not to stare at Rileigh's face, at her *eyes*, as he nursed his cup of coffee.

"And the rest of your day consists of?" he asked her.

"Taking Mama to church and trying to talk Jillian into going along. And you?"

"Slightly similar. I'm going to go have a come-to-Jesus conversation with Clive McCutcheon."

Chapter Eight

THE WOMAN at McCutcheon's home, perhaps his wife, perhaps not, told Mitch that Clive was at work at the Haggerty Brothers Sawmill on Pendleton Road.

Mitch went to the sawmill and parked his cruiser out front. It was an old business, had likely been there for maybe a hundred years, passed down through the Haggarty family for generations.

He went into what he assumed was the office and approached the woman at the desk, where the nameplate identified her as "Nguyen Hoang, receptionist."

"I'd like to see Clive McCutcheon. I understand he is here working this morning. It's official business."

The woman picked up a hand-held walkie-talkie and pushed the button.

"Mr. Haggarty, the sheriff is here and he wants to talk to Clive. Should I send him down?"

"No, he'd have to get suited up. I'll send Clive to the office."

Mitch assumed 'getting suited up' meant donning some kind of gear required by OSHA regulations.

"He won't be long," Nguyen said. "Please have a seat while you wait."

She was a pleasant woman with a round face, a bright smile, and a voice that seemed to have a hint of laughter in it.

McCutcheon didn't keep Mitch waiting long. He came stomping in the back door of the office area — literally stomping to get the sawdust off his shoes. He was wearing blue coveralls with "Haggerty Brothers Sawmill" stenciled above one pocket and "Clive McCutchen" stenciled above the other.

"Mr. McCutcheon." Mitch approached the man with his hand extended. McCutcheon ignored it.

"You came here to talk to me because of what happened to Jody Hatfield last night, ain't you?"

"I am."

"Wasting your time and mine. I get paid by the hour and talkin' to you's costing me money. I don't know jack shit about what happened to that bastard."

"Why don't we step outside where we can talk privately." Mitch didn't wait for McCutcheon's response. Just turned and went back out the front door. McCutcheon stomped after him.

Mitch tried to visualize McCutcheon as the running back who had caught all those passes that Jody Hatfield threw to beat Knox County 35-0 in the state championship football game. But it was hard to envision. The man standing in front of him had a pronounced beer belly and looked way older than his twenty-six years. If Mitch had to guess, he would suspect that Jody Hatfield, Travis Bramley, and Clive McCutcheon were juicers when they were in high school. They had that sort of deflated look that accompanied age and lack of exercise after a person had taken steroids to enhance their strength.

"Mr. McCutcheon, where were you last night?"

"Ain't none of your damn business where I was last night."

"Sir, we can do this one of two ways. Either you can answer my questions civilly, or I can load you up in the back of that cruiser and take you down to the station, which will cost you a lot more time than telling me what I want to know here and now."

McCutcheon held up his hand. "I was home last night, all night."

"So, it was Saturday night, and you weren't out ..." Mitch couldn't help his eye going to McCutcheon's beer belly. "... drinking beer with your buddies."

"I went out for a while."

"Where did you go?"

"The Rusty Nail over in Gatlinburg."

"Who did you go with?"

"Tom Hagey, Willis Stephenson, Lamont Phillips. A few others."

"I'll need the contact information for the men you said you were with last night."

"They're in the phone book. Look 'em up."

"Are they all members of the McCoy's gang?"

"It ain't the 'McCoy's.'" McCutcheon spit the words out. "It's 35/Zip. That's how bad we beat Knox County. Thirty-five to nothing."

"Were all of those men members of 35/Zip?" Mitch asked.

"Some of them."

"What time did you get to the Rusty Nail?"

"Ah, must have been maybe eight o'clock. Maybe a little later."

"And when did you leave?"

"Hell, I don't know. It was Saturday night. I got drunk."

"So, you don't know what time you left the Rusty Nail last night."

"Nope. You can go over to Gatlinburg and talk to Smitty. Maybe he can tell you. At some point, he quit serving me beer."

"How did you get home if you were so drunk?"

"I drove home."

"You were too drunk to know what time it was when you left the bar but not too drunk to drive home."

"You didn't catch me at it, so you ain't got no dog in the fight."

Mitch marveled that the number of people who were arrested for driving under the influence in the mountains was about the same as it was in the city. But he could not understand how in the world people managed to keep a car on these narrow, winding, twisting, almost vertical roads while sober, let alone drunk.

"What did you do when you got home?"

"Hell, what do you think I done?"

Mitch thought that perhaps the correct answer was either A) he had thrown up about half of that beer, B) he had passed out, or C) he and the woman Mitch met had gotten chummy.

"I asked you a question, Mr. McCutcheon. What did you do when you got home?"

"I screwed my girlfriend, then I went to sleep."

Two out of three.

"So, you're saying that late last night and early this morning, you were home in bed asleep."

"Yeah, I was home in bed asleep."

"When was the last time you saw Jody Hatfield?"

"Oh, I seen him in the distance now and then. Flip the bird every time I do."

"When was the last time you talked to him?"

"I ain't said a word to that son of a bitch in years ... until the Fourth of July."

Two days ago. "What did you talk about on the Fourth of July?"

"Let's just say we got into it at Smoke Creek Park."

"You and Jody Hatfield had a fight two days before he was killed?"

"Me and Jody ... and a few 'close personal friends.'"

"Your gangs fought?"

"In a manner of speaking. We'd have killed some of them bastards if the law'd let us be."

"Didn't you all play on the same high school football team together?"

"Hell yeah."

"And Jody Hatfield was the quarterback, so he threw the passes you were catching. Right?"

"Right. So, what's your point? Just because I was able to drag those piddly ass passes out of the air and score doesn't make us blood brothers."

"People tell me that you were friends at one time."

"We was."

"So why aren't you friends anymore?"

"That ain't none of your business."

"It's my business if the two of you parted ways on unfriendly terms."

"You could call it that."

"That being the case, that would give you a motive to—"

"Hell, if I'd wanted to kill Jody Hatfield, I'd have done it a long time ago. I should have done it a long time ago.

Whoever did kill him, I want to find that man and shake his hand."

"You still haven't answered my question. Why aren't you friends anymore?"

"I caught the bastard fooling around with my woman, okay?" Clive snapped. "And I beat the shit out of him. Broke his nose, messed up that 'pretty-boy' face."

Pretty boy. Travis Bramley had said Jody Hatfield's face had been ripped off because he was "a pretty boy."

"How long ago was that?"

"Hell, I don't know. Sometime the summer after we graduated. I come in and there that bastard was, caught them in the act!"

"Who was the woman?"

"Her name was Lauren Coleman. Me and her had been going together all through high school. Then I find out my best friend has been screwing around with her behind my back. I'd ought to have taken a shotgun and blown his brains out."

"Let's circle back around to where you were last night."

"I done told you where I was. You don't b'lieve me, go ask them other people. You can ask my girlfriend. You can go to the Rusty Nail and ask Lamont or Tom."

Mitch knew every one of those witnesses would cheerfully lie through their teeth to protect Clive McCutcheon.

Except perhaps the bartender. According to Rileigh, he was a straight-up guy. Mitch just might be able to establish that McCutcheon had been at the bar. Gus hadn't yet given him a time of death — just sometime last night. Mitch needed more specifics.

"Are you through messing around with my day? I'm gonna get docked for the time I was off. I'll send your ass a bill."

"If you didn't kill Jody Hatfield, do you know who did?"

The big man threw his head back and roared with laughter. He finally coughed and spluttered to a stop, shaking his head. "Who would like to see Jody Hatfield dead? Every damn member of 35/Zip. Add to that all the husbands whose wives he screwed around with. And all them wives he dumped. And all the customers he's cheated with bad weed. Shit. The list is real long. Like I said, are you done?"

Mitch looked then at McCutcheon's hand. "That ring's not a high school ring, is it?"

McCutcheon held his hand up to display the ring. "Hell no, it ain't. This here is a 35/Zip ring."

"Does every member of your gang have a ring like that?"

"Most of them, yeah. Why?"

"The gang ring that Jody Hatfield wore was not on his body when it was found."

McCutcheon looked genuinely surprised. "Why the hell not?"

"I suppose because whoever killed him took it off."

"Well, it wasn't me. I don't want his stupid ring. The 35/Zip rings are way better than them dumbass 'Smoked 'Em'rings." He held his ring up in the light. It had several stones of various colors. "Our rings have the score of the game! They're symbols that say, 'We won!'"

Mitch remembered that Travis Bramley had used those same words about the Smoked' Em rings— that they symbolized, 'We won!'

"Each of them colors means something different," Clive added.

"For example?"

"Ain't none of your business. That's private information for our club members."

But Mitch had to agree. The 35/Zip ring was far more attractive than the ring Travis Bramley had shown him yesterday.

"You can go back to work now. Just know that if I have more questions, I will come talk to you again."

"You poor bastard," McCutcheon said, shaking his head. "I'd hate to be the fella who had to plow through all the people who had motives to kill that bastard, Jody. That there's going to be looking for a shiny needle in a bale of hay."

Gus called with the highlights of the autopsy report on Jody Hatfield's body while Mitch was driving back into town. The time of death was somewhere between midnight and three a.m., a time when Clive McCutcheon's alibi was at best squishy.

"The cause of death was a stab wound to the heart made by a knife blade no more than an inch wide," Gus said. "I know the width not from the wound it made but because if it'd been any wider, it wouldn't have fit between the ribs."

"What can you tell me about the murder weapon?"

"Could be as fancy as an Egyptian dagger filched from the tomb of Tutankhamun or a common butcher knife you could buy in the housewares section of Walmart. Safe money's on a long carving knife."

"So, there's nothing about the cause of death that'll help us find the killer."

"I didn't say that."

"What did you say?"

"I said the murder weapon is common; the manner of death isn't."

"A stab wound to the heart? You see it on every other cop show on TV."

"And cop shows are such reliable purveyors of accurate information."

"So, stab wounds to the heart really aren't common?"

"Stab wounds *near* the heart happen all the time. The blade cuts into a major artery in the chest that leads to the heart, causing massive external and internal bleeding precisely because the heart is undamaged and still beating, pumping the blood out. Unconscious before you hit the floor, dead in four minutes. But if it's the heart itself that takes the kill shot, it will react one of two ways to an injury. It will keep pumping rhythmically, or the wound will trigger fibrillation — random contractions, like the heart's having a seizure."

"But you're saying Jody Hatfield died from a stab wound *in* the heart... and that's rare?"

"It's damned hard to stab the heart because it lies right behind the sternum and is partially covered by ribs. The tissue that connects the ribs to each other is tough, and then the blade has to cut through the heart's own shield, the fibrous covering of the pericardium. The killer certainly had above-average upper body strength.

"And in order to kill a person, the wound would have to be more than a simple puncture. The heart contracts and relaxes, and it will seal up a hole when it contracts, so there's only bleeding when it relaxes. You could survive a long time with a punctured heart."

"Would a butcher knife make a simple puncture?"

"Oh, the hole in Jody Hatfield's heart was no puncture. It was catastrophic. His heart was slashed, almost cut in two."

"*Slashed?*"

"Yep, ripped open from left to right ... which means the killer is right-handed, there is that."

Before Mitch could comment, Gus went on.

"Mitch, whoever killed Jody Hatfield knew what they were doing. At the very least, they had an above-average understanding of human anatomy. Maybe they even *practiced*. The knife entered the body between the fourth and fifth ribs on the left with the blade angled up and then ripped sideways."

"Holy shit."

"The result would have been what you see in the movies — blood spurting out under pressure, splattering the killer and everything around him."

"Was Jody instantly unconscious?"

"Dropped like a rock, if he was standing up when he was stabbed, but I don't think he was. Given the blood splatter pattern, I think he was lying on his back at the time."

"He didn't put up a fight?"

"There's no evidence he resisted. No defensive wounds of any kind, no cuts on his hands and arms."

"Knocked out?"

"No contusions on the skull."

"Drugged?"

"Drunk on his ass and a little weed, nothing fancy."

"So the killer just said, *Hold still while I stab you*?"

"Something like that."

"That makes no sense at all."

"Finding the evidence is my job. Making sense of it is yours."

"So ... then his face was removed?"

"It sounds and looks — and if he'd been alive at the time, it would have *felt* —absolutely horrific, but it wasn't very hard to do. Cut the scalp, get your fingers under the skin, and pull down."

"Have you ever seen anything like that before?"

"Nope. You, my friend, get the Kewpie Doll for most original murder."

Chapter Nine

JILLIAN REFUSED to go to church with Rileigh and Mama that morning. Rileigh wasn't surprised, but she was disappointed. She had been hoping that as time went by, Jillian would relax and go out more often in public. Go to the movies, the grocery store, Walmart. But Jillian was content to stay at Mama's and go nowhere and see nobody. She felt safe there, not threatened. Apparently, everything beyond the front porch was scary.

Rileigh couldn't blame her, given what she'd gone through. But Jillian was never going to have a rich, full life, the life she deserved to have, the life that had been stolen from her by Aunt Daisy, if she refused to engage with life at all.

Rileigh had been putting the full-court press on Jillian to go to therapy. And Jillian admitted she needed it. She simply wanted to kick the can farther down the road every time the subject came up.

"Maybe next week." But next week came, and she put it off again.

When Rileigh and Mama got home from church,

A Friend Like You

Jillian was in a dark place, non-communicative. She didn't ask how church was or who Mama and Rileigh had seen. She helped Mama get lunch ready, but not with any degree of enjoyment. Even Mama picked up on it, and Mama was certainly not the queen of sensitivity. She had looked a question at Rileigh several times during lunch when both of them caught Jillian just staring out into space, moving her food around and around on her plate, but not eating anything.

Mitch had called a couple of times during the day. He had gone to question Clive McCutcheon at his job at the sawmill. McCutcheon's alibi was that he had been at the Rusty Nail Bar in Gatlinburg when the murder was committed, or at least he thought he had. Mitch had talked to Smitty, the bartender there, who said Clive had been in the night before and had gotten totally shit-faced drunk. But Smitty didn't know what time he left.

Being drunk, in Mitch's eyes, was almost as good an alibi as being with other people. What had happened to Jody Hatfield had not been the work of a drunk man... but then, heavy drinkers were often able to sober up faster than the average bear.

Rileigh tried to pretend that she wouldn't have preferred to question Smitty with Mitch than attend church with Mama.

Jillian spent the whole of Sunday afternoon in her studio, painting. Mama and Rileigh tried to stay out of her way at times like that because they believed that the painting was therapeutic. Now Rileigh sat in bed trying to read, but she couldn't concentrate. Finally, she got up, tiptoed down the hall to check on Jillian, and found her asleep. Then she went into Jillian's studio and looked at the picture she had been painting. Jillian wanted to keep her paintings private, and Rileigh and Mama had respected that privacy. Occasionally, she would show them some still life, but mostly, she took the paintings out into the backyard, broke up the frames, tore the canvases, and set the pile on fire. Rileigh had helped her do that a time or two. She had even gone into the house and gotten marshmallows.

Rileigh switched on the light in the studio. The most current painting was still on the easel, the paint wet. What Rileigh saw in it was disturbing in a way she couldn't put her finger on. It wasn't anything recognizable, an apple or a tree or, for that matter, a demon or a monster. It was just colors and lines and shapes, but they were all dark colors. There were no pastels, no sky blues, no green like the mountains in the morning, just swirling black funnels, brown blotches with jagged edges, and red, lots of red. Not the candy apple red of a new Corvette, shades of blood red — the bright red of fresh blood, the dark red of dried blood. Inside Jillian's head must be a very dark place with nothing but jagged edges. No softness, no happiness, no sunshine, no color of any kind, just dark.

Rileigh went back to her room for her phone, then returned to Jillian's studio and took pictures of the canvas and several other canvasses leaning against the wall. She realized she was invading her sister's privacy, breaking her word that she would stay out of Jillian's studio unless invited. But she had a mind to take the photographs to a woman she knew who might be able to interpret what they meant.

When Rileigh was a police officer in Memphis, she had arrested a couple for child abuse, and in the course of the investigation, she met a woman named Dr. Aaliyah Al-Masri. Dr. Al-Masri was a psychiatrist who had been called in to find out whether the bruised and battered little girl, who refused to speak a word to anybody, had been sexually as well as physically abused. Dr. Al-Masri had spoken to the child kindly, didn't pressure her to talk back, then gave her crayons and a piece of paper and asked her to draw a picture.

When she returned, the psychiatrist looked at the picture and told the prosecutor, "In my professional opinion, this little girl has been sexually abused." She said the picture was evidence and explained that art allowed the subconscious mind to take over, and all of the things the child was hiding from her conscious mind showed up in her art. Both Rileigh and the psychiatrist had been called to testify at the trial and had wound up spending a couple of hours together in the witness waiting room. It was a little like being in time-out with Georgia, stuck with their noses in opposite corners of the storage room when they were in kindergarten — she and the doctor had emerged as friends.

Dr. Al-Masri had moved to Knoxville, so Rileigh hadn't seen her in years, but she intended to take the photographs of Jillian's artwork to the psychiatrist and ask her what she could tell about Jillian's state of mind. Since Jillian was unwilling to go to therapy, perhaps Dr. Al-Masri could help Rileigh understand how she should respond to her sister's reclusive behavior.

Rileigh went back into her bedroom and slipped between the still-warm sheets. She lay in the dark, guilt and hope warring in her chest as she tried to go to sleep.

Chapter Ten

TANISHA JEFFERSON LOOKED at her watch and wondered for the thousandth time where Derek could be. He had been playing golf with some buddies on Sunday afternoon and said he'd been loading up his clubs when he got a call from the answering service saying that someone had called in with a dental emergency. Since he was on call tonight, he'd agreed to meet the patient at his office. But that had been four hours ago. He could have pulled out all the patient's teeth in that amount of time.

Derek always turned his cell phone off when he was working because he wanted to set an example for the dental hygienists and other technicians in the office to show that having a cell phone on at work was not acceptable for *any* employee. It was a little harder to get patients to comply with the rule. But it was certainly easier if you could point out that you had turned your cell phone off, too. With his cell turned off, there was no way to reach him. She'd dialed the number of the office and gotten the answering service at least half a dozen times. So, Derek was either busy or ... yeah, or *what?*

What could he have gotten so involved in that it took four hours?

Just then, the baby kicked really hard, banging her in the rib cage. So hard she almost groaned out loud. Not that it hurt. Oh no, there was nothing in that sensation she would label "pain." But it was startling sometimes. She wondered how in the world a baby in the womb could kick that hard.

Tanisha didn't know if she was carrying a boy or a girl. Apparently, she was quite an anomaly, an expectant mother who did *not* want to know the sex of her baby before it was born. Yeah, there were perfectly good reasons to find out. Not the least of which was curiosity. But she believed knowing in advance took some of the magic out of it, some of the glorious mystery. So, she had told the people doing ultrasounds not to tell her. She and Derek had names picked out for both sexes. Next week, she'd begin her last month of pregnancy. And Derek had agreed that he would no longer keep his cell phone turned off when he was at work. He said that he would not go anywhere without his cell phone turned on. But that was then, and this was now, and she wanted him to come home to supper.

At some point during the last couple of hours, her annoyance had turned to concern, and in the last half hour, the concern had morphed into fear. Finally, she couldn't take it anymore. So she had — she didn't like to call it "waddling," but that's really how she walked now. No, she had "walked ponderously" to her car, gotten in, and driven to Derek's office. She parked around back where the employees parked, leaving the good spaces out front for the patients. Using her key, she let herself in the back door, opened it quietly, and listened. She didn't want to come upon Derek unexpectedly. Some of the procedures that he did were very delicate, and surprising him in the middle of them could be catastrophic. She listened and heard nothing, not the sound of voices or the "burring" sound equipment made when he was working. The vacuum/water sprayer was on, she could hear that, and it was always turned off after hours.

She went down the hallway from the back door. Derek's office was on the right, and she glanced in, but the light wasn't even on in there. He had come in to do some kind of emergency procedure, not to hang out and play Candy Crush on his computer.

She made her way down the aisle between the cubicles. There were six of them. She passed the first, which was empty, as was the second. Then she saw something dark spilled on the floor in front of the third. What in the world? What had somebody spilled that they'd just left there?

She didn't lean over and examine it, though, because leaning over to do anything, given that she didn't bend at the waist anymore, was uncomfortable. But the smell was familiar.

Blood.

Tanisha stepped into the doorway of the cubicle and followed with her eyes the trail of blood back into the cubicle.

Nothing for Tanisha Jefferson would ever be the same again.

Lying on his back in a puddle of blood was Derek, and something ... an elevator, the icepick thing he used to lift a tooth up so he could grasp it with pliers to pull it ... the end of an elevator was sticking out of his left eye.

She didn't command her legs to carry her to where Derek lay. They did it unbidden, and then her knees collapsed out from under her and hit the floor hard, sliding in the blood. She reached her hands toward his face tentatively, but she was afraid to touch him. When she did touch his skin, it was cool. That was not the warm cheek that she kissed every morning as he was listening to the latest podcast. Not the cheek that she'd kissed this morning when he leaned over her to say goodbye.

At some point, Tanisha started screaming.

She was unaware of screaming until her throat was so raw she couldn't make any more sound. That's when she noticed the vibration on her wrist. Her Apple watch. Derek had insisted she turn on "fall detection" in the emergency SOS app. He was like that, so caring and concerned for her welfare. Had always been, even before she got pregnant.

As she looked at the watch, the vibration turned to a buzzing sound, and she realized she had not done what you had to do to deactivate the falling app. Particular motions always set it off, like flipping a sheet out to put it on a bed. Then she had to tell the watch that no, she hadn't fallen, she was fine. She hadn't done that. After a while, if you didn't do that, the app on the phone dialed 911 and sent an emergency crew to investigate. She stared at it dully, not comprehending what the flashing meant. In fact, she wasn't comprehending anything right now. The world spun around her, and she understood with a sense of gratifying relief that this was a dream. This hadn't really happened. This wasn't real. She had fallen asleep in that comfortable recliner, waiting for Derek to come home and—

Bang, bang, bang!

Tanisha Jefferson looked up. She was sitting on the floor in a puddle of blood beside her husband, who was ... who was ... was...

Someone was banging on the door, and she started

screaming again, making very little sound because she was so hoarse. But screaming was all she could do. It was the only reasonable response to the horror.

Then, there were people in the room. She didn't know how they had come in because she hadn't gone and opened the door. Suddenly, there was a man crouched beside her, telling her that she needed to move out of the way because he—

Tanisha lost it. She shoved at the man. He was down on a knee, off-balance, and he fell sideways. She threw herself over Derek's body and told the people in the room to leave her alone, to go away, that she didn't want them here.

The man spoke kindly and softly. She didn't know what he was saying, but it didn't matter because nobody was going to touch Derek. No way in hell was Tanisha going to let anybody touch her husband.

Chapter Eleven

IT DIDN'T FEEL like she had slept more than five minutes when Rileigh was jarred awake by the sound of her cell phone ringing. Her eyes popped open, and she felt around frantically on the bedside table to get to it and answer before it had a chance to ring again.

As she grabbed it, she saw the caller ID was Mitch. Her heart sank. He wouldn't be calling her at three o'clock in the morning to ask for her recipe for bean dip. If he was calling now, there was a crisis, and she feared that he would tell her someone else had been murdered as brutally as Jody Hatfield had been.

"Hello?" She said quietly.

"I'm really sorry to—"

Rileigh interrupted him before he got the words out. "What's wrong? What's happened?"

"Another murder."

Rileigh couldn't help a groan escaping from her lips. "Oh no. The Hatfields went after somebody that fast?"

"Not one of the McCoys. Not one of the Hatfields. Not anybody you'd expect."

"Who then?" Rileigh asked, throwing her legs over the side of the bed and feeling around on the cold hardwood floor for her house shoes.

She heard the reluctance in his voice when he continued. "It's Derek Jefferson."

"*Dr.* Jefferson?"

"Yep. Dr. Jefferson has been murdered."

"Oh, Lord."

Derek Jefferson was Rileigh's dentist. Perhaps he was Mitch's dentist, too. The nicest man you ever met. She couldn't imagine a possible motive for murdering him.

"His wife is pregnant, Mitch. She—"

"I know she's pregnant. She's why I need you."

Rileigh was already out of bed, shucking out of the oversized t-shirt she slept in and digging out a pair of socks from her drawer.

"She's the one who found the body," Mitch said.

"Oh, no."

"And she won't let anybody near it."

"You mean she found the body and called 911, but now she won't—"

"She didn't call 911. Her watch has an app on it that summons help if you fall down."

Mitch didn't have to describe what the app did, but she let him keep talking just because she couldn't quite get her breath and she was looking for a mate to a sock that had a hole in it.

Mama had an Apple watch with that app on it, and she hated it because she said it went off too easily. She claimed that all she had to do was change the sheets on the bed to activate the alarm, signifying she'd fallen down. There was something about the motion of snapping a sheet out over the mattress that set it off every time. Rileigh tuned back into Mitch's voice as he finished the explanation. "So, she didn't cancel the emergency call, and it summoned help. Stephanie dispatched Billy Crawford, who went to the location and found Dr. Jefferson's car parked behind the building and his wife's car parked beside it. There were lights on inside, and he knocked on the door, but he could never get anybody to answer. Finally, he went around to the side of the building and broke out a window, unlatched it, and climbed in."

"And when he got inside?"

"Billy said that Mrs. Jefferson was sitting on the floor holding her husband against her big pregnant belly. Blood everywhere. When Billy tried to touch Dr. Jefferson to see if he was still alive — she wouldn't let him near, screamed, and got hysterical. And Billy was afraid … I mean, she's pregnant, he didn't want to…"

"I get it. You're hoping I can talk her off the ledge. I'll be there as fast as I can."

Rileigh finished dressing and then went down the hall as quietly as she could. She didn't think that her mother and sister had been awakened, because she had caught the phone after it had rung only one time. But it was also possible that Jillian had heard it and had simply stayed in her room rather than coming to investigate. It hadn't gone real well between the two of them the last time Rileigh was called out in the middle of the night.

All the way into town, Rileigh was trying to figure out what could possibly be going on. Last night, Jody Hatfield was murdered, and somebody removed his face. Tonight, somebody had killed the dentist. Dr. Jefferson. Could they possibly be related? But how could they be unrelated? How much of a coincidence would that be?

She pulled into the parking lot of the dentist's office, which was now ablaze with rescue squad vehicles. There were red and blue and white lights flashing, making ugly shadows in the trees. She went into the building and spoke to Billy, who was stationed at the door. He nodded his head down the hallway, and she could see the rescue squad members standing around looking into one of the cubicles.

Mitch stepped out of the cubicle when he heard someone greet Rileigh. He came to her and spoke softly.

"She's no better than she was to begin with. She's in some kind of zone somewhere. She still won't let anybody touch Derek's body."

"And you're sure he's—"

"Oh, he's dead, all right," Mitch interrupted. "There's something that looks like an ice pick sticking out of his eye. Gus is on his way."

Rileigh steeled herself with a big breath, then stepped around the corner into the cubicle where Tanisha Jefferson sat on the floor with the body of her murdered husband pulled as far into her lap as she could get it, given that she was at least eight-and-a-half months pregnant.

Rileigh spoke quietly, "Tanisha. It's me, Rileigh Bishop."

Tanisha did not appear to have heard her, so Rileigh walked into the room and knelt down on the floor, keeping a good six or seven feet between them. "Tanisha, Tanisha, can you hear me?"

The pregnant woman turned her eyes slowly toward Rileigh, who could see that she was in severe shock. Tanisha just looked at her, said nothing, just looked.

"Tanisha, you need to let the EMTs see to Derek."

Tanisha shook her head no like a frightened child and hugged his limp body up against her. "No," she said, "nobody's touching him, no."

Rileigh suspected that in Tanisha's mind if she let anybody touch him, it would become real. Somebody else would know about it besides her, and she could no longer deny a reality so painful she couldn't face it.

Rileigh moved closer to Tanisha and knelt down on the floor about two or three feet away. She reached out her hand and touched Tanisha's shoulder. The woman jumped, but it was a surprised jump. Not a wanting-to-get-away jump. Rileigh left her hand on the woman's shoulder, establishing the connection. Then she eased herself down onto her backside so that she was sitting next to Tanisha. She shot a glance at the body in her arms.

"Tanisha," she said quietly, "tell me what happened."

"He didn't come home," Tanisha said, her voice hoarse and ragged. "He was supposed to come home."

"Why was he working on a Sunday night?"

"He wasn't supposed to be working. He got called in."

"Called in, why?"

"Somebody called the answering service and said they had a dental emergency, and Derek's on tonight. He was playing golf, and he just went straight from the golf course to his office. He said he'd be home for supper."

Tanisha said all of that in a kind of dreamy voice. Like it wasn't real to her, not yet.

"Then he didn't come to supper, right?"

"He never showed up. He was an hour late and then two and then three. He had been gone so long that he couldn't possibly have been treating a patient for that long."

"Did you try to call him?"

"He turns his cell phone off when he's working. It's a thing he has." She burped out a little sound that might have been the beginning of a chuckle being strangled into a sob. "Next week, he promised me that he would keep it turned on 24-7 no matter where he was because next week, I'll be …" She looked down at herself, at her belly, at the husband she clutched. And she started to cry. "Oh God. Oh God, please, no. This isn't real."

Rileigh continued to talk, kept her voice soothing. It didn't matter what she said because Tanisha wasn't listening. The woman cried; Rileigh talked. Minutes ticked by. Then Rileigh summoned Mike, the EMT standing in the doorway.

"Tanisha, honey, you have to let us see to Derek."

Tanisha only cried harder. The EMT knelt on the other side of the body from Rileigh and reached out his hand to take hold of Derek's shoulders. He pulled, and for a moment, Tanisha held on tight, wouldn't let him move. But then she relaxed, crying harder as he pried Derek's body out of her arms and rolled him over onto the floor.

There was very little room with the chair, Tanisha and Rileigh, and the body on the floor. So Rileigh scooted out of the way to allow the EMT to take her place.

"Mrs. Franklin, my name is Mike. I'm worried about you. You need to get up off the floor now. You're too far along to be sitting like you are."

She looked at him blankly as if she had no idea what he was talking about.

"Let me help you up," he said. He leaned over and took hold of her arms. Rileigh got up to help, and the two of them got Tanisha Jefferson to her feet.

She stopped crying momentarily and looked back at her husband.

"He came down here to treat a patient. What happened?" Tanisha made eye contact with Rileigh. The pleading look in her eye was absolutely heartbreaking. "What happened?"

Rileigh shook her head. "I don't know, sweetheart, but we'll find out."

Chapter Twelve

WHEN GUS ARRIVED at the crime scene, Rileigh looked up and saw him rushing down the small hallway between the cubicles and the offices.

He didn't greet her with black humor — *I'd have dressed up if you'd told me it was a black-tie murder* — like he usually did to ease the tension of the horror they saw every day.

He didn't greet her at all. Didn't greet Mitch, either. Just made a beeline down the hallway, got to the third cubicle and looked inside. He made some kind of sound, some kind of "ah" groan like he'd taken a blow to the belly. Then he turned his back on the room and stood motionless, shaking his head.

"Gus, are you alright?" Mitch asked.

"No, I'm not alright, I most definitely am *not* alright." His voice was quaking. "I was playing golf with Derek this afternoon, not six hours ago."

"I'm sorry, Gus."

"When I got the call to come to this address, I didn't even think about Derek. I'd just seen him. I assumed it was one of the other dentists, a hygienist, the cleaning lady, or some random stranger — anybody. But when I pulled up in the parking lot, I saw his car."

Rileigh put her hand on his arm. "Maybe you need to sit down for a minute."

"No," he said and exhaled a huge sigh, blinking his eyes as if to hold back the tears that wanted to flow. "No, I'm good."

He turned again and looked at the body lying on the floor. "What was Derek doing down here tonight in his office — do you know?"

"What little we could get out of Tanisha was that he had gotten a call from his answering service that there was some kind of dental emergency, and he was the dentist on call."

Gus groaned again and leaned back against the door frame.

"I saw him get the call," he said, shaking his head. "We were loading up our clubs in the trunks of our cars after the round, and his cell phone rang. He picked it up and just stood there, listening, didn't say a word. He just clicked off, waved at us, and said, 'I'll see you next Sunday.'"

Gus' voice cracked on that last word, and he turned away. "I'll be back. Give me a minute," he said. He went down the hall into the bathroom and closed the door behind him. Rileigh could hear the water running in the sink.

"Do you think he ought to be the one to do the autopsy on his friend?" she asked.

Mitch shrugged. "I don't know if he ought to or not, but knowing Gus..."

Rileigh finished the sentence for him. "He'll do it anyway."

The two of them stood silent, looking at the body on

the floor. The EMTs had moved out of the cubicle to clear the crime scene for Gus.

Gus came back down the hall, drying his face with a paper towel. He went into the cubicle and knelt down on one knee. His eyes raked the cabinets, the floor, the dental chair, and the instruments.

He pointed to a cup lying on the floor. "You need to bag that, Mitch. Might have the murderer's prints or DNA on it."

Mitch had already put on gloves. He pulled out a plastic evidence bag and carefully put the cup into the bag.

"So, the killer used a weapon of opportunity." Gus indicated the thing that looked like an icepick protruding from Derek's eye. "That's a dental instrument, an elevator — you use it to pull a tooth. The killer picked it up and killed Derek with it."

"Meaning the killer didn't come here intending to commit a crime, didn't bring a weapon with him," Mitch said.

"I was assuming the call was a ruse to get him down here," Rileigh said. "You don't think so?"

Gus was still down on one knee, examining the body as he spoke. "When the dentist's office is closed, an answering service answers calls. Derek told me it's just a machine that takes emergency calls, then summons whichever dentist is on call. Men get punched in the face, or kids fall out of a tree after regular business hours." Gus swallowed. "Derek was a damn good dentist. He's been here his whole life, took over his father's practice when the old man retired. Derek started working in the office as a hygienist when he was in high school and came on full-time when he graduated from dental school. He genuinely cared about his patients' welfare. It wasn't just a job to him."

Gus shifted gears.

"So you're saying that the EMS was summoned by Tanisha's watch ... oh, God," he said, as realization hit him, "that means she found the body, right?"

Mitch nodded.

"Is she all right?"

"As all right as you can be when you find your husband dead on the floor," Mitch said. "If you're asking about her condition, she didn't go into labor, but she's understandably freaked out. I got the telephone number for her mother, who picked her up a few minutes ago. I'll go by tomorrow and see if there's anything she has to offer to the investigation. But I doubt that there is. He didn't show up for dinner, and when he didn't, Tanisha went looking for him."

"You don't think he called her and told her who he was meeting?" Rileigh asked.

"He didn't know who he was meeting," Gus said. "The answering service just summons him with a recorded message of some kind. He finds out who they are and what their problem is when he gets here."

"But there's a record of who called the person at the answering service, right?"

"It's not a person, it's a machine."

"There has to be some kind of paperwork somewhere," Rileigh said.

"Derek would have filled out an intake form with all the information you give a doctor's office — name, address, phone, dental insurance. But if the patient was in pain, he'd have waited to do that until *after* he treated them." Gus looked from the floor to the chair and back to the floor.

"From the blood splatter," he indicated the blood on the side of the chair and on the floor next to the chair, "it would seem to me that whoever killed him was *in the chair* at the time. I think it's likely that Derek was leaning over, treating the patient, when they grabbed an elevator off the tray and stabbed him through his eye."

"So, you're saying there was a real dental emergency, that someone came here needing a dentist, and that after they got here, while he was treating them, they decided to kill him," Mitch said.

"Absent any further information, that's the only scenario I can think of."

"But why would you kill the dentist after he fixes what's wrong with you?"

"If it were anybody but Derek, I'd make a joke," Gus said, but there was no humor in him now. He scrubbed his hand down his face. "Crimes of opportunity are sloppy. If you simply decide to kill somebody and then do it, you can't take the care that a murderer does when he's planned it out. There ought to be more evidence."

Mitch indicated the syringe on the tray and the dental instruments.

"If he stuck all that in the killer's mouth, there should be plenty of DNA evidence. Both blood and saliva."

But unless the killer was in some national DNA database, it wouldn't help the police find him. It'd just help prove the case when they did.

Rileigh watched as Mitch pulled out evidence bags and carefully placed each instrument in one, then sealed it.

As Mitch worked, he asked Gus, "Do you know if he had any enemies?"

Gus barked out a sad laugh. "Derek was the nicest human being you ever met, a genuinely good guy. Once, he hit a ball into the rough, went to it, took a couple of practice swings, then hit it onto the green; beautiful shot, six inches from the cup. He had a gimme for par, and that hole was a bitch. Except not. When we'd all putted out, he put down a bogie on his scorecard. I tried to correct him, and he said one of the swings looked like a practice swing, he'd actually been trying to hit the ball and whiffed it. Called an extra stroke on himself!"

"Two bodies in three days," Mitch said, shaking his head.

"You don't think this has anything to do with the death of Jody Hatfield, do you?" Rileigh asked.

"Whoever killed Jody planned to do it. Intended to do it. Brought along the knife to stab him with. Somehow, got him to meet them in the storage room and killed him there," Gus said. "This is a totally different MO, indicating a different killer."

"I don't believe in coincidences," Mitch said.

"Neither do I. But I can't see how these two crimes fit together."

Gus let out a long sigh.

"Derek was so excited about the baby. He knew it was a little girl." Gus' voice almost broke. "Tanny didn't. She had told the ultrasound people she didn't want to know. But afterward, Derek went back and found out. He talked about how he planned to do silly things, like buy her lacy dresses that girls these days hated and probably never wore. But he said maybe she'd play baseball and climb trees. He hoped she'd bring home a frog—" Gus stopped himself. "And now that little girl's going to grow up without a daddy."

Chapter Thirteen

It was mid-morning before Rileigh turned off Bent Twig Road into Mama's driveway. She got out of the car and walked slowly to the house. She felt so bad for Gus. Derek had been a good friend, and to come upon his body like that was so sad.

When Rileigh stepped into the living room, Mama looked up. She had been sitting on the couch, doing what passed for knitting for Lily Bishop: knitting needles and yarn and a ball, a lump of tangled something that Lily thought was a scarf or Afghan, or didn't care that it wasn't. Either way, she seemed to just enjoy the process.

Mama put her finger to her lips, jumped to her feet, and took Rileigh by the arm, dragging her back out onto the front porch.

"Jillian's out feeding the chickens, but I want to be sure she can't hear," Mama said.

"What happened?" Though Rileigh thought she knew what had probably happened.

"She had one of them things again. You know, you told me about them things, them PSD ...*whatever* things."

"Oh, I'm sorry, Mama."

"I don't know what caused it. We were doing the dishes from breakfast and just talking, and she picked up a soapy glass, and it slipped out of her hands and fell to the floor and broke. She reached down to start picking up the glass ... and then she was gone. It's like she wasn't there. She stood up and went running out of the kitchen, out into the backyard, and hid behind the chicken house."

"What did you do?"

"I went running after her and I seen her hunkered down behind the chicken house, and I could tell she was hiding. That's when I remembered what you said about PTSD and how a person who had it thought they were somewhere else, doing something else that they'd done before, and it was bad. She must have been hiding." Mama swallowed. "She must have got away, and she was hiding, and she was scared to death. I wanted to run up to her and grab her up in my arms, but I remembered you said not to touch her."

Mama paused, then repeated, "So, I just walked over to where she was hunkered down behind the chicken house. And I done what you said."

As Mama began to describe her actions, Rileigh went from surprised to stunned to something like slack-jawed wonder. Mama hadn't just remembered what Rileigh had told her to do. She'd remembered *exactly* what Rileigh had said and quoted it back to her verbatim. It was like listening to Buddy describing the cars in the school parking lot after the school festival.

"'*You tell her who you are. Remind her that she's safe where she is.*' You said to say something like, 'Jillian, it's Mama. It's me. Mama. You're here with me and Rileigh at home, in the mountains. And you're safe here.'"

Mama said she squatted down on the ground beside

Jillian, which must have been a feat to behold since she could barely bend over at all because of her arthritis.

Mama continued: "You said, *'If she has her eyes squeezed shut, ask her to open her eyes and keep asking her until she does.'* You told me that with her eyes shut, she was locked in unreality. What I was s'posed to do was help her gradually realize that she was here and not there."

Hearing her own words echoed back to her with such precision gave Rileigh an odd feeling.

"I kept telling her to open her eyes, and it was like she couldn't hear me, so I kept saying it until finally she did."

Mama continued, "Then you said, *'Ask her to look around the room and tell you the colors she sees or name the objects she sees.'*"

So Mama had pointed to the chickens and asked Jillian what they were doing —and kept asking until Jillian said, "Pecking in the dirt."

"I knew she actually saw the chickens then," Mama said. "I knew she'd come back. She stood up, and then she helped me up 'cause I was stuck down there all squatted like that. And she hugged me. Then she just turned and went on into the house. I didn't know what to do then. How do you go on with normal after that?"

"Mama, I am so proud of you!" Rileigh went to her mother and hugged her. "You did just what needed to be done to bring her back."

"Well, it ain't like I had no choice," Mama snapped, "since *you* wasn't here to help me. Why wasn't you here to help your sister when she needed you?"

Rileigh groaned.

"You know Dr. Jefferson?"

"Sure, everybody knows Dr. Jefferson. What about him?"

"He was murdered last night."

"Murdered?" Mama's hands flew to her mouth as she

shook her head. "Oh, you can't mean it, not nice Dr. Jefferson?"

"Yeah. And Tanisha was..." She let out a breath. "Tanisha found the body, and it was really ugly, Mama."

"Why, Tanisha's pregnant, about to have that baby any day now."

"Right. Tanisha found Derek dead on the floor in his office building this morning, but when the EMS got there, she wouldn't let anybody touch him. So Mitch called me and asked if I could come down and talk to her."

Mama let out a sigh. "I guess you had to go then, it being Tanisha and all."

Rileigh took her mother's shoulders in her hands, "Whenever I go somewhere like that, it's always *somebody's* mother, somebody's friend, somebody's son or uncle or father. When I go to help Mitch with a murder, it's because somebody died, and everybody matters."

Mama sat down heavily on the porch rocking chair. "It's been a hell of a morning, hasn't it?"

Rileigh almost choked. Mama never cursed. So, apparently, it had indeed been a hell of a morning.

Then the screen door squawked, and Jillian came out onto the porch. Rileigh thought she looked a little pale but otherwise normal.

"When did you get home, Rileigh?"

Rileigh told her where she'd been and why.

"Derek Jefferson was the nicest young man you ever met in your whole life." Mama shook her head sadly, then got up out of the rocking chair and announced that she was going to go feed the chickens.

Jillian had just fed the chickens, but it would do no good to tell Mama that. But they wouldn't complain about a surprise afternoon snack.

When Rileigh and Jillian were alone on the porch,

Jillian said quietly, "I had another PTSD episode this morning."

"I know. Mama told me. She said you dropped a glass, then ran out and hid behind the chicken house." Rileigh said nothing more. If Jillian wanted to continue, she would. If she didn't, Rileigh wouldn't ask.

"It was the broken glass." She looked knowingly at Rileigh. "Two other girls and I had decided to try to escape. We were in a place where we had a reasonable chance if we could just get out of the room. They left the windows open, with the screens nailed shut. That evening at dinner, I purposefully dropped a glass on the floor, and as I was picking up the pieces, I pocketed a sharp shard that we hoped would be sharp enough to cut through the screen."

"Was it?"

Jillian nodded.

"We used it to slice through the screen near the bottom, then pushed it open from there until we could squeeze out." Jillian took a breath. "We ran, split up, and figured we would give them three different people in three different places to catch rather than all of us together. I didn't make it very far at all. There was a cabana behind the big house, and I ran to it. I was edging around the back of it when I heard screaming. I knew that they had caught either Yvette or Sharla. And I froze. Crawled into the undergrowth in the bushes behind the cabana and sat there like a rabbit waiting for the dogs to run me down."

She said the last part with obvious rage. Rileigh could understand rage tangled up with fear. She'd felt that in battle. But she'd had an army with her, she had been armed, and she had chosen to go there on purpose. None of that was true of the poor kid that Jillian had been when they took her.

"What did Mama tell you?" Jillian asked.

"Just that she found you there and did what I told her to do."

Jillian looked at her questioningly.

"After the first one, I told her you'd have more. Everyone always does. I told her what it was best to do when someone had a PTSD episode in your presence."

"I hate this for Mama," Jillian said and balled her hand into a fist. "I hate that she has to do this for me."

"You can hold up right there, sister of mine. Our mother is so glad to have you home that you could run up and down Main Street in the Forge with your clothes on fire. And she'd be happy to follow along with the fire extinguisher."

There was silence then. Jillian pushed the swing back and forth.

"About counseling …" Rileigh said.

Jillian let out a sigh. "Yeah, I know, I need to do that."

"But it's a can you keep kicking down the road. I am here to testify that the farther you kick it down the road and the longer it takes you to finally open up, the harder it's going to be. Take it from someone who knows."

Jillian looked at her. "Will you go with me?"

"Wouldn't miss it for the world."

"Do you know somewhere I could go?"

The phone book was full of psychologists and counselors. It wouldn't be hard to find one. The trick would be finding a good one.

"Let me do some checking around. I have someone in mind."

Chapter Fourteen

"MOTHER'S DAY Out is the greatest invention since disposable diapers," Georgia said, leaning back in her seat in the Red Eye Gravy Diner, slurping up a double chocolate cookies and cream milkshake with whipped cream and a cherry on top.

Mother's Day Out was an event organized by local churches. Once a month, for a small fee, Mothers could bring their children to the church where volunteers looked after them — made Play-Doh castles with them, built houses out of blocks, read them stories, anything to keep them happy for three hours while Mama ... well, while Mama did whatever she wanted. Many mothers just went home and took a nap.

But Georgia didn't want a nap. She wanted a cheeseburger. She'd just gotten off a lose-twenty pounds-in-twenty-days diet — she'd lost ten — not the traditional low-carb diet where she was allowed to eat sixty carbs a day, but some vegan cleanse, where she was only allowed to eat twigs and bark. She'd spent nineteen of the twenty diet days fantasizing about cheeseburgers.

"When I die, I want to slide into home plate in heaven with the taste of a cheeseburger in my mouth," Georgia said, grinning across the table at Rileigh.

"What are you going to do with the remainder of your three hours of glorious freedom?"

Georgia looked at her watch and got a mock-stricken look on her face. "No, it's only two hours now. Well, rats. Guess that means I can't go to Nashville and take in some cultural sites, like a museum or an art gallery."

"You hate museums and art galleries." Rileigh took a large bite out of her own cheeseburger. "What do you really want to do?"

Georgia sighed. "I think when I leave here, I'm going to go to the grocery store because going to the grocery store with the kids is a lot like having a root canal without novocaine. Then I'll go home and take a nap."

Cookie appeared at their table, notepad in hand. "You ladies want anything else?" Rileigh noticed a bandage on her left arm near her hand.

"Cut yourself?"

"Nope. Frozen pork chop, hot grease … ouchie. Ever get a grease burn?" She sighed, then rolled her eyes and continued dramatically, "They are the *worst!*"

"I think we're good," Georgia said. "Thanks."

Cookie twitched her way back across the room.

"You think that ass is real?" Rileigh asked.

"How can an ass not be real?"

"That's what Mitch said. If you can get breast implants, you can … never mind."

"What's on the Rileigh Bishop To Do list today?"

"I'm going to go see a shrink."

"It's about time. When was it exactly that you realized you're crazy?"

"You'd have to be twice as funny as you *really* are to be

half as funny as you *think* you are." That hadn't come out quite right, and Georgia cocked her head to the side.

"That sounds like Bilbo Baggins's birthday party speech -- 'I don't know half of you half as well as I should like, and I like less than half of you half as well as you deserve.' The hobbits didn't know if it was an insult or not."

Of course, Georgia could quote it verbatim. They'd both read Lord of the Rings so many times they could quote huge chunks of it from memory.

"It was an insult."

"Lame."

Rileigh nodded. "Lame."

"No points."

Rileigh dropped the banter. "This afternoon, I'm going to talk to a psychiatrist I know, Dr. Aaliyah Al-Masri, about Jillian. I met her when I worked for the Memphis PD, and we sort of clicked. I'm hoping she'll take Jillian as a patient."

"All the way to Memphis this afternoon?"

"She has an office in Knoxville now. I called to get Jillie an appointment, and they said she wasn't taking any new patients at the moment. But the receptionist mentioned she was conducting seminars at some kind of symposium in Gatlinburg today. I'm going to pop over there and see if I can talk her into taking Jillian's case."

Rileigh and Georgia looked up as the bell on the diner's front door jingled.

"That's Clive McCutcheon," Rileigh said.

"How do you know him?"

"He's probably the prime suspect in the murder of Jody Hatfield."

Georgia leaned over. "Yeah, I guess he would be, as the head of the McCoys. It's a shame. They used to be friends. Or at least they were when my sister was in high school."

McCutcheon sat down at the bar, and Cookie fell all over herself to get to him, leaning close so he could get a bird's-eye view of that cleavage.

Rileigh shook her head. Well, at least there was one thing to be said in Cookie's favor. She appeared to be an equal-opportunity flirt. If it wore pants, she flirted with it. Whether or not she ever made good on any of the obvious offers, Rileigh had no idea.

"Which sister?"

"Abby." Georgia took another bite of her burger and continued to talk around it. "She was in the same class as Jody Hatfield, Clive McCutcheon, and Travis Bramley from elementary to high school. She said they started being assholes in first grade."

"So they weren't particularly nice human beings, even in grade school."

"Hell no. They were a pack of wolves. The quintessential bullies. There was one kid, I can't remember what his name was, that Abby told me about. Small, red hair, freckles, big, thick glasses. They tormented that kid. Tripped him and swatted him with a wet towel in gym class. He walked around with a perpetual wedgie for six years. He should have just mailed them his lunch money so he wouldn't have to suffer through the beatings when they took it. And in high school—"

"Please tell me you're about to recount the heartwarming story of how the redheaded kid grew up to be tall and strong and beat the shit out of them when they were teenagers."

"Nope," Georgia said. "That kid moved away after eighth grade, so they had to go looking for new prey."

Georgia paused to suck up a straw full of chocolate ecstasy.

"There was this one girl, oh gosh, she was a freshman, and every time Abby came to babysit — Liam was two then, and Eli was just a baby — she'd tell me about this girl ... Stella something, I think. She moved away after her sophomore year."

"Why'd they single her out?"

Georgia took another bite of her cheeseburger, rolled her eyes in her head to signify that she was eating heaven between two buns, then continued. "Let's just call a spade a spade. She was fat. I mean, she made Abby look like a Barbie doll, and in high school, Abby was only... you know... kinda chubby."

All the girls in Georgia's family were "full-figured." But after Abby got married and had children, she'd ballooned up to be the biggest of the lot.

Rileigh cast a glance at Clive McCutcheon, sitting at the counter. He had turned to watch Cookie wait on two of the other guys from the sawmill that he had come with. They were sitting at a table by the window, captivated by her flirting. Usually, beautiful girls let the guys come to them rather than the other way around. Most girls who looked like Cookie wouldn't give the time of day to a beer-bellied guy with a bald head like Clive McCutcheon and his not-ready-for-prime-time friends, but Cookie was all over every one of them. When she came back to the counter to turn in their orders, she leaned over Clive and whispered something in his ear ... and the grin that lit his face would have melted a glacier. Rileigh rolled her eyes.

"That girl is a sunflower, and every male in a fifty-mile radius is a bee," Rileigh said.

"I remember what her name was," Georgia said.

"Whose name?"

"The freshman girl those guys picked out as their victim. It was *Sheila*, not Stella — don't remember her last name, though. And Abby said it wasn't just that she was fat. She was pimply-faced."

"Every teenager is pimply-faced."

"Apparently, she had that kind of acne that makes your face look like ground meat."

Rileigh winced as Georgia continued. "But even if she'd been thin, with good skin, she was just ... unattractive. Had a big nose, wore glasses with thick lenses, had big ears, like, Dumbo ears that even long hair wouldn't hide. Abby said one time she saw Jody in the hallway, and Sheila was getting her books out of her locker, and when Sheila turned around, there he was. He's still good-looking, even now— I mean, he was before somebody ..."

Rileigh waved her hand dismissively and Georgia went on with her story. "But in high school, Jody was an Adonis. He put his hands on either side of her and started nuzzling up against her neck."

"Did she try to push him away?"

"I don't know. I wasn't there, and Abby didn't say. But apparently, he staggered backward and pretended to be sick. Squirted out onto the floor and all over her shoes, whatever he'd been holding in his mouth, a soft drink or something. He pretended to heave and heave, like making out with Sheila was so sickening, he threw up."

"That's awful!"

"Oh, they were brutal. Chanted every time they saw her, 'Piggy, piggy, piggy. Oink, oink, oink.' Did all kinds of awful things to her. She was their primary target, but they had other victims. If you were new or different in some way, God help you. They stole this Korean kid's clothes in the dressing room, then shoved him out into the gym full of people in his underwear. I think it was Kai Tadaka's brother. They tripped him so often, made him spill his tray in the lunchroom that he started bringing his lunch from home and ate at his desk during study hall."

"What assholes!"

Georgia took a final slurp on her milkshake.

"They started in on Sheila when they were juniors, and she was a freshman. And the next year, dear Lord, that was the year they won the state championship. They weren't just jocks, they were absolute royalty at school. And everywhere else, too. They got away with terrorizing their neighborhoods, pulling pranks that were *not* funny. They were untouchable, could do no wrong. It had to have been the peak era of their whole lives."

Georgia nodded at Clive. Cookie was still leaning toward him, cleavage half an inch from his face.

"He was fit, big and tall, with broad shoulders, flat abs, and big muscles. He was the biggest of the three of them."

Now, his belly hung out over the front of his pants so far that he probably had to lift it up to fasten the buckle on his belt.

"If those guys have behaved as adults the way they did as teenagers, half the county probably had a motive to kill Jody Hatfield."

The door to the diner opened, and in strode a young man, tall and muscular. He looked around, scanned the crowd, spotted Clive McCutcheon with his back to him at the bar, and started toward him.

Chapter Fifteen

THE MAN who just walked into the diner grabbed Clive McCutcheon by the shoulder and spun him around on the stool. "You're Clive McCutcheon, aren't you?"

"Uh-oh," Rileigh said, tensing.

"And you're—"

But McCutcheon never had a chance to finish the sentence. The man slammed his fist in a vicious uppercut that caught Clive under the chin and knocked him backward off the stool.

Cookie, who had been standing inches from him, leapt back. Her elbow caught a pitcher of water and sent it spiraling down to the floor. It was metal, so it didn't break; it just bounced and spewed water everywhere.

Obviously, this was one of Jody Hatfield's brothers — probably Buster, the one on the oil rig in the Gulf of Mexico. The one in Germany couldn't possibly be home yet. Rileigh looked around for Big John. She'd seen him earlier, so she knew he was in the building, but he wasn't in here now.

Clive tried to get to his feet, but as soon as he got up on

all fours, Hatfield's brother reared back and kicked him in the side. Must have cracked a rib, and Clive went sliding on the slick floor toward the tables. He slammed into chairs and tables, toppling some and dropping uncleared dishes to shatter on the floor.

Rileigh was surprised by what happened next. She wouldn't have believed somebody Clive's size and shape could recover and move that fast. He leapt to his feet and went charging at Buster Hatfield, punching him in the stomach with a blow that knocked the breath out of him. Buster fell backward, hit a table, and sent everything on it flying—napkins, ketchup, salt, and pepper shakers.

Clive was growling insults as he stood over Hatfield, who lay on his back on the floor. He grabbed Hatfield by the front of his shirt, dragging him upward, then landed a massive fist on the side of his face and knocked him back down again.

Then he reached out and picked up a steak knife off a nearby uncleared table — and *that* dragged Rileigh into the fight.

She had not interfered before because, in Black Bear Forge, fistfights weren't all that uncommon, and she knew that Big John would soon make an appearance and put an end to it. But when Clive grabbed the knife, Rileigh leapt to her feet and pulled the pistol out of the holster on her belt. With the gun in a two-hand grip and trained on Clive, Rileigh said, "Clive, put the knife down *right now*. Drop it!"

He hadn't even noticed her before, but now he whipped in her direction.

"You stay the hell out of this," he said. "This ain't none of your concern."

"You're damned right it's not. It's fine by me if the two of you beat the shit out of each other, but you are *not* going to use a deadly weapon. That is *not* fine by me."

"Shit," he spat the word out, then threw the knife on the floor. It slid away from Buster Hatfield, who had gotten to his feet by then, and as soon as Clive dropped the knife, Buster launched himself at Clive. Rileigh backed off, pointed her pistol toward the floor, and just then, Big John burst through the doors leading into the kitchen. He must have been out behind the building because he usually didn't take this long to break up a fight.

Reaching over and grabbing the baseball bat out of its rack behind the bar, he held it in his right hand as he slammed through the double half-doors that led out into the dining area, then banged the bat down on the top of one of the tables. It made a thunderous *whap* sound, and both the fighting men looked in his direction.

"This fight's over, boys."

"I ain't gonna—" Buster began, but Big John didn't let him finish.

"I said the fight's over. The next person who tries to throw a punch, I'm gonna bust your head open like a cantaloupe. You hear me?" He marched toward them, his eyes flashing, the baseball bat raised in his right hand, ready to slam it down on anyone who decided to challenge him. Rileigh holstered her weapon and watched both men backed away from Big John, who he held out his hand to Clive. "Twenty bucks."

Clive looked at him. "What?"

"I said twenty bucks to pay for the chair you broke," Big John said, nodding to a broken chair.

"I wasn't the one who—"

Big John held out his hand to Buster Hatfield and said the same thing. "Twenty bucks."

"I ain't paying you nothin'—"

Big John took a menacing step in Buster Hatfield's direction, lifting the baseball bat higher.

"I ain't gonna ask again. Twenty bucks. Both of you."

Both men reached into their hip pockets and pulled out billfolds. Clive snatched two ten-dollar bills and threw them at Big John, then turned on his heel and marched out the front door.

Buster Hatfield reached up and wiped the blood off his nose and split lip. He cut his eyes toward the parking lot, where Clive was getting into a car with the other men from the sawmill. "What if I ain't got twenty bucks?"

Big John didn't answer. He just raised the baseball bat an inch or two higher.

Hatfield threw a twenty-dollar bill on the table. "I'll catch him later. That son of a bitch killed my brother."

"Not my problem," Big John said. "Settle your differences somewhere else."

Clive's buddies had gotten up from their table and left. Hatfield turned and headed for the door. Rileigh watched him go, sure there'd be no further altercation in the parking lot because now it was three to one. She could hear Buster Hatfield yelling obscenities at Clive as the sawmill crew drove away.

Everyone in the diner relaxed back into their chairs.

Cookie came around and helped clean up the mess of water on the floor and straightened the tables. Big John picked up the broken chair and hauled it back through the doors into the kitchen area.

Rileigh sat down across from Georgia, whose eyes were wide.

"What?" Rileigh asked.

"Would you really have shot that man?" Georgia asked.

"It wouldn't have come to that," Rileigh said. "Big brutes like that are used to using their strength and size and pure meanness to lord it over other people. They always back down when they see a gun."

"You didn't answer my question," Georgia said, her voice small. "I asked, would you have shot him?"

"If Clive'd gone after him with a knife, I wouldn't have had any choice. But I'd have shot him in the leg. That would have taken the steam out of him."

Rileigh didn't like the look on Georgia's face, and she realized that Georgia had probably never imagined what it was like for Rileigh as a police officer or a soldier. This was the first time she'd seen Rileigh in action, and clearly it was upsetting.

"Hey, look, Georgia, you're freaked. Don't be. Let's calm our nerves with another milkshake. What do you say? I'm buying."

Turning around, she called to Cookie, who had straightened up the mess by then and was back at the other end of the counter.

"We need two new milkshakes — another vanilla and …"

She looked to Georgia. Georgia's face relaxed then. "I want a large Royal New York cheesecake milkshake with extra strawberries."

Chapter Sixteen

As Rileigh drove away from the Red Eye Gravy Diner and headed toward Gatlinburg, she made a bet with herself. She would give Georgia maybe two weeks before she gained back the ten pounds she had worked so hard to lose. You didn't celebrate the end of a diet with a cheeseburger and two milkshakes and have much hope of keeping the weight off.

Rileigh had always been slender, sometimes had to struggle to keep her weight up, not down. She knew it was hard on Georgia, in a constant battle with the body type that ran through her family. Impossible to tell how much was genetics and how much was environment, but every one of Georgia's sisters was overweight. Georgia was the thinnest of the bunch, and that was because she spent all day chasing five kids.

The drive to Gatlinburg was spoiled by road construction that routed Rileigh through Pigeon Forge, which wasn't one of her favorite places. The crush of tourists and ticky-tacky souvenir shops — places that sold a gazillion different flavors of ice cream and bags of saltwater taffy and "homemade" fudge and, of course, the requisite rubber tomahawks and fake fur coon-skin caps — all of it in the shadow of King Kong climbing up the side of a building. It pretty much overwhelmed the senses. Why would anybody drive for hours and hours to get to the most beautiful mountain range in America — the Great Smoky Mountains — and then spend all their time in town buying junk?

Of course, the tourist industry was the lifeblood of the economy. There wasn't much you could do in the mountains except love them. You couldn't farm there, raise livestock, mine coal, or build factories, distribution centers, skyscrapers, or universities. Generations of young people had left to make a living somewhere else. At least some of them got to stay at home now to provide services to the tourists.

Rileigh turned off the crowded streets of central Gatlinburg and wound her way back to a building called the Vicksburg Adult Learning Center, where the symposium she planned to crash was being conducted. She parked and went inside, passing a registration table set up near the front door that dispensed name tags and conference information packets to the attendees of the conference. She called out, "Just came to see a friend," as she walked briskly away before they could ask her who the friend was and if the friend was expecting her.

Then she orbited up and down the hallways of the building, looking at the small placards that had been placed beside the doors of rooms where the seminar was being conducted. She was gratified to see the topic of the seminar that Dr. Aaliyah Al-Masri was conducting: "Using art in the diagnosis and treatment of mental illness."

She looked at her watch. If the seminar was an hour long, it would be over in just a few minutes, so she leaned against the wall beside the door to wait. She soon heard movement inside the room, chairs scooting on the floor and voices murmuring, just before the door opened and people began to file out. She had a prepared speech ready to give when she stepped into the room and found a woman in a dark brown hijab gathering up her things.

"Hello, Dr. Al-Masri," she began. "You might not remember me. My name is—"

The woman turned around, and a broad smile wreathed her face.

"Rileigh!" she cried. "*Forget* Rileigh Bishop? Good luck with that! What are you doing here?"

Rileigh relaxed. She had felt a connection to the woman when they had worked that case together in Memphis. Sometimes, you just clicked with strangers — folks with whom, given time and circumstances, you would have built a deep friendship.

"The way you can read body language, it won't do me any good to make something up, will it?"

The woman's smile broadened. "Probably not. But it might be entertaining if you want to give it a shot." She paused. "How was it you put it ... 'If you're feeling froggy, jump.'"

Rileigh felt herself smile all the way down to her toes.

"Here, walk with me, I don't have another seminar today," Dr. Al-Masri said. "Let's find a place, have some coffee, and get caught up."

They made small talk as they walked to the little cafeteria, with the psychiatrist insisting Rileigh, "Ditch the *Dr.* Al-Masri ... it's just me here, Aaliyah." They got coffee from the table that had been set up for conference attendees with Styrofoam cups and little packets of creamer and sugar. Rileigh hated those little packets because she couldn't drink coffee unless it had a bucket of creamer in it, and it took forever to open all those little containers. When she left the table, it looked like somewhere a small child had just eaten. Grabbing a handful of tiny creamers and sugars, Rileigh led them to a table in the back and set to ripping the tops off the creamer cups while Aaliyah sat down in the chair opposite her with a cup of black coffee.

"I know what happened in Memphis," Aaliyah said, calmly and straightforward, no awkwardness, just friendly concern. "I hated that for you."

"I don't know if you know that I resigned."

Aaliyah nodded. "I tried to keep up with the story as it unfolded, and when the media vultures finally found a new piece of carrion to rip apart and left you alone, I called the department and asked for you, but you had left."

"I came back home. I'm from the Smoky Mountains."

"You told me that. Black Bear Forge?"

"I remember you said to me once — I don't remember what we were talking about, but you said ..." Rileigh paused to get the wording right. "'Home is the place that, when you have to go there, they have to take you in.'"

"*I* said that? Well, good for me. It's probably not original, but it is insightful. I need to write it down, so when the university forces me to write my memoirs, I'll have something to say."

Rileigh dumped one tiny tub of creamer after another into her cup.

"My excuse for coming home was to look after my mother, who has dementia, but the truth—"

"The truth in long johns with the butt flap down?"

Rileigh laughed. "*I* said that? Yeah, I guess I did. Not

particularly insightful, but definitely colorful. And my aunt is waaay crazier than my mother, as in homicidal — she's locked up in a psychiatric hospital. She … you don't want to hear this story, but she tried to kill me with a chainsaw."

"Don't want to hear it? Of course, I want to hear it!"

"I'd be glad to tell it to you, embellishing it with all kinds of exaggerated details to make it gorier. But some other time, maybe. I have something else I'd like to talk to you about."

"If it trumps a homicidal aunt with a chainsaw …"

"This story matters." She took a deep breath. "My sister Jillian …" And that's as far as Rileigh got because she didn't know how to condense the awful into a few concise sentences that would describe it well. She let out the breath. "It's a long story, and I'm definitely not going to tell you all of it. I'm hoping that maybe someday Jillian will. My sister disappeared when I was seven years old. Vanished in a puff of smoke on the day before her wedding, and nobody saw her again for twenty-seven years."

"Ok, that trumps a homicidal aunt with a chainsaw."

"She came home about a month ago, and we discovered that at age eighteen, she had been kidnapped by a sex trafficking ring and had been taken overseas and sold various times to various men for various purposes. And she finally got away."

"Oh my God."

"As you can probably imagine, she's not doing very well emotionally."

"There'd have to be something terribly wrong with her if she could go through something like that and come out the other side without a mark on her. You want me to help her, right?"

"Yes. I called your office, and they said you weren't taking any new patients, so I decided to see if I could catch you and talk you into—"

"I'm not taking any new patients, but I would be glad to talk to your sister if she wants to talk to me."

"She knows she needs to talk to a therapist, but she keeps kicking the can down the road every time I bring it up. She had a PTSD episode the other day that was pretty ugly, though, and I got her to agree to see someone."

Rileigh reached into her pocket and pulled out her phone. "I thought perhaps it would help her to have something to do, so I bought some paints and canvases. These are pictures of some of her paintings." She handed the phone to the psychiatrist, who flipped from one picture to the next to the next. When she was finished, she handed the phone back to Rileigh.

"There is so much anger and so much pain in those paintings."

"And if she keeps pretending it's not there?"

"People who've gone through that much pain and trauma for years generally spiral downward into depression because they have stuffed down rage every day of their lives, and they're afraid to let it out. They're afraid if they ever let go of it, if they ever set it free, it will tear up the whole world."

"Depression ... and then...?"

"I'm not going to lie to you, Rileigh. There is a significant incidence of suicide among survivors of that kind of trauma. I will tell my secretary to slot her in sometime after hours. She needs to start unpacking that load she's carrying around *now.*"

Rileigh reached across the table and took her friend's hand.

"Thank you, Aaliyah." Rileigh didn't intend to tear up.

It happened so quickly she couldn't keep her eyes from welling. "All I want for Jillian is a chance at a normal life."

"It won't ever be normal," Aaliyah said. "That doesn't mean it won't be a good life, but you don't come back to normal from the place where she is. I think I can help her, though. I'll try."

Chapter Seventeen

CLETUS PUGH HAD GOTTEN up early Tuesday morning to come in to work because he knew he wouldn't be able to use that lawnmower until he put a new blade in it.

The last time he'd used it, he'd hoped that maybe he'd get a couple more mowings of the football field. Maybe not the whole field, but at least up to the fifty-yard line. But the more he'd thought about it last night, the more sure he was that he was just putting off the inevitable. He was going to have to change out that blade sometime, and he might as well do it now so it wouldn't take all day to mow the field. A new, sharp blade would make cutting it easy. Mowing with the dull one was like chewing on that grass with dentures.

But the thing was, he hated to have to take that damn thing apart to put a new blade on it. He didn't like doing mechanical things. He was the school district's groundskeeper, and he'd been hired to mow the grass, trim the bushes, and edge around the sidewalks. He hadn't been hired to fix the equipment when it broke down. But if he didn't fix it, it'd take him forever to find somebody else to do it. And in the meantime, that grass would grow so tall, he'd need a bush hog to cut through it.

It was about sunrise when he parked in front of the equipment barn at the high school, reluctantly dragged his toolbox out of the back of his pickup truck, and went inside.

"I just want you to know I ain't happy about having to do this," he said to the green machine sitting silent in the shadowy shed.

Cletus talked to his equipment. If he didn't talk to his equipment, who the hell was he gonna talk to? He wasn't married and didn't have no kids. He liked to go to the Rusty Nail in Gatlinburg every now and again, have some beers, shoot some pool. But he was mostly a solitary man, and that was fine by him. He'd picked it. The thing about talking to a lawnmower was that the lawnmower didn't talk back. It didn't make nasty remarks. It didn't argue with you. It just sat there, mute, and listened to what you had to say.

"I knew this morning I was gonna have to fix you. And I'd be mighty appreciative if you would let me get them screws loose easy. I don't like having to wrestle them things. You wouldn't like it neither, if you was me."

He kept talking to the machine as he took it apart piece by piece. He got down to the blade, then affixed the new blade he'd gotten about a month ago in its place. It took him more than an hour, but that was all right because he couldn't get out and mow until the dew was off the grass anyway. Mowing the football field was his favorite part of the job as a groundskeeper. Mowing on the playgrounds at the elementary schools meant he had to make his way around swing sets and monkey bars and all kinds of other play equipment that had them rubber mat things under them, which wasn't easy to do on a great big riding lawnmower. What he always ended up doing was coming back with a smaller mower and cutting all the places he couldn't get to with the big one.

But the football field? That was just one big swath of grass, and he could go back and forth across it without having to dodge nothing.

He always started between the goal posts under the scoreboard: Bears and Visitors. Got the end zone looking good, then started down the field. He went back and forth across it instead of long-ways down it, cutting between the white stripes, tried to leave as much of the paint as he could for them to use as a guide when they painted the stripes again before the first game.

He had just made his first turn when he glanced up and saw something lying out in the middle of the field. He wasn't sure what it was. His vision had gotten bad, so bad he probably shouldn't still be driving. But how the hell else was he going to get around if he didn't drive? Call an Uber?

He didn't need cheaters like most people his age. He could read just fine. It was things far away he couldn't see well, and that was what made it hard to drive.

Cletus cut all the way across the field, made a turn, and started back, looking over at the big lump in the middle of the field, close to the fifty-yard line. A bag of something, maybe. Whatever it was, he was going to have to move it when he got to it.

Cletus talked to the lawnmower as he chugged along. He'd had a lot of pieces of equipment in his life, and this was by far the crankiest, most annoying, so he let her know it.

"Every time I turn around, I gotta fix something on you. This thing's broken, or that thing's broken. This other piece has come loose. You're pathetic."

He had a chainsaw, though, that he dearly loved. And when he talked to it, it was like he was talking to his girlfriend. He'd say sweet things, enjoyed sharpening the blades on it, loved the rumble and roar. Mostly, he loved how that blade would eat through anything he touched, screeching and carrying on while it sent pieces of wood and sawdust flying every which way. My goodness, it was like a dance.

He got to the end of the row, swung around, and headed back. He could see the lump a little bit better, but still couldn't make out what it was. And he had to concentrate on his driving. You could see the mow marks on the field from the bleachers, and it was a matter of personal pride to Cletus that they were always straight as them white lines.

Who'd put something in the middle of a football field? Hell, it was probably them damn teenagers. Maybe they'd been partying out here. He hated it when they did that. They messed up the grass, something awful. Left beer bottles and the like all over the place. After the last time they made a mess, the sheriff's department took to making nightly swings around the school to make sure there wasn't nobody vandalizing nothing.

He got to the edge of the field, whipped the lawnmower in a U-turn, and started back across, closer now to whatever was laying on the fifty-yard line. He squinted at it, tried to see it better. It looked like a bag of something, maybe a trash bag. But it didn't look like there was trash scattered everywhere.

The lawnmower grabbed hold of something that was

lying on the ground. He heard it whirring around in the guts, then it flew out the side like a missile. If he'd been standing there, whatever that was, a piece of a can or whatever, would have cut his leg off.

"You worthless piece of owl shit," he told the lawnmower. "Don't you know you could hurt somebody doing stuff like that?"

On his next pass, he was closer to the lump, and he eyed it suspiciously because it seemed to be the shape of... of...

He wouldn't let his mind go any farther than that until he got to the side of the field, turned the mower around, and headed back. Now, he was close enough to tell. He gawked at what was unmistakably ... *a body*. When he was even with it, he reached down and killed the engine on the lawnmower, sat on the seat, breathing hard.

Then he got up and walked across the grass to the fifty-yard line. He slowed down as he got closer to the thing that was obviously somebody lying on his back on the fifty-yard line. He kept walking slower and slower. Didn't want to see, but he had to see.

Finally, he got close enough that his old eyes could make it out clear. There was blood everywhere. Cletus's eyes roved from the feet up across the chest, up to the face.

Cletus gasped, couldn't breathe, couldn't scream. He stumbled backward and fell down, then turned around and crawled across the grass back to the lawnmower on all fours.

He'd left his cell phone in the tray beside the lawnmower seat, and he climbed up onto the seat, gasping and crying as he grabbed the phone. Took him three tries to dial 911, but when they answered, "Yarmouth County Emergency Services," all he could say was, "Oh god... oh my god..."

"Sir, what's your name?"

"Cletus Pugh."

"What's your emergency?"

"There's a dead body laying on the fifty-yard line at the football field …and it ain't got no face!"

Chapter Eighteen

RILEIGH HAD to weave in and out among the cars that had converged that morning on the high school football field. You would have thought there was a game. The sheriff's deputies had kept them back off the field, but there was a huge crowd, people actually sitting in the stands. They had come to see the show. Mitch called them looky-loos and rubberneckers — people who enjoyed seeing the misery of others — but Rileigh was a little more charitable. She understood that people were curious, and news had blown through the county like flames through a wheat field that a body had been found on the fifty-yard line at the school. It wasn't surprising that people wanted to come have a look.

She passed by Deputy Tony Hadley, cast an eye around to the spectators, and rolled her eyes. He mimicked the gesture. Mitch stood in the center of the field with Gus, who was down on one knee beside the body. Two deputies, Beau Mullins and Billy Crawford, stood a good distance from the corpse, preserving the crime scene since there was nothing to attach police tape to.

Rileigh had heard the rumors about the condition of the body, that it had no face. But she still wasn't prepared for what she saw when she got there. There was literally nothing but destroyed tissue from his hairline to his chin. No face, no skin. But they had no trouble identifying the body. He was wearing a Haggerty Brothers Sawmill shirt with his name stenciled above the pocket.

She had steeled herself for the sight, but still ... *holy shit!* There'd be no need for an autopsy to determine the exact cause of death. It was obvious. Clive McCutcheon's throat has been sliced literally ear to ear, the wound so deep that the spinal cord was visible. Not trusting her voice quite yet, she pointed toward the horror and looked a question at Gus.

"I'm thinking sulfuric acid, but I'll have to test to be sure. Nobody hauled this body out here," Gus said. "The crime was committed here. Look at the blood. Look at the scuffle marks. Not to mention the fact that Clive McCutcheon is a chunk. I don't know how anybody could have hauled his body here by themselves, and there are no track marks for a truck, a four-wheeler, not even a wheelbarrow."

"Somebody came out here with Clive McCutcheon and cut his throat here on the fifty-yard line, then poured sulfuric acid on his face," Rileigh asked.

"That about covers it," Gus said.

"Who found the body?"

Mitch pointed to an old man sitting on a riding lawn-mower at the edge of the field.

"Cletus Pugh and he's pretty torn up about it."

"Can't say I blame him."

The three were silent, all mulling over variations of the same thought. Rileigh was the first to give it voice.

"First Jody Hatfield, and now, Clive McCutcheon. Both of them, minus their faces. What does that tell us? You remember what Travis Bramley said about Jody — that somebody ripped his face off because he was a 'pretty boy'?"

"McCutcheon called him that, too, when I questioned him," Mitch said. "But I can't imagine anybody ever called Clive a pretty boy. If he ever was, he's sure not now."

"Sulfuric acid is unfortunately easy to come by and pretty much untraceable. You can buy it at Home Depot and Walmart."

"How much would it take to do that much damage?" Rileigh asked.

"You could put enough in a water bottle to have destroyed all that tissue."

Rileigh couldn't help it. She had to look away.

It wasn't that she'd never seen anything ugly before. You didn't do two tours in combat and not see every conceivable destruction of the human body. But even so, the man lying there with absolutely nothing recognizable from his chin up was hard to take.

"Both Clive and Jody were killed where their bodies were found," She said, mostly to have something to focus on besides Clive's missing face.

"Rival gang leaders," Mitch said, "so there's no lack of people with a motive to kill both of them."

"I can put a name on the top of the list of Clive McCutcheon suspects." Both Mitch and Gus looked in Rileigh's direction. "Georgia and I were at Red Eye Gravy yesterday having a cheeseburger."

"I'm going to have to try that place out," Gus said. "Everybody I know tells me it's got the best cheeseburgers they ever ate."

"You won't get an argument from me," Rileigh said. "Clive McCutcheon was there, sitting at the bar."

"Let me guess," Mitch said with something of a grin. "Flirting with the new waitress, Cookie, right?"

"Now, how could you possibly know a thing like that?" Rileigh said in mock wonder.

"If he was male, she was flirting with him."

"That settles it," Gus said. "I gotta get my ass to that diner for a cheeseburger ... and to take a look at the scenery while I'm eating it."

"Beautiful scenery," Rileigh said, "But I think you just about have to get in line behind every other man in Yarmouth County."

"Let's get back to the subject," Mitch said. "You were telling us that you and Georgia had been in the diner while McCutcheon was there."

"Yep. And one of Jody Hatfield's brothers showed up. The one who works on an oil rig off the coast of Louisiana, I think. Buster."

"He got home first."

Rileigh nodded. "He came in the door, walked up to Clive, and started swinging."

"And Big John didn't break it up?" Mitch asked.

"He wasn't in the diner right then. I think he was out in the back, taking the garbage out or something. Everybody in the place was waiting for Big John to show up. Meanwhile, they're knocking down chairs and tables, throwing punches. The usual fare until Clive picked up a knife off a table."

"Uh oh," Mitch said.

Rileigh said, "Yeah, and at that point, I had to get involved."

"You got involved?" Gus said.

She lifted her t-shirt and pointed to her pistol in her

waistband. "I was armed. And I couldn't very well stand there and let somebody get murdered."

"So you pulled a gun."

"Yeah, I did."

"I would have paid cash money to see that," Gus said and grinned, revealing his Madonna Gap.

"Well, I would have charged admission if I'd known you'd find it so entertaining," Rileigh said. "Clive dropped the knife, and Big John showed up then with his baseball bat and threatened to crack heads. He got both of them to pay him $20 for the damage before he kicked them out. McCutcheon had come with some other guys from the sawmill, and they left with him. Otherwise, the brawl probably would have continued in the parking lot."

"So, Buster Hatfield's number one on our list of suspects."

"I'm betting the autopsy will show that the same kind of weapon was used this time as was used on Jody Hatfield."

"A knife with a long, sharp blade," Rileigh said. Mitch had told her about the autopsy report.

"We have Jody Hatfield killed Saturday night in the storage room at the diner and his face torn off. And we have Clive McCutcheon killed out here on the fifty-yard line last night, and his face melted off," Gus said.

"And Dr. Jefferson," Rileigh said carefully. Gus flinched at the name.

"Do you really think these murders are connected to Dr. Jefferson's?" Mitch asked.

"It was a totally different MO," Gus said. "A crime of opportunity. Whoever killed him hadn't meant to kill him when they got there. At least they didn't bring a weapon."

"Both Jody's and Clive's murders were premeditated," Mitch continued. "Somebody planned it out even to the point of bringing along a container of sulfuric acid to destroy Clive's face afterward."

"Yeah, it's hard to believe the same person committed all three murders."

"But it's equally hard to believe the coincidence of three murders in as many days," Rileigh pointed out. "That's a lot of random mayhem in a short period of time."

"Maybe I can turn up something on the autopsy," Gus said.

Rileigh thought about the fact that Gus had had to perform the autopsy on Derek Jefferson and was grateful that this victim had not also been a personal friend of the man who would have to determine how he'd died.

Gus nodded, and the EMTs, who had been waiting with a rolling gurney on the side of the field, rolled it over and began to load up the body.

"The problem with the gang-killing theory is that I can't come up with any obvious inciting incident," Mitch said. "These gangs have been rivals ever since they were formed. Five, eight years ago. Maybe longer. And now, suddenly, they're committing murder. Why now? Something set these gangs on a killing spree."

"Maybe," Rileigh said, considering, "or maybe it didn't start out as a gang thing. Somebody murdered Jody and ripped his face off for some unknown reason. And the other gang retaliated — destroying Clive's face just because Jody's was destroyed, in revenge — so two different killers, tit for tat vengeance."

"Wait a minute," Gus said. The EMTs loading the body stopped, and Gus leaned over and wiped the blood off McCutcheon's right hand, revealing that he was wearing a ring on his little finger.

"The person who killed Jody took his ring, but McCutcheon's gang ring is still there," Rileigh said.

"McCutcheon was a member of 35/Zip, right?" Gus said.

"Yes."

"Then we've just ruled out the possibility of two different killers."

"How so?"

"*This* ring is a Smoked 'Em ring. Dollars to doughnuts says it's Jody's. Travis Bramley said Jody's ring was different from the others, that it had rubies on both sides of the words." The ruby stones were a deeper red than the blood on the ring. "Which would explain why it's on Clive's *little* finger. It wouldn't fit on any other finger because his hand's too big. And it's the only ring on either hand."

Rileigh frowned. "The killer took Jody's ring after he killed him, and put it on Clive McCutcheon's body after he killed him, and then took Clive's 35/Zip ring?"

What was the point of that?

"If we're dealing with a single killer, that suggests the killer might not be a member of either one of the gangs," said Mitch.

"Try to convince them of that. There are what? Twenty-five, thirty guys in those gangs?"

"Easily that," Rileigh said. "I think the Hatfield gang is considerably larger than the McCoys. This could become an all-out war."

"Could that be the point?" Gus mused. "Somebody's trying to pit one gang against the other to start a war? But who'd benefit from a gang war?"

They all were silent as they watched the EMTs wheel Clive's body off the ball field.

Mitch turned to Rileigh. "I have to go notify McCutcheon's family of his death." He paused. "His girlfriend's already been here, got here right after I did. I think she was high on something. We had to restrain her, eventually had to sedate her, and call her sisters to come to get her. So, I'm on the hook for his parents."

"And you probably want some company," Rileigh said.

The two of them turned and walked off the football field together.

Chapter Nineteen

MITCH LOOKED OVER AT RILEIGH, who sat in the passenger seat of his cruiser as they headed toward the address given to them for Clive McCutcheon's parents. He was surprised at how grateful he was to see her there.

Nope, not grateful. It wasn't gratitude at someone helping him perform a difficult task. He was simply glad she was there. He enjoyed her company. It seemed that whatever he was doing, it was better if she was there with him.

The implications of that might be pretty huge if he let himself think about them, but he didn't. He just settled back in the seat and enjoyed.

He could tell that Rileigh's mind was on the case. And that was fine because then she wasn't aware of his constant glances in her direction. Didn't notice, but if he hadn't had to drive to keep that cruiser on the road, he might have just flat-out stared at her.

He didn't have the luxury of that kind of inattention.

"So, here's what we've got," Rileigh said, finally looking over at him. "We have two murders, two gang leaders, same MO with both, killed with the same weapon — we're assuming unless Gus finds something different in the autopsy. And both of them had their faces removed in some way. The faces are the key, but I can't figure out where the lock is."

"There's some kind of message in the faces being removed. It mattered a lot to the killer to do that. It was difficult and gruesome with Jody, and it had to be planned out in advance with Clive. Why go to that much trouble when you could just kill them? Obviously, it was about removing the faces. Why would you want to take away somebody's face?"

"Remove their identity?" Rileigh guessed. But that didn't make sense because the killer had left Jody's wallet and Clive's shirt with his name embroidered on it with the bodies.

"What was it that set the killer off?" Mitch mused as if she hadn't spoken. "There must be some inciting incident, something that's changed recently because these guys have hated each other ever since they got out of high school. But the worst that ever happened was a fistfight, maybe a broken nose or jaw. Certainly not premeditated murder. So, what happened?"

Rileigh shook her head. "No idea."

"We need to do some digging into the lives of the victims to figure out what triggered somebody to kill them both."

"Maybe that's the key," Rileigh said. "*Both*. They're rival gangs. But something pissed off somebody enough to kill the heads of both gangs. So, we're talking an equal-opportunity murderer here, not one of the gang members."

"What about Dr. Jefferson?" Mitch said.

"You got me on that one," Rileigh said. "Like Gus said,

it was a crime of opportunity. It wasn't premeditated. And nothing about the MO fits the killer of the other two. It really seems like the killer didn't decide to murder Derek Jefferson until he got there."

"Obviously, the person who killed him was the person who called the answering service with a dental emergency. But we checked the answering service. It's AI-operated. Not a human being involved anywhere. The calls are not recorded. So, someone called and said they had a dental emergency. And the artificial intelligence told the caller to go to Derek's office at a particular time."

Mitch piloted his cruiser around a hairpin turn, then drove up an incline at an absolutely ridiculous grade and promptly dropped down on the other side of it.

"Let me guess," Mitch said, certain he could smell the brake pads on the cruiser smoking, "There's no radio service here."

"Probably not," Rileigh said.

Mitch flipped the switch on the mic on his shoulder and got nothing but static.

Rileigh shrugged and looked at her cell phone. "I got one bar, so maybe, maybe not. For all the 'unlimited 5G network' hype, there are pockets of real estate in the mountains that are black holes."

Mitch turned off the highway onto the road leading to the McCutcheon's house and immediately stopped at a gate. Cattle grazed in the field behind the fence, and beneath the gate was a cattle guard — a surface of metal pipes above a shallow pit that cows refused to cross because it felt too unstable beneath their hooves.

Rileigh got out of the cruiser and opened the gate so Mitch could drive through. Then Rileigh closed the gate, got back into the cruiser, and they drove another seventy-five yards or so to the house. It was an old house with a wide front porch bounded by a railing. The porch was equipped with rocking chairs and the requisite porch swing.

The family was already gathered at the McCutcheon's home, and the hostility in their eyes was palpable. Mitch and Rileigh were not welcome here, which was fine by Mitch. All he wanted was to deliver the news and leave. This family didn't need any more grief.

He and Rileigh stepped up onto the porch and a large man with arms that were only possible through a lot of workouts and a lot of steroids stepped forward to bar their path to the door. "What are you doing here?"

"I need to speak to Mr. and Mrs. McCutcheon, please," Mitch said.

"They don't need you to tell them what happened. They know somebody done murdered Clive. They know who done it, too."

"I'll ask you to step aside, please, sir. It's my job to inform the family of the death of Clive McCutcheon."

A woman opened the door behind him.

"Leave him be, Dion," she said, gesturing inside. "Come on in and say what you got to say, then get the hell out of here."

Rileigh and Mitch entered the house, which was crowded with people. It didn't matter where you happened to land on the rungs of society in the mountains, what color you were, or how old you were. The traditions were pretty much the same. Close your eyes, and this crowd could have been the people at Chloe Malone's house after she was kidnapped or at Georgia's house when Mason was taken. Though culture and circumstances had tried to rip these communities apart and make these people hate each other, the core traditions remained the same.

Unlike Jody Hatfield, Clive McCutcheon had lived

with his girlfriend in their own home. But someone who lived here had small children because the yard was strewn with little kid toys. Mitch had heard someone say that Clive's sister lived at home with her three children.

"May I speak to Mr. and Mrs. McCutcheon, please?" he said to everybody and nobody.

"Mama don't want to see nobody. Sure as hell don't want to see the sheriff, and neither does Papa. Just say what you got to say and go," snarled a small young woman with a newborn baby in her arms.

"Unless they're *unable* to talk to me, I really would like to speak briefly with the McCutcheons," Mitch said.

Mitch was polite beyond reasonableness when faced with hostility. He'd been trained that way. Law enforcement officers understood that often, the people you spoke to mirrored your behavior and attitude and spoke to you the way you spoke to them. If you were nasty, they got nasty. But as often as not, if you were polite, the people you spoke to were at least civil.

"Go get Daddy," said a woman sitting on the couch. Suddenly a young man burst into the room. He was about eighteen, maybe twenty. Thin but muscular. A kid you could imagine playing basketball, he was quick like that.

"What the hell happened to my brother?" He screamed at Mitch and launched himself at the sheriff. Mitch simply fended him off while family members grabbed his arms to hold him away.

"We don't know what happened to your brother," Mitch said.

"They said somebody put acid in his face. Is that right?"

"I know it's right. I talked to Cletus Pugh, and he seen," someone else muttered.

"Is it right? I just want to know, is it right?" The young

man said, struggling to get away from those who held his arms.

"Yes, that's accurate," Mitch said. There wasn't any sense in trying to soften the blow. They already knew what had happened, and even if they didn't, they'd find out soon enough when they went to the funeral home. "Someone put some kind of acid — the coroner believes it's sulfuric, but he's not sure — on his face after he died."

"Why?" The young man screamed. "Why would they do a thing like that?"

"I don't have any idea," Mitch said. "I wish I did, and if you have any idea, I'd like to hear it. What possible motive could somebody have for doing a thing like that?"

Mitch felt a bit of a shift in the mood of the room. As if in response to what they could see was genuine confusion and concern on his part, the hostility cranked down a notch or two. Not gone, but not quite as close to the surface either.

"We been talking about it," said a man who was standing in the kitchen door with a beer, "and we can't come up with any possible explanation other than just pure meanness."

Mitch knew this might be dripping water into hot grease, but he said it anyway. "Whoever killed Jody Hatfield two days ago destroyed his face too."

The people in the room knew that. Surely, they did. But it appeared that they hadn't put it together with what had happened to Clive until Mitch said that. They looked at each other and started muttering.

"Why?"

"What the hell?"

"No, really, that's a—"

"So, you're saying that the same somebody killed both of them?" the man with the beer asked.

"We don't know that. But we do know that Jody's ring, his gang ring, was taken off his hand after he was killed, and we found it on the little finger of Clive's hand."

"You sayin' Clive killed Jody?"

"No, I don't believe he did," Mitch said and felt the tension in the room lessen again. "That ring didn't fit on Clive's hand."

"He's a sight bigger than that puny Jody Hatfield," someone else said.

"But somebody put Jody's ring on Clive's hand." Mitch said, "I suspect after he died. Then they took his ring."

That caused an explosion of rumbling conversation.

"His gang ring? Somebody took it?"

Mitch nodded. "I haven't had time to ask his girlfriend if perhaps it's at home and he wasn't wearing—"

"He never took it off," snarled the young man who was still being restrained. People had holds on both his arms, but he wasn't pulling toward Mitch any longer. "He wore that ring every day. I don't believe I've ever seen him take it off."

"So that means the killer took it," Mitch said. "And replaced it with Jody's ring."

"Those sick bastards," the young man spit out. "Making a mockery of 35/Zip. Taking his ring. Putting that filthy, Smoked 'Em ring on his hand instead. Those sick bastards."

"But you have to admit it doesn't make sense that someone from the Hatfield gang killed Jody and took his ring," Rileigh said. It was the first time she'd spoken, and it appeared that nobody had noticed her until then, standing slightly behind Mitch. "Smoked 'Em is his gang, isn't it?"

There was only silent rumbling.

"None of it makes any sense," Mitch said. "Just know that I will do everything I can to find—"

"I don't know, and I don't care who killed Jody Hatfield," said a voice from a doorway to Mitch's right. An old man stood there, bent with age. "I just want to know who killed my boy Clive."

"Are you—" Mitch began, but the man waved him to silence.

"I'm Clive's Pa, and you come to tell me he's dead. Fine. You done your job. Now, get out of my house."

Mitch nodded and turned to go, but the young man was suddenly in front of him.

"Leroy, leave him be," someone said to the boy. Mitch tensed, but Leroy didn't raise his hands. Just got in Mitch's face.

"Know this for true, I'm gonna kill me the son of a bitch who killed my brother. I'll find him, and I'll kill him."

Mitch didn't respond, just turned to the others in the room. "I'm sorry for your loss," he said and then ushered Rileigh out the front door.

Chapter Twenty

WHEN RILEIGH SLID into the passenger side of Mitch's cruiser, she didn't know whether to say anything or not. She couldn't decide. What she wanted to say was to tell him what a wonderful job he had done at the McCutcheon's. He had done all the right things, but it was way more than that. The whole was greater somehow than the sum of the parts. It was the strength of his character and maybe the genuineness of his concern that had changed the attitudes of the people in that room. While they hadn't been expecting a "you in a heap a'trouble, *boy*" sheriff with an attitude, they had been expecting cold and uncaring. Instead, Mitch had treated them with concern, respect, and empathy. People respond to that, and those people did.

But Rileigh didn't know if that was too personal a thing to say. She knew that she was perhaps the only person who noticed it and understood the dynamic. Certainly, Clive McCutcheon's relatives didn't.

But they had a different opinion of Sheriff Mitchell Webster when he left than they had when he arrived.

A Friend Like You

"After I drop you off at your car, I'm going to have a conversation with Buster Hatfield, the young man you and Georgia saw in a fight with Clive yesterday," Mitch said.

He hadn't called Rileigh and asked her to come to the football field. She'd just heard about it and went to see if she could help.

But she wasn't his deputy, had no official role to play in this investigation. There was no reason for him to ask her to go with him to talk to Buster. Or anyone else.

"And then?" she asked.

"The suspects, in this case, have to take a number and take a seat. Next up will be Travis Bramley, who swore vengeance for Jody Hatfield's murder."

"Jillian and I are going on a hike this afternoon if it doesn't rain." Rileigh glanced up at the sky as if that would tell her anything. She could only see one tiny swath of it. There could be a thunderstorm, a tornado, or a hurricane on the other side of the mountain, and she wouldn't know it.

"How is Jillian getting along?" Mitch asked.

"Well. There's good news and bad news. The good news is that I've convinced her to go to therapy, and I've made an appointment."

"Good job!" he said. "But when you say the good news, that implies there's bad news. What's that?"

"Bad news is she had another PTSD episode the other day. And Mama was home alone with her."

"How'd Mama do?" he said.

"She was ... amazing. I never dreamed she'd remember anything I told her to do if that happened, but she remembered everything."

"Your Mama's all that and a bag of chips," Mitch said. "Even though the bag is shy a few chips."

"She would do anything, up to and including laying down her very life, to help Jillian."

"Did Jillian tell her what was going on inside her head?"

"No, and just like I told her, Mama didn't ask. But later, Jillian told me. She said that the trigger had been picking up a piece of broken glass off the floor."

Rileigh closed her eyes and squeezed them shut tight before she continued.

"It's so awful and ugly you want to scream. What she flashed back to was a time that she and some other girls had tried to escape, using a piece of broken glass to cut the screen on the window."

"How far did they get?"

"She only made it a short way from the house and then hid in the bushes, afraid to keep running."

"My God," Mitch said. "I can't even fathom that."

"Neither can I. If I thought about it, if I let myself dwell on what happened to her every day and every night for all these years, I think I'd lose my mind. But I can't wallow in that kind of thinking, not when Jillian is trying so hard to get back to normal, to have a real ordinary life after so much of it has been stolen." Rileigh let out a long breath. "So I grit my teeth, I smile, and I tell her that the two of us are going to go to that shrink's appointment together. And today, we're going to go for a hike in the woods."

They drove along in silence for a time. Then Rileigh asked Mitch, "How's Gus doing? *Really* doing?"

"He's hanging in there. He called me with the autopsy report, and he was holding on to himself so tight I might as well have been talking to an automated attendant. He's been over to see Tanisha, and she's falling apart. They'd wanted this baby for so long. And now Derek is dead."

A Friend Like You

"There's no motive for that," Rileigh said, shaking her head. "Nothing makes sense."

"It wouldn't do much for tourism in Yarmouth County if the average person booking a rental home knew the murder rate here," Mitch said.

"Yeah, but it's not like it's crime-related murders. All of these are personal stuff."

Mitch looked at her and raised an eyebrow.

"Well, OK. There were three tourists who died when Sarah Park threw gasoline on them and lit a match. Hard to forget that."

"I think the key to solving these murder cases lies in finding out everything we can about those two guys. Not just now but also when they were connected to each other back in high school. Along with Travis Bramley, who is the last man standing from their trio."

"Does that mean you think he might be the next target?"

"Yeah ... if he's not the killer, it seems like a logical progression, don't you think? If I were Travis, I'd watch my back."

"Georgia says all three of them were the ultimate assholes in school."

"How'd she know what they were like? She wasn't in their class."

"Georgia's got so many relatives, she knows somebody in every graduating class from Yarmouth County High School in the last thirty years. Her sister, Abby, was in the class of 2016 and went to school with all three of those guys from elementary school on up. She said that they were consistent and predictable. They were assholes and bullies every time life gave them an opportunity. And since they were bigger and probably tougher than most of the other people in the class, and there were three of them, they pretty much ruled supreme."

"You know, that doesn't surprise me," Mitch said.

"She told me stories about some kid whose lunch money they stole so often; he should have just mailed it to them and saved himself the beating. And there was a girl who was a freshman, I think, that they just treated abominably. Their neighbors put up with vandalism, pranks, and all manner of ugliness. And, of course, when the Bears started winning football games, they weren't just the biggest and toughest guys around. They were also football heroes. So add to the fear of their strength and reprisals some kind of idiot hero worship for their football exploits. They were gods."

"It's been my experience that guys like that never get over that kind of notoriety. Their egos are so artificially inflated. Then suddenly it's over, the cheering fades, and they find themselves in the stands, not out there making glory runs toward the end zone."

"None of the three of them ever adjusted to that," Rileigh said. "They couldn't let it go, clung to it, lived in those glory years in their minds, and never had careers or families. Just lived suspended there as they got older and fatter. And more pathetic."

"I'm going to dig around in their pasts," Mitch said. "But none of it helps us find the killer of Derek Jefferson."

Rileigh shook her head, "What kind of person does a thing like that?"

Chapter Twenty-One

MITCH WASN'T EXPECTING a warm welcome when he went to the Hatfield house looking for Buster, and a warm welcome was exactly what he didn't get. He knocked on the door, and the woman who opened it didn't look grief-stricken, just pissed off. Jody's mother, he guessed.

"Ma'am, if Buster isn't here, who's driving that pickup truck out there with Louisiana tags?"

She wasn't expecting that question. "Well, it's... I mean it b'longs to Buster, but he left it here and went off somewhere with somebody. I don't know where."

He noticed then that she had no teeth at all on the top and maybe none on the bottom either.

"You're telling me he's nowhere on this property, right?"

"That's what I'm telling you."

"So you wouldn't mind if I had a look around for myself."

"Hell yes, I'd mind. You can't search my property 'less you got a search warrant." She was proud of herself for knowing that.

Mitch let out a long-suffering sigh. "If it's got to come to that, I suppose I'll have to go get one. But, of course, when I get a search warrant, there's no telling what else I might find when I start digging around trying to find Buster."

That was a bald-faced lie, of course. If he got a search warrant, which he couldn't because he had absolutely no grounds for one, search warrants were specific. You were allowed to go looking for a certain thing, not just generally toss the house and see if you could find something illegal.

He doubted very much if the toothless woman standing in the doorway knew that, though, and he was guessing the Hatfields just might have something or other on their property they didn't want the county sheriff to see.

"Go on, then," she said with a shooing motion. "You don't need to get no warrant. Buster's in the barn out back. He's been out there all day. Won't talk to nobody, won't take nothing to eat. Just out there."

Mitch drove his cruiser around to the barn, which was fifty yards or so from the house. It was a big old barn. Obviously had once been a tobacco barn — painted black, with a high-pitched roof where the tobacco would have been hung. But he doubted that there had been any tobacco grown here in twenty years, so the barn had likely been repurposed for some other use. They probably put livestock in it now or maybe stored equipment in there.

He got out of the cruiser, and as he approached the barn, he heard a *Bang!* Instantly, his hand went to his weapon, but that bang didn't sound like a gunshot.

Bang.

He heard it again.

Bang.

That was the sound of a hammer hitting a nail.

Bang. Bang.

Though it was clear whoever was inside was building something, Mitch opened the door carefully and peered inside. The interior was dark because the big bay doors weren't open. The only light came from slits up on the sides of the building, put there to let the air circulate when it had been a tobacco barn. Those slits cast bright arrows of sunshine into the dark interior, lighting up the dust motes hanging in the air.

In the dim light, Mitch could see a figure standing near the back of the barn between two sawhorses. A wide board had been stretched across the sawhorses and the figure was hammering nails into that board. Not building anything, just hammering nails. *Bang. Bang. Bang.*

Mitch opened the door and walked into the barn, left it open so there'd be more light and so it wouldn't seem like he was sneaking up on the occupant.

Bang. Bang.

"Are you Buster Hatfield?"

The man didn't spin around like you'd expect someone to do when they'd been startled. He froze in place, then his shoulders slumped a little.

"Yeah, I'm Buster Hatfield. What do you want?" His voice was gruff, his words slurred. It was amazing he could hit any of those nails with a hammer if he was as drunk as he sounded.

"I'm Yarmouth County Sheriff Mitchell Webster, and I have a few questions for you."

"Why don't you go question them other people?"

The man turned around slowly and looked at Mitch, dropped the hammer onto the floor, then unexpectedly sank down to his knees beside it.

"You didn't come out here to talk to me about Jody because you don't give a shit about Jody. You come here to talk about that McCutcheon guy, the fella who probably killed Jody. Or maybe it was one of the others of them. There's a whole gang full, and it sure was one of 'em killed my brother."

He picked up the hammer that was lying on the boards of the barn floor and began to bang it rhythmically on the boards.

Bang. Bang.

Mitch took a couple of steps forward.

"Mr. Hatfield, we're doing everything we can to find out who killed your brother."

"Bullshit," Hatfield said without looking up, "Don't nobody care that Jody's dead except me and my family and the other members of Smoked' Em. We're going to find out who killed him if we have to kill every damn member of 35/Zip to do it."

He sank down off of his knees, then fell back onto the floor and sat his feet out in front of him, leaned back against the leg of one of the sawhorses.

"You didn't know my brother, did you?" he asked.

"Never met him," Mitch admitted.

"I know there was folks had things against Jody. He was wild and he could be mean as a snake. But he took care of me when I needed it, and I won't never forget it."

The man closed his eyes and kept talking.

"When I was a little kid, I was the youngest. My brothers was all tougher and stronger and meaner than I was. Jody was the oldest, and he kept the others off me. It was hell on a biscuit to be me when Jody wasn't around."

Mitch walked forward and squatted down so that he was more on an eye level with Buster Hatfield.

"I tried to take care of my kid brother," Mitch said. "I tried to protect him."

"It wasn't so much my brothers, it was Papa that Jody

had to protect me from. Papa beat the shit out of me." Buster shook his head. "Every chance he got."

"I can relate to that," Mitch said.

The man's eyes roamed up to Mitch's face, trying to focus on him, but he was too drunk.

"When I was just a kid, seven, eight years old maybe — way too old to be doing it — sometimes, I'd wet the bed. When Papa found out, he'd yank me up, take out his belt, and blister my ass. Left bruises I could feel for weeks. I got where I was afraid to go to sleep. I had a little room up in the attic by myself. It had a slanted low ceiling, so couldn't nobody be comfortable in it but a little kid.

"One night, I woke up in the dark and seen I'd wet the bed, and I was terrified. I didn't know what to do, so I run to Jody's room. He and my other brothers had bunk beds. I woke him up, shook him, and whispered, 'Jody help, I wet the bed.'"

"He rubbed his eyes and sat up, and I said, 'You know what Papa's going to do when he finds it.'"

"'Well, he ain't going to find it,' Jody said and got out of bed. He went to my bedroom, stripped them wet sheets off, got fresh ones from the linen closet and put them on. Then he took them stinky wet ones into the laundry room, stuck them in the washing machine, put in some soap, and turned it on. I mean, it was the middle of the night, and Papa or Mama or one of the other kids could have walked in on us at any time, but nobody did. We got away with it. We washed the sheets, dried 'em. They was still damp, but we folded them and put them in the linen closet under a bunch of others. Then Jody told me to come back to bed with him, to sleep in his bed. He was afraid I'd wet again, and all that work woulda been for nothing. So I slept with him.

"After that, every night I'd go to bed in my bed up in

the attic, and then I'd come downstairs and crawl in bed with Jody and sleep with him. I never did wet the bed while I slept with Jody. The other brothers picked up on it after a while. But they didn't say nothing because they knew Jody'd beat the shit out of them if they did."

The man looked up into Mitch's eyes with tears running down his face.

"Jody done that for me for years, 'til I was old enough to control my bladder and not piss on the sheets. And then … I remember it was an Easter Sunday morning, and Mama rousted us out because she decided the whole lot of us was gonna go to church. We were Chri-easters."

Mitch knew the term — Catholics who only went to church on the two holy days in the year.

"Everybody was running around trying to find matching socks and underwear that didn't have holes in it. I asked Jody to help me tie my tie. He got behind me and was pulling on it, trying to get the knot square, and I said, 'I think I'm okay now.'"

"He didn't know what I was talking about.

"'You know what I mean.' I said, and I didn't look at him. That's why I picked then to tell him, because I didn't want to have to look into his eyes when I said it. 'I'm going to be sleeping in my own bed tonight.'"

"'You sure about that?' He said, 'I'm sure.' I tried to laugh a little bit, but I couldn't pull it off. 'If I screw it up and Papa comes after me with that belt, I ain't gonna let him beat me.'

"Jody didn't say nothing, wondering if I could defend myself if Papa took after me. And I guess he decided that I could and he didn't need to worry about me, or that if I couldn't, he'd come to my rescue … or that I really was old enough not to wet the bed anymore. After that, I never slept with him no more. Then he moved out of the house, and my other brothers moved out, and it was just me. Daddy only ever come after me one more time after that. He was drunk, and I dropped something or spilled something, I don't know what it was. But he come at me with his fists and I was near big as he was. Papa ain't very big. He makes up in meanness what he lacks in size. I grabbed him by the collar and slammed him up against the wall, and I said, 'Don't you ever raise your fist to me again, old man, or I will beat you to death.' And he never did hit me after that."

Buster lifted his head, and his jaw quivered as he spoke. "But as God is my witness. I believe that old man would have beat me to death if it hadn't been for Jody. I think he'd got so mad at me for wetting the bed that he'd just lose it and keep hitting me and hitting me until I was dead. I'm here today because of my brother Jody. And somebody's done killed him."

He banged the hammer on the floor again. "Murdered him."

Banged it again. "Somebody ripped his face off!"

He banged the hammer again and again and again.

"I will find that son of a bitch, and when I do, I'm gonna beat him to death." He banged the hammer on the floor, then held it out toward Mitch. "I'm gonna beat him until there ain't no bone in his whole body that ain't broke."

Then Buster's chin hit his chest, and he started to cry. He didn't hear Mitch say, "Thank you for your time, Mr. Hatfield," before Mitch turned and left the barn.

Chapter Twenty-Two

MITCH HAD SPENT most of yesterday evening trying to track down Travis Bramley, the second in command of the Smoked 'Em Street gang, who had charged into the diner screaming and making threats about what he would do to the McCutcheons when he caught Jody's killer.

He would have been the first person Mitch went to talk to as a suspect if it hadn't been for the fight Rileigh had witnessed between Buster and Clive yesterday. But after talking to Buster, he'd moved Clive's brother off the suspect list altogether.

Mitch didn't have any luck tracking down Travis Bramley that night. Finally, he gave up and went home.

But shortly after he came into the office Wednesday morning, the dispatcher forwarded a call came that indicated the whereabouts of Travis Bramley — an accident, and one of the cars involved belonged to Bramley. Though when Mitch arrived at the scene, a ranting Travis Bramley maintained it had been no "accident."

He zeroed in on Mitch as soon as he saw him approaching the site where Bramley's vehicle had left Bergamot Drive and would have tumbled end-over-end down the embankment had it not been for a lone pine tree that stopped the fall.

"It's about damn time you showed up," Bramley said. "I got forced off the road. I damn near got murdered."

There were other deputies standing around, but Bramley had demanded to see Mitch, which was fine with Mitch because he wanted to talk to the man anyway.

"They tried to kill me."

"They who?"

Before Bramley could launch into a tirade, Mitch held up his hand. "Specifically, who? A name."

"I didn't see specifically who," Bramley said. "This black truck come at me around that bend on my side of the road and it was either take to the ditch or hit him." He paused. "I should have hit him. He never even slowed down."

"Is it possible that it was just an unfortunate accident?" Mitch said.

"Unfortunate accident, my ass. It was one of the McCutcheons. You know that, and I know that. They come after me because they're pissed about somebody killing Clive."

"Actually, that's exactly what I'd like to talk to you about — somebody killing Clive McCutcheon."

Bramley burst out laughing.

"No shit. You think it was me? You think I was the one that somehow got Clive to go out on the fifty-yard line so I could murder him? Good luck with that theory."

"Where were you last night?"

"Where the hell you think I was? Home in bed."

"Are there any witnesses who could testify to your whereabouts?"

"S'pose you could ask the mattress."

He laughed at his own attempt at humor, then shook his head.

"Hell no, it wasn't me killed him. I would have, as God is my witness, I would have." Bramley paused.

"Why didn't you?"

"Because I ain't sure it was him done it, that's why! One of 'em done it, and one of 'em's gonna pay. But I ain't gonna kill every single 35/Zip until I happen to accidentally get the right one. I want to know who killed Jody! I want to look that son of a bitch in the eye and then choke the life out of him."

"And you don't think it was Clive McCutcheon?"

"I didn't say that."

"So, you *do* think—"

"I don't *know!* Ain't you listening? I don't know that it was Clive McCutcheon. I figured it had to be him at first, ripping off Jody's face so he wasn't a 'pretty boy' anymore. But when I cooled off and started thinking — Jody fooled around with lotsa women who belonged to other men. He loved the challenge of it, taking risks made it more fun. Every one of them men probably wanted to mess up his pretty face. And he's been seeing some woman on the sneak for a couple months now. I don't know who she is, but maybe he got caught. I've had my ear to the ground. Them guys are so stupid, they go to the bar and get drunk and brag, and I've been listening. "

"And you're saying you're hearing that Clive McCutcheon isn't the killer?"

"I didn't hear nothing that told me anything *for sure* about anybody. But the killer knows I'm looking. That's why he tried to run my car off the road. If I knew who was driving that black truck, I wouldn't be standing here jabbering with you. I'd be out beating the bushes to flush him out so I could strangle him." Bramley let out a frustrated breath, "But I don't know. I didn't see nothing."

He gestured off down the side of the embankment where his pickup truck was lodged up against a pine tree twenty feet below the edge of the road.

"Now, how in the hell am I gonna get that truck back up here on the road?"

"You got triple-A?" Mitch asked.

Bramley sneered. "And I ain't got the insurance that little green frog sells, neither, or the duck, or the guy who wrecks things and is all bunged up. I ain't an insurance/Triple-A kinda guy."

He looked around then as if to see if he recognized anybody in the small crowd of people who had stopped to look or had come out as part of the rescue squad summoned when the call came in.

"If you're looking for a ride back into town," Mitch said, "I'm on my way, and you're welcome to ride with me."

"I don't need your help," Bramley snapped.

"Suit yourself," Mitch said. "Six miles, lots of hills — you're gonna work up a sweat."

Mitch turned and started back toward his cruiser.

"All right, dammit," Bramley called after him. "My phone's in my truck. Drop me off at Red Eye Gravy, and I'll get somebody to pick me up there."

"This is your lucky day," Mitch said. "That's where I was headed."

Mitch and Bramley rode along together in silence for a few minutes, Mitch trying to decide which of several questions he had in mind to ask the man. It had been Mitch's experience, at least so far in Yarmouth County, that people tended to be real. He didn't think any of the "suspects" he'd talked to so far was clever enough to pretend emotions they didn't feel. Buster Hatfield, and now Travis Bramley. Neither one of them was faking — they weren't that sharp.

"Have you put it together yet in your head?" Mitch asked.

"Put what together?"

"That of the three star players on the football team that won the state championship in 2016, two of them are dead — and that leaves you the last man standing."

Bramley looked like perhaps he hadn't put that together in his head yet, but he took the news with equanimity.

"Fine, bring it. I'd love for some son-of-a-bitch to try to kill me. See how that works out for 'em."

"Do you think the same person killed both Jody and Clyde?"

"I don't know who killed Clyde McCutcheon, and I don't give a shit. All I care about is finding who killed Jody and making the bastard pay."

When Mitch pulled his cruiser into a parking space in front of the diner, Clyde immediately got out and stomped toward the door, hollering over his shoulder. "Thanks for the ride."

"Oh, I was coming here anyway," Mitch said. Then he nodded to Rileigh Bishop, who had just arrived as Bramley entered the building.

Rileigh parked and came to stand with Mitch. "Did I see Travis Bramley get out of your cruiser?"

"Yep, I gave him a ride into town." She raised an eyebrow. "He says somebody tried to run him off the road this morning."

"Do you believe him?"

"I think he believes it, but I'm not convinced he's right."

Mitch and Rileigh went inside and sat together at the

same table where they had sat the night Jody Hatfield was murdered. It was funny how people did things like that, went to the same table, the same pew, the same armchair. Creatures of habit.

Reba Simmons came to take their order. Cookie was busy behind the bar flirting with Travis Bramley.

Rileigh shook her head. "I swear I've never seen a woman who was attracted to every single man on the planet the way that girl is."

Mitch smiled. "I'm just glad not to be in her sights right now. It's like being on a bare stage by yourself in the spotlight. I don't know if the same thing happens to women that happens to men, but it's awkward when some woman throws herself at you, and you don't quite know how to throw her back."

"I guess it's easier for women," Rileigh mused. "Some guy makes a pass at me, and I'll break his arm."

Mitch laughed. "You wouldn't do a thing like that."

"Watch me."

Mitch opened his mouth to ask if Gus had gotten in touch with her to say he'd be late when Gus opened the door and stepped inside. The dynamic duo became a trio then. Mitch had invited the other two to brainstorm a way to narrow down the list of suspects, reasoning that three heads were better than one.

Chapter Twenty-Three

IT HAD BEEN GUS' idea for them to meet here at the diner. He'd said he was tired of listening to everybody talk about the new waitress, and he wanted to get a look at her himself. For Rileigh's part, she would have preferred to go somewhere else. It was getting old, watching Miss Perfect-Ass throw herself at every male who came through the door.

Rileigh watched Gus' face as he crossed the diner to sit down with her and was surprised that he didn't trip over something since he was not looking where he was going. His eyes were fixed on—drum roll, please! — Cookie.

Gus sat down at the table, barely giving Rileigh and Mitch a glance.

"I thought you had to be exaggerating." He nodded with his chin toward Cookie. "But if anything, you didn't quite do her justice."

"Didn't do her justice?" Rileigh cried.

"You never mentioned the dimple."

"She has dimples?"

"Dimple. Singular. On her right cheek. Didn't you notice?"

"No, I missed that part," Rileigh said. "I must have been putting on my catcher's mitt ..."

"Catcher's mitt?" Gus asked, distracted.

"Getting ready for the imminent wardrobe malfunction."

Mitch rolled his eyes. The remark blew right by Gus.

Though Reba Simmons was waiting on them, as soon as Cookie spotted the newcomer at Rileigh and Mitch's table, she abandoned Travis Bramley at the bar and made for the fresh meat.

"Hello there, you're somebody I don't know," she said to Gus, leaning over to give him a cinematic view of the Twin Peaks.

"Aren't you going to introduce me?" she said. To Mitch, of course. It was as if Rileigh was invisible.

"Gus," Mitch said, "This is Ashlie Neal—"

"Just call me Cookie."

If she says, 'Everybody likes to nibble on a cookie,' I—

Mitch interrupted Rileigh's thought.

"And this is Dr. Gus Hazelton."

"Doctor? Great! Can you tell me a five-letter word where the second letter is Y and that means infant avian?"

"What?" Mitch and Rileigh both said with the perfect unison of a Greek chorus.

"It's in a crossword puzzle. I love word puzzles, cryptograms, word search, rebuses."

"What's a rebus?" Rileigh asked.

"You know ... where you have a picture, and you have to figure out the phrase it represents. Like a picture of a head stacked on top of a pair of high heels."

She paused, looking from Mitch to Rileigh to Gus, all of whose faces were blank.

"Head over heels," Cookie squeaked. "Doncha get it? But this avian thing has me stumped." She leaned even closer to Gus, shoving her cleavage into his face. "Surely, you know it ... *doctor.*"

"Sorry," Gus said, flustered. "All the blood just drained out of my head."

Another customer came in then and saved poor Gus from almost certain suffocation. It was a woman, so Cookie didn't break her neck to get to her. The woman started toward the counter. Rileigh recognized her and gasped, leapt to her feet, and hurried to her.

"Mrs. Considine?" she said, and her favorite teacher of all time turned to her and gave her a bright smile.

"Why Rileigh Bishop. I haven't seen you since ... oh, I think there was a Democrat in the White House, wasn't there? That nice young man with the two daughters."

Rileigh ushered the woman back to the table. Somewhere between fifty and a hundred years old — no way to tell— she was tiny and frail, like a baby bird. She had a mound of white hair at her neck in a bun and skin that looked like tissue paper that had been crumpled and then smoothed out. Her eyes were bright blue, vibrant and alert, and her smile showed the perfect teeth of a double set of dentures.

"I'd like you to meet Mrs. Edna Considine," Rileigh said. "She was my high school English teacher. The best teacher I ever had."

Mitch invited Edna to sit with them, but she declined.

"I only escaped long enough to get a milkshake."

"Where have you been, Mrs. Considine?" Rileigh asked.

"My children moved me to Florida," she said. "It's awful. They have cockroaches as big as mice, and they can fly!"

"Palmetto bugs," Gus said. "I've seen them as big as puppies."

"It's my own fault they kidnapped me," she said, shaking her head. "I did something silly — picked up Bob's car keys when he came to visit and put them in my sock drawer. I don't know why I did that. I'm sure it's a sign of dementia, and I'm okay with that. When you get to be my age, dementia can be fun. But I never dreamed they'd decide I couldn't take care of myself. The next thing I knew, I was listening to seagulls outside my window — such rude birds — instead of meadowlarks and sparrows. But I make them bring me home as often as I can. I have become quite adept at guilt trips." Edna smiled at Mitch and Gus. "So, which one of you is sparking with Rileigh?"

"*Sparking?*" Rileigh said, although she was pretty sure she knew what her former teacher meant — and she couldn't help flushing a little.

"I use as many antiquated words as I can work into a conversation, trying to keep them alive. I know what it feels like to be outdated and behind the times."

"We're here to talk about a case we're working on." Rileigh ignored Gus' smirk and Mitch's sudden fascination with his phone.

"Oh, poo. I'm old. I'm not dead. You're a pretty young girl. And I don't see wedding rings on the fingers of these fine young men." She leaned close to Rileigh and said quietly. "One or the other of them — safe money's on the sheriff — has the hots for you, Rileigh girl."

Then, the old woman headed for the counter to get her milkshake.

As soon as Mrs. Considine was out of earshot, Mitch looked up from his phone with a wry smile. "I see why she was your favorite."

"Perceptive woman," Gus added.

Rileigh wasn't sure why she felt like she had to defend Mrs. Considine, but she did, "That woman made a difference in the lives of every student she taught — and there were hundreds. She kept teaching for another twenty years after retirement age. She let us read wonderful things — Lord of the Rings and C.S. Lewis. But even if she'd stuck to the standard fare like Great Expectations, I would have loved her because she didn't just look at you, she *saw* you. She saw who you were under the pimples and the bad hair and the football jacket."

"Cygnet!" Cookie squealed. "That's it, that's the word. A baby swan." They all turned to look at her. She was talking with Mrs. Considine, who'd obviously solved the riddle.

Rileigh continued. "I was in her class when I was deciding to join the military, and I couldn't talk to anybody about it, not even Georgia. She didn't want me to leave Yarmouth County. Mama certainly wouldn't have wanted me to go somewhere and get shot at. Then, one day, Mrs. Considine asked me to stay after class. When we were alone, she said she didn't want to talk to *me*, but she thought maybe *I* wanted to talk to her. She could tell something was wrong. And I just blurted out that I wanted to join the Army, and everyone I knew would be pissed when they found out. She smiled and asked just one question — why? And for the first time, I had to actually tack words onto the yearning I was feeling. I'd never had to explain it to anybody, so I didn't really have it all that clear in my mind. But as I laid it out in front of Mrs. Considine, I understood. As far as I can remember, she didn't recommend whether I should do it or not. She just listened. When I got home on my first leave, I took her a box of chocolates. But when I came back home last summer, she was gone." Rileigh grimaced. "For her sons to drag her off to Florida just because it's convenient for them ... that sucks. I would never do that to Mama."

"I'm glad you had someone who was there for you," Mitch said. "Must've been hard to leave everyone behind, knowing they wouldn't understand why you were going."

Rileigh nodded, realizing that she'd never really understood how much Mrs. Considine had mattered to her until she'd seen her walk through the diner's front door today. The woman had only been a part of Rileigh's life for a couple of years, but Rileigh wouldn't be the person she was today — wouldn't be sitting here about to discuss a murder right now — if it wasn't for Mrs. Considine's kind, perceptive presence.

She hoped that the guilt trips kept working and that she'd see her former teacher come back for many more milkshakes.

After a moment of thoughtful silence, Gus cleared his throat and brought the conversation around to the murders.

"There were no surprises in Clive McCutcheon's autopsy. The cause of death was exsanguination — both the right and left carotid arteries and the left and right interior jugular veins were cut clean through with a very sharp knife."

"A butcher knife or carving knife?"

"Like the one used on Jody Hatfield, yes. Though it could have been a larger knife, a hunting knife perhaps since it didn't have to fit between the ribs. The acid the killer used to dissolve his face was high-concentrate sulfuric ... and the ring on his finger was Jody Hatfield's." He paused. "His blood alcohol level would have felled a bull elephant, which more or less solves the why-didn't-he-fight-back riddle. He was too drunk to stand upright, let alone defend himself."

"Was Jody Hatfield that drunk?" Rileigh asked.

"Just about."

"I might have come across a possible 'inciting incident,'" Mitch said. "It didn't happen in Yarmouth County, so that's why it didn't come out sooner. Seems members of both gangs were at Smoke Creek Park on the other side of Gatlinburg for the Fourth of July fireworks show last week. I haven't had time to do my own investigation, but from the eye-witness-accounts of a crowd of people who 'didn't see a thing,' Jody Hatfield set off some kind of bottle rocket, and it flew crooked, crashed back down close to where he'd set it off — almost landed in Travis Bramley's lap. And Travis got into a fistfight with Jody over it."

"Fighting among the members of one gang — now that tangles up the Christmas tree lights," Gus said.

"There may be more. Rumor has it that there was already trouble between Travis and Jody over drugs. This is where the information really gets sketchy. Supposedly, the reason both gangs were at Smoke Creek Park at the same time was they were meeting with somebody."

"*Both* gangs?"

Mitch nodded. "It's all rumor, but there's probably at least a kernel of truth in it. Word is, somebody approached both gangs about selling drugs. Jody said absolutely *not*, but Travis thought it was a good idea. If Travis made a deal behind Jody's back—"

"You think Travis was getting ready to stage some kind of coup?" Rileigh asked. "If he was, he deserves an Academy Award for his performance the night we found Jody's body."

"*Who* approached them about drugs, do you know?" Gus asked.

Mitch shook his head. "Because every time I turn around, I hear rumblings about a 'mysterious drug cartel.' If there is such a thing, and they approached *both* gangs, that would be one more reason for the two gangs to be at each other's throats. Maybe the 'why now?' is about eliminating the competition."

Chapter Twenty-Four

"We ain't homeless, are we, Beetlejuice," Sophie said to the mutt perched atop her belongings in the shopping cart. Sophie had a home. She had lots of homes, more homes than most people actually, if you thought about it. She just didn't stay in any of them very long.

"We're multi-homed, that's what it is," she told the dog.

Sophie wandered slowly down the alley pushing the grocery basket filled with her possessions and the dog she loved better than life. Beetlejuice was probably part poodle and part boxer, and maybe had some golden retriever in there somewhere. She found him when he was a puppy. He had a face that was real sweet. It looked like he smiled at her, like his mouth turned up when he liked something. His fur was curly like a poodle, apricot colored and his tail was too, except for the white strand of fur that hung off the end of it. When he wagged his tail, it looked like he was waving a flag. She'd named him Beetlejuice from that movie that she never did see, mostly called him B.J. They'd been together for six years now.

Sophie liked to think of her shopping cart as a mobile

home, since she took it with her from one of her homes to the next. Her home on Monday nights was a screened-in porch on the back of the Fellowship Hall of the Methodist Church. And on Tuesday nights, she usually stayed behind the dry goods store. Herbert Oliver ran the store, and when it got cold in the wintertime, he'd leave that back door unlocked so she could get into the storage room in the back.

"I'm thinking about maybe spending tonight back behind the courthouse." There was big bushes back there and if you tunneled in behind them, it was warm and cozy. "What do you think, BJ?" The dog cocked his head to the side. She loved it when he did that. Looked like he understood every word she said. "Yeah, I agree. Behind the courthouse it is."

Sophie never did know what time it was because she didn't have no watch, but she liked to get up real early, She got woke up where she was sleeping last night in that bus shelter by a car driving by that didn't have no muffler. It rumbled and roared, woke her up and set BJ to barking. It had still been dark, but once she was up, she was up.

Casting her eye over the dumpsters on both sides of the alley, she looked for useful items, things she might need, things she just kind of liked to have. She found clothes sometimes. iIf she liked them, she'd put them on over top of what she was already wearing.

There had been a time when Sophie Krueger had had a house like everybody else, a house with a foundation and doors and windows and a backyard. But she didn't like to think about that very often. Didn't want to be yearning and hankering for something that was gone and she couldn't have it anymore.

After Willard died, she realized he'd done gambled away every dime they had, hocked everything, and mortgaged the house to the hilt, and she wound up with a handful of nothing. When she couldn't pay the mortgage, she wondered where she'd go, fretted about where she'd live, scared about it. Then she seen on television this woman walking down the street, pushing a grocery cart that was full of things. And she thought she could do that, put what mattered to her in a basket and roll it along with her. Walk along and smell the flowers, smile and laugh at everybody. Most of the time, it was a good life.

Oh, there was those that said she was crazy, and she probably was. She seen things other people didn't see. Spirits-like, that come up out of the ground and through the grates down to the storm drains in the streets, but they couldn't talk to her through the aluminum foil she'd put in the floppy hat she wore all the time.

Black Bear Forge looked after their own and Sophie was one of their own, so she didn't want for food very often. Oh, she was skinny and there was things she'd like to eat that she never got anymore, but she wasn't starving and she had enough to feed BJ. If the store manager of McDonald's seen her digging around in the dumpsters, a lot of times he'd come out and give her food. She thought it made him sad, looking at an old woman digging for scraps, but in most ways that mattered, Sophie Krueger was fine with her life.

She pushed her shopping cart with its wobbly wheels toward the dumpster on the left side of the alley behind the doughnut shop. From the dumpster on the right, which was behind the pizza parlor, she caught a whiff of something that smelled like spoiled marinara sauce or cheese going bad. But bad smells didn't bother her. They was just a part of life. Good smells and bad smells. Hot days and cold days. That was just the cycle of it all.

The brick wall at the far end of the alley suddenly lit

up with headlights as a car pulled into the alley. Sophie ducked down behind the dumpster, peeked out around it, and that car pulled up right across from her, right next to the dumpster on the other side of the alley. Somebody got out of the car, but with the streetlight behind them, they was just a silhouette. She seen them go around to the trunk, open it and drag something out of it, something big and heavy. She couldn't see what it was, but it was huge.

BJ was growling like he always done when folks was around that he didn't know.

"Shh!" she told him. "Be quiet!"

But the little dog didn't mind very well. He just kept growling. Sophie moved around quietly to the other side of the dumpster, trying to get a better look at what somebody was dumping that they didn't want nobody to see. It was something big. Maybe it was something she could use.

Peeking around the other side of the dumpster, the streetlight wasn't in her eyes no more and she seen what it was that was bein' unloaded out of the trunk of that car. And she couldn't breathe. She couldn't think. She couldn't move. It was a body. It was a *dead body*, had blood all over it. She wanted to scream, but she couldn't do that. If she did, the person dumping the body would know she was there.

Soon's the body was lying flat on its back, the person who'd dumped it picked up a hammer and started hitting it in the face. Hitting it and hitting it, smashing the face, again and again, blood and gore flying every which way.

That's when B.J. went from growling to barking.

"Shh! B.J., be quiet! Shut up now! Hush!" Sophie hissed. But once that dog got going, there wasn't no shutting him up. He was going to bark until he was done barking. Sophie hunkered down behind the dumpster against the wall, out of sight.

Maybe that person who was dumping that body would

just think there's a little dog over here. Sure, that's what they'd think. Nothing but a little dog —

And then the shaft of light from the streetlight was blacked out. Somebody was standing over her, all backlit, a silhouette. B.J. kept barking as loud as he could.

"Yap, yap, yap, yap!"

Sophie made a little squeaking sound, pitiful.

"I ain't gonna say nothing," she told the silhouette. "I didn't see nothing at all."

And there was B.J. yap, yap, yapping.

The figure took a step toward her. Then time sort of did a funny hopping thing. It froze. Everything seemed to happen in slow motion. Sophie saw the silhouette of a hand raise up in the air. The hand had a hammer in it. And she knew that hammer was gonna come down on her.

She shook her head no and tried to say no. Tried to beg. But her mouth felt too dry to speak. B.J. kept yapping and yapping. Sophie Krueger didn't want to die, she wanted to live.

As the hammer began to come down, all she could do was whimper. "Please don't hurt my dog. Please—"

The world went black.

Chapter Twenty-Five

DOUGLAS BAXTER FOUND the bodies and called it in. By the time Mitch arrived on the scene, Baxter had already told his story to Deputy Mullins and Deputy Rawlings. Mitch crossed the alley to where the man stood with his arms wrapped around himself, almost hugging himself.

"Hey, Doug."

Baxter looked up. "Hey, Sheriff."

"You wanna tell me what happened?"

"No, I don't want to tell you what happened. I don't want to have lived what happened." Doug shook his head and tried to stand up straighter. Doug owned the confectionary shop, Doug's Doughnuts. The bodies had been found in the alley behind it.

"I just heard that little dog barking. I figured it was Sophie's, but her dog doesn't usually bark that much."

Doug was a tall, thin man who Mitch had always suspected would have made a good basketball player if he'd been able to see well enough. The coke-bottle-thick lenses on his glasses gave him an amphibian look. Mitch had heard that Doug had detached retinas and all kinds of other eye issues.

Baxter took his glasses off, wiped his eyes with the back of his hand, then cleaned his glasses on his shirt sleeve and put them back on.

"Sophie Krueger comes around the dumpsters all the time. If I find her out here, I box up a couple of donuts for her. I don't like her crawling around inside the dumpster. People shouldn't have to do that for food." He let out a sigh and continued. "I hadn't seen her in a few days. When I came into work this morning and after I got the place opened up, I heard some yapping coming from out in the alley. It sounded like Sophie's, except B.J. doesn't usually bark."

He cleared his throat. "B.J. stands for Beetlejuice. That's the dog's name."

Baxter continued. "So I turned on the alley light and looked out the back door. There was B.J. yap, yap, yap, yapping on the other side of the dumpster. But something was ... wrong. I don't see very well, but the dog didn't look right, and then I saw there was something smeared all over it like it'd rolled in something. I thought, 'Oh, God, it's rolled around in paint. What a mess it's going to make.' So I went out into the alley, looking for Sophie. And when I got closer to the dog, I could see its coat was smeared with red."

Baxter took his glasses off again and wiped them at his eyes with the back of his hand before putting them back on.

"I took a few more steps and saw a foot sticking out from behind the dumpster." The man shook his head. "I shouldn't have looked. Why'd I give myself that image to carry around for the rest of my life? I should have just dialed 911 as soon as I saw that foot. But I thought for a second that maybe it was Sophie, that she'd fallen and needed help. So I took two more steps and … 'Oh, God, oh, God,'"

Baxter wrapped his arms around himself tighter and hugged.

"There was blood everywhere, just everywhere, and that little dog was sitting in it, barking and barking. I wanted to run away. But when I turned around, I saw … I saw the other body and…"

He had to stop to gather himself.

"I reached in my pocket and grabbed my cell phone, but my hands were shaking, and I dropped it, made a big ole crack in the face of my iPhone. I picked it up, walked to the end of the alley, and called 911, and that poor little dog just kept yapping and yapping."

"Did you see anyone around the bodies?"

"I didn't see any cars or any people. Your deputies already asked me about that."

"I know, but I like to hear it myself."

Mitch told Baxter he could go, then stood in the middle of the alley, looking at the bodies on opposite sides. The man's body was laid out flat on his back, and his face was gone, completely *gone*. Looked like it had been pulverized with some blunt object, a hammer maybe. He was unrecognizable but easily identifiable because of the vitiligo that had splotched his face and arms with white — Travis Bramley. Mitch turned and looked at the old woman curled up on her side between the dumpster and the wall and the little dog that sat beside her, yapping.

He called out to Deputy Mullins, "Call somebody at the animal shelter to come down here and get this dog."

"Yes, sir," Mullins said,

It seemed pretty clear to Mitch what had happened. The old woman had stumbled upon the murder in progress, so the killer had killed her, too. Looked like he had beat her to death with whatever he'd used to kill Bramley.

Gus would have to make an official ruling on the cause of death when he did an autopsy because Mitch couldn't see any wounds on Bramley's body, not on his chest or his neck, anyway. Just the head wounds, his face smashed beyond recognition.

Mitch thought about Buster Hatfield and what he'd said to Mitch the day before. Buster had said that if he ever found out who killed his brother, he'd beat him to death with a hammer and not leave a single bone in his body unbroken. He had remarked that Bramley was causing trouble for Jody. And word had it that Bramley might be trying to take over the Smoked' Em gang. Could Buster have discovered that Bramley killed his brother and beat Bramley to death with a hammer?

But it didn't fit what Buster said. Buster had said he wouldn't leave a single bone unbroken. But Bramley's body seemed to be untouched. Just his face, which the killer could have pounded in after stabbing Bramley. Or shooting him. Or poisoning him.

First Jody, then Clive, and now Travis — it didn't fit that Buster had killed them all.

Mitch shook his head, annoyed by the sound of the little dog yapping, wishing the animal shelter would get here and take it away. He hadn't known the homeless woman, though he'd heard of her and had seen her around. Apparently, she was a harmless old lady that the town kind of looked after, and she made sure she had a place to stay and something to eat. And someone had beaten her to death.

This case just got uglier and uglier.

Gus came striding down the alley toward him, and

Mitch was grateful for the man's presence. Not that he believed he'd be able to shed much light on what was happening, but it was good to have somebody share the burden of figuring it all out with him.

Like Rileigh had in the past. He missed having her as his deputy.

Because she'd been more than just a deputy.

And that was why he couldn't ask her to share this with him. Even though he knew she would willingly drop whatever she was doing if he called.

Why did it have to be so complicated?

"Two bodies for the price of one this time," Gus said, looking from one to the other.

"That's Travis Bramley," Mitch said, pointing to the man lying on his back. "And that—"

"Is Sophie Krueger," Gus finished for him.

"Do you know her?"

"Sure ... everybody knows Sophie. Or *knew* Sophie."

Though Mitch couldn't imagine a circumstance in which Gus would have had a conversation with a homeless woman, he was still mildly embarrassed that it sounded like he was the only person in town who didn't know her.

Gus turned around in a slow circle, taking in the bodies on the opposite sides of the alley next to the two dumpsters.

"Doesn't take a rocket scientist to figure out what happened," Mitch said. "Sophie was in the wrong place at the wrong time."

"But we have a change in modus operandi," Gus said.

"The other two murders were committed on the site where the bodies were found. But this murder was committed somewhere else, then the killer brought the body here."

"And you can tell that how?"

"Just an educated guess, but it appears to me that Bramley has been dead for longer than Sophie. She's only been dead an hour or two. He was killed late last night. So, Sophie must have caught the killer dumping the body, and he killed her, too."

"I talked to Jody Hatfield's brother yesterday, Buster, the one who threatened to kill whoever killed his brother. I found him out in the barn, drunk on his ass. He had a hammer in his hand, and he threatened to find whoever had killed Jody and beat the killer to death with a hammer, break every bone in his body."

Gus raised an eyebrow.

"Is that how Travis died?" Mitch asked.

"Maybe. I'll need an autopsy to be sure. But from what I can see from simple observation, there aren't any other wounds on his body, just his head."

"So why dump the body *here?* I don't see anything significant about this place, do you?"

"No. Might simply be a dump site of convenience. It's in an alley, it's dark."

"Yeah, but that seems awfully random for a killer who seemed to have everything else all planned out. Just driving around town with a body in the trunk, looking for a place to dump it?"

Gus shrugged. "And then poor Sophie was back here dumpster diving and saw."

The little dog continued to yap, and Mitch tried hard not to be irritated by the sound. Then it occurred to him that perhaps that's what got Sophie killed. "Maybe Sophie was trying to hide, and the dog barked and gave her away."

Mitch knelt down beside Travis Bramley's body and picked up his hand. "Check this out."

There was a mark on his finger where a ring had been, but no ring.

"So the killer stole his ring — what for? What's the point the killer is trying to make with the rings?"

Mitch stood. "I have no idea." He sighed. "But now I have another death notification to deliver." He looked at his watch. "And it's not even 10 o'clock in the morning."

A splat of water hit Mitch on the top of the head. It was starting to rain.

Chapter Twenty-Six

EDNA CONSIDINE SAT inside the little bookstore off Westmoreland Street in Black Bear Forge and watched the rain falling outside. The name of the bookstore was Sawa Sawa Books, which the new Kenyan owner told her meant "all good, no worries, just fine." Edna hadn't brought an umbrella, so she'd just had to sit here and wait until it was over. That was fine with Edna. There was no better place to while away a half hour or so than in a bookstore.

"It has started to rain out there," said Kipsang Mwangi.

"It has indeed," Edna said.

"I have an umbrella, dear lady. Should you wish to borrow, I would be honored to lend."

"No, thank you. I'm supposed to meet my son at the bank. I'm in no hurry to get there." She looked out again at the rain and smiled. "Rain's different here than it is in Florida,"

"How so?" Mr. Mwangi said. "Only I have been there once, to a horse race, and I lost my pants."

"Lost your shirt?"

"Yes, so sorry, my shirt."

"Everything's different here than in Florida," she shook her head. She thought about her little town home, a " planned community" called The Palms. Every one of those little ticky-tacky houses reminded her of the houses in a Monopoly game — all of them just the same. Edna had to write her house number in The Palms on the back of her hand when she left so she could find it when she went back.

In her arthritis-gnarled hands, she held a copy of the book she had just purchased — The Gap by Ninie Hammon. Greta Mazokawitz, the only friend she'd made in Florida, had told her the book had "way too many characters to keep track of" and a "sprawling, convoluted plot." Greta had been just about to give up and stop reading when it suddenly became so riveting she stayed up all night to finish it. The last book Edna had stayed up all night to finish was Paradise Lost, and she doubted this Hammon woman was in the same league with John Milton, but she'd give it a try.

Edna listened to the rain, inhaled deeply to smell the pleasant aroma coming in the open window. She concentrated, tried to memorize the scent.

She remembered the first few weeks she'd spent in Florida, how she'd sit in the living room looking out that picture window. Picture windows were meant for houses in a place where there was something beautiful to look at through them. Not just a mirror image of your own house across the street, with somebody sitting in the opposite picture window looking back at you.

Sometimes, she'd look out that picture window and imagine she was looking out over the mountains at twilight, watching darkness *happen* — a progression of images unlike anywhere else in the world. As the sun slid toward the horizon out there on the flat, the shadow of the mountain would travel from one side of the valley to the other every day. Within that shadow were other shadows. The shadows of the trees and the rocks and the bushes. And those shadows simply got darker as night fell, grew thicker and ran together — smaller shadows joining other small shadows to make larger shadows. And as you watched, the light ebbed out of the world almost magically, leaving behind the darkness of all those shadows holding hands.

She shook her head. Mornings in The Palms was a musical time, and she could hear the hinky-tinky melody of the wordless tune playing in her head.

All around the mulberry bush the monkey chased the weasel. The monkey stopped to pull up his sock ...POP goes the weasel.

It was the song that blared out the speakers of the ice cream truck as it made its way among the Monopoly houses. She had been there three years now, and she had never once seen a child run out to that truck with money. She wondered how the man made a living since nobody had cash money anymore. You couldn't go beg Mama for a quarter to get an ice cream. Mama didn't have a quarter. Mama had a credit card. Or Mama had an iPhone wallet or some other techie thing Edna didn't understand. But whatever it was, it *wasn't* something you could go hand to the ice cream man and trade it for an ice cream sandwich. She found that loss infinitely sad.

The rain was lightening up now, just dribbling out of the overcast sky. The clouds would probably blow away by the time she walked the length of Westmoreland Street to the bank where she was supposed to meet her son.

Her visit was almost over, and then they would haul her back to ugly, hot Florida where roaches as big as mice had wings. She would never get used to palmetto bugs. *Never!*

They symbolized all that was ugly and crass and too hot and foreign to her. Roaches with *wings*.

Tucking the book under her arm, she turned back to smile at Mr. Mwangi.

"I'll be going now," she said. "I don't know when I'll be back."

She never knew when she'd be able to come back to the mountains. Only one of her sons still lived in Tennessee, in Knoxville. And it was obviously an imposition of the highest order to ask that he drive her forty miles to Black Bear Forge so she could walk up and down the streets of home.

"Take care of yourself, dear lady," he said. "I am waiting to see you again. Too soon, I hope."

She smiled at that. "Too soon would be fine with me."

Edna stepped out onto the sidewalk. It was still spitting rain, but there were awnings stretching out from the storefronts on the other side of the street. She stepped down off the curb onto the asphalt to cross over.

She had taken three steps, maybe four, wasn't even in the middle of the street, when she heard a grinding sound. She didn't understand why her computer-operated hearing aids had chosen to amplify that one sound. They were supposed to make speech easier to understand by blocking out background noises. She couldn't tell that they did either one. She'd had trouble understanding what that sweet girl in the diner this morning had been saying, had to concentrate and watch her lips to guess what she'd been saying.

Edna glanced in the direction of the grinding noise, and that's when she saw it bearing down on her. It looked enormous, like the front end of an 18-wheeler, though it was just the bumper and chrome on the front of one of those SUVs that everybody drove now.

That was the sound her hearing aid was picking up, the sound of that engine revving as it came toward her. Her old eyes weren't what they'd once been, but her vision was a lot better than her hearing. She looked through the rain-slicked windshield at the person driving the dark-colored SUV. And something inside Edna Considine ripped, tore loose in horror at what she was looking at.

Edna wasn't afraid. In fact, her dying would certainly be a relief to all of her children, so they didn't have to fool with hauling her back and forth to the mountains whenever she wanted to see them.

Not afraid. But sad. Sad at the face she could see. Sad at the look on that face.

Edna didn't feel the impact when the chrome bumper plowed into her. The force flipped her body up and over the vehicle, and she landed with a sickening splat sound on the street behind it. As the vehicle sped away down the street, Edna Considine's sightless blue eyes remained open, the sockets slowly filling with rainwater.

Chapter Twenty-Seven

MITCH ASKED the dispatcher to repeat the call sign and the message that went along with it. That's what the numbers were for, to disguise messages, delivering awful news so that the average person on the street listening to the radio band wouldn't know that officers had been dispatched to a fatal fire or a fatal accident. But Mitch had been here long enough to know as well as anyone that it didn't matter how disguised the radio calls went out. The telephone tree transmitted every bit of information about every situation to anybody who wanted to hear it.

But he did want to be the one to tell Rileigh. So he called her.

Rileigh answered the phone with, "What's up?"

"So, you haven't heard?"

"I don't like the sound of that. Anything other than Travis Bramley, no." Mitch had called earlier to tell her about finding the body. "Mama and Jillian are out in the backyard messing with the rose bushes, so Mama's telephone tree connection is temporarily out of service. What is it?"

"Rileigh, I'm really sorry to have to tell you this. The woman you introduced us to yesterday, Edna Considine. She was just struck and killed by a car on Westmoreland Street."

"What?" Rileigh cried. "You can't be serious." He heard her struggle to take it in. "Struck ... and killed?"

"Yes. A hit and run."

"Tell me what ..." She'd obviously had the air kicked out of her.

"All I've gathered so far is that she was struck by a dark-colored SUV that continued down the street, turned the corner, and disappeared."

"Oh, my God."

"I'm so sorry."

"Out-of-state plates? Tourist?"

"Don't know yet."

"I'll be right there."

Mitch thought to say, *No, don't come.* But, of course, he couldn't say that. Wouldn't say that. Not only did she have a right to come, but she would be a lot of help. She always was.

He just didn't have the right to assume that she would.

"I just have to jot down a note for Mama and Jillian telling them where I'm going."

A note. Mitch got it. That way, she wouldn't have to work her way through the inevitable protests.

She didn't say goodbye. Just disconnected.

* * *

RILEIGH COULD BARELY BREATHE. She had so much enjoyed seeing Mrs. Considine yesterday, loved how healthy she looked, how totally "with it" she was even though she must have been in her nineties, surely. Who knew?

And now...

Rileigh shook her head to clear it. Grabbing a piece of notebook paper, she jotted a note.

"Mom and Jillian, I have to go. Mitch needs my help. I'll be back in time to take Jillian to her psychologist appointment."

Then she ran out the door, leapt into her car, and hurried to Black Bear Forge.

The accident site was controlled chaos as word spread through the crowd that the person lying under somebody's black raincoat on the asphalt in the middle of the street was Edna Considine.

Rileigh rushed up to Mitch. She knew her eyes were pleading with him to tell her that it wasn't so, that he'd been wrong, that it was somebody else. Though she knew none of that would happen, she couldn't help that last-second hope, that grasping at straws before the final blow falls. He met her as she stepped off the curb into the street, and he put his arm around her shoulders. She found that surprisingly comforting. Surprising in the way that it surprised her when he opened a door for her. And it felt good in the same way that felt good.

"I'm sorry," he said. He was holding an umbrella absentmindedly over his head, and it covered her, too. Though the heavy rain had gone from rain to sprinkle to mist. And now it was just the basic smokiness in the air that gave the Smoky Mountains their name.

"What happened? What do witnesses say?"

"There weren't but a couple of people out on the street. It had just stopped raining. Henry Perkins had his back turned, heard the impact, and turned to see the vehicle speeding away down the street. A tourist from Oregon was on the sidewalk nearby, examining a flowerpot she was thinking about buying. She looked up at the sound of the impact and saw a vehicle drive away. Another couple of tourists from Omaha were facing the street but looking at their phones."

Rileigh was fighting tears and ground her teeth to keep from crying.

"The couple from Omaha say the vehicle that struck her was dark red. The tourist from Oregon says it was dark blue. Henry swears it was black. They all concur that it was some kind of SUV."

"So, nobody saw the actual accident."

Mitch pointed up at the traffic cam on a pole nearby. "There are traffic cams every two blocks, so it should have been captured on that camera. I'm just waiting for Billy Crawford to get down here so we can see what the cams recorded."

Rileigh had allowed herself to indulge in a short cruise down Denial River on her way into town. But standing there on the wet street, looking at the lump of a body under the black raincoat, denial was no longer an option. She didn't want to do it, but she stepped to the body, knelt down on one knee, and lifted the coat off the face.

It was Edna Considine. There was not a mark on her face, but her glasses were gone. Rileigh looked around, couldn't see them lying anywhere. Maybe she hadn't been wearing them. And her beautifully perfect hair was mussed a little. Other than that, there was no evidence at all that she had been run down. Rileigh didn't need to look at her other injuries, just gently placed the raincoat back over her face.

When she stood back up, Mitch put his arm back around her shoulders and she stood there, liking the strength of his grip, feeling the warmth of him through her shirt.

Chapter Twenty-Eight

GUS ARRIVED at the accident scene shortly before Billy Crawford made it there with his iPad and worked his electronic magic to get into the system so that they could view the traffic cam footage on it. Gus crossed the street to stand with Rileigh and Mitch beside the body and patted Rileigh on the shoulder.

"I'm sorry," he said. "I know you cared about her."

"It's just crazy. It's like your worst nightmare. It's like every time we turn around, somebody's dying or murdered."

She grabbed hold of herself before she continued because she could hear the sharp edge of incipient hysteria in her voice, and she couldn't let that out into the world. If she let herself think about the horror of this poor little old lady lying crushed on the asphalt, she might cry. And aside from being very unprofessional, she didn't want to cry. She stood beside the body lying on the street under Mitch's upraised umbrella, even though it wasn't raining anymore. It felt good to be up close to Mitch, so she just didn't move as she watched a series of memories play in her mind's eye.

Mrs. Considine sitting at her desk with her hands folded primly in front of her as Rileigh gushed about how glad she was that she'd been assigned to read Lord of the Rings, that she thought it was the best thing she'd ever read ever, ever, *ever*. And Mrs. Considine smiled that little smile of hers that showed up in the crinkles around her eyes.

Mrs. Considine handing out essays that the class had turned in the Friday before. She had walked up and down the aisles, handing each student their essay, looking them in the eye, and speaking a word or two. When she got to Rileigh, she gave her the essay and said, "Good job." Rileigh looked down to see that she'd made an A on the essay— about choosing a career in the military.

Mrs. Considine, the day Rileigh had walked across the stage on graduation night. She shook hands with the principal and walked off the other side of the stage to rejoin the other students in her row, who would then file together back to their seats. Halfway to her seat, she saw Mrs. Considine standing off to the side, out of the way of the marching students in their flowing gowns and those stupid hats with the tassels. And as Rileigh passed by, she took Rileigh's hand, squeezed it briefly, and said, "Good luck, dear."

Mrs. Considine had stood in that spot just so she could have that brief contact with Rileigh — because she knew she was the only person in the world Rileigh had told that she'd be leaving for basic training in two days. Rileigh would have to go home from graduation to tell Mama and Aunt Daisy the news. And she wasn't looking forward to it. But that brief encounter with Edna Considine bolstered her courage. It gave her confidence that even though nobody in her life would like her decision, Edna Considine thought it was a fine choice of careers.

Billy Crawford finally rolled up in his cruiser, got out, and stood with Mitch beside the body.

"Do you want to go somewhere where we can sit down and look at this?" Billy asked.

"No," Rileigh blurted out. He hadn't asked her. But she didn't want to just walk away and leave Mrs. Considine's body lying there on the wet asphalt. "We can look at it here, can't we?"

"Yeah, we can look at it here," Mitch said. "Call it up."

She tried to concentrate as Billy explained the procedure for accessing the traffic cams remotely and pointed out that they couldn't simply call up this particular one. They would have to view the cams' footage in order, starting with the one on the far end of the block.

So they peered at the snowy screen of Billy Crawford's iPad and watched traffic pass down the street from the north end to the south end, turning off on Benjamin Street beside the bank or on Collier Street beside the Charlie Parman Insurance Agency. They watched it begin to rain.

They watched the rain come down harder and harder until it was bouncing on the street like little silver balls. But that part didn't last long. And afterward, it faded away to mist.

The order in which they were looking at the cameras was not the direction from which the vehicle that struck Mrs. Considine had come. They'd have to look at those cameras after they had looked at this one. When they finally got to this traffic cam and turned on the footage, Rileigh steeled herself for what she would see.

Rileigh's eyes were fixed on the sidewalk in front of Sawa Sawa Books as the door opened and Edna Considine stepped out onto the sidewalk. She looked up into the rain and lifted her face to it. And maybe she smiled. The footage was so grainy, the picture so bad that it was hard to tell.

Then she stepped off the curb into the street, took another step or two—

Rileigh still gasped in shock as the black vehicle came out of nowhere, struck Mrs. Considine, and threw her body up into the air, then continued down the street to the corner and turned.

Over the course of the next hour and a half, Rileigh stood in the street with Mitch, Gus, and Billy Crawford and watched the accident from every angle it could be seen on any of the traffic cameras. The one two blocks away that recorded the car from the back was smudged with something, most likely bird shit, and the picture was blurred, though the accident itself was clearly displayed in the window of the furniture store across the street, which mirrored the accident, reflecting the black SUV striking Mrs. Considine and throwing her body into the air like a rag doll.

They were mostly silent as they watched, occasionally pointing out this detail and that. Rileigh let it sink into her consciousness slowly.

From the first moment they saw the dark vehicle, it was clear they would not be able to identify the driver. The SUV had smoked glass windows and windshield. Coming toward the camera, the windshield was a slick silver mirror, and there was no license plate on the front. The view of the vehicle leaving the scene was from the cameras two blocks away, blurred and too far to clearly see the license plate number or even determine the state.

Rileigh wouldn't let herself tack words onto what she saw. She grabbed hold of the words behind her teeth and waited for the others to say something.

Finally, Mitch spoke and said what Rileigh was

thinking and probably what Billy was thinking. Certainly, it was what Gus was thinking.

"Did you see it swerve?" Mitch said. It was a simple question. But it was the only question that mattered.

"Yeah," Rileigh said. "I saw it swerve."

"How about you, Gus?" Mitch asked. Gus nodded. Mitch hadn't asked Billy yet, but he nodded as well.

"It didn't swerve *away* from her," Mitch said, his voice emotionless. "It swerved *toward* her."

The others nodded in agreement.

"So was the swerve accidental or ..." Gus let the question dangle. Nobody had a definitive answer. With the available information, there was no way to tell *for sure*.

Rileigh had been in something like shock. She recognized the feeling. Time had stopped as they watched one traffic cam after another showing the same thing. The vehicle swerving. Only slightly. But undeniably swerving *toward* Mrs. Considine. Not *away from* her.

The ambulance crews came then to gather up Mrs. Considine's body. When Rileigh stepped back, she lifted her head up to the sky. It was blue and cloudless, the slice of it she could see. If it had been raining, she'd have felt the tiny drops on her face like Mrs. Considine had. The last things the old woman ever felt. And Rileigh's sigh was something like a sob.

That was when her eye fell on Mitch's watch. But it couldn't have been right. She lifted her own watch and looked at it. Five o'clock. That couldn't be right. She couldn't have been here for three hours!

But she had been. She'd been here since two o'clock. And Jillian's appointment with the psychologist was at four-thirty. Rileigh was supposed to take her. Rileigh was supposed to go *with* her. And Rileigh hadn't shown up.

Chapter Twenty-Nine

RILEIGH RUSHED to her car and leapt in, promising herself she wouldn't drive ridiculously fast on these wet roads to get home, knowing she wouldn't keep the promise. She pulled out her cell phone and thought about calling and explaining, but it was way too late to explain to Jillian and Mama. And she didn't want to do that on the phone anyway. She wanted to do it face-to-face, but she did need to call Dr. Al-Masri's office. She explained to the receptionist that she had made an appointment for Jillian Bishop at four-thirty today. Something came up, and they'd missed it.

"Yes, it's a special appointment. Dr. Al-Masri penciled it in personally."

Rileigh felt her belly sink. "Yes, I know. Dr. Al-Masri was very kind to give us a special appointment..." The polite "something came up" sounded like she'd decided at the last minute she'd rather stay home and watch Family Feud.

"There was a traffic accident, a fatality, and I was called in by the sheriff to work it."

"Please hold the line," the woman said. Rileigh drove wildly down the slick streets.

Aaliyah Al-Masri's voice came on the phone. "Rileigh, I was looking forward to meeting—"

"I'm really sorry. I really am. It was just—"

"Regina said something about a fatal traffic accident? Are you all right?"

"Yes, I'm fine. This afternoon, an old woman, a former teacher of mine, was run down by a hit-and-run driver."

"Oh, I'm sorry."

"I don't think it was an accident." Rileigh didn't know she believed that until she heard the words come out of her mouth. They had the ring of truth. "I believe it was intentional. It was murder."

"Oh, Rileigh. You knew her?"

"Knew and *loved* her. I got involved in looking at the footage from the traffic cameras and lost track of time. I'm really sorry. Now I'm going to have to go home and explain to my sister that after I twisted her arm up behind her back to get her to agree to go to counseling, I missed the appointment."

"It's fine, Rileigh. We can work something out. How about on Monday, late afternoon. My last appointment will end at six. Can you come after that?"

"Yes. Absolutely. Thank you so much. You've been so very kind."

"It's nothing, Rileigh. And remember, as you're beating yourself up over this —whether she admits it or not, your sister is secretly grateful she got to put it off."

Rileigh smiled at that. Aaliyah Al-Masri didn't miss a trick.

When Rileigh found Mama and Jillian in the kitchen, Mama looked as angry as Rileigh had ever seen her.

"Where have you been, child?" she demanded. "You promised you'd take Jilly to that doctor. You's the one wanted her to go in the first place. And then you don't even show up."

"Mama, Jilly, I'm really sorry."

"That job of yours, always out there running around…" Jillian said.

She looked into Jillian's eyes. "I'm really sorry, Jilly."

"You get up in the middle of the night and go out into dangerous situations. And you're not even a police officer. The sheriff calls, and you go running off and don't even think—"

"It wasn't that I didn't think." Rileigh turned to her mother. "Mama, Mrs. Considine, was run down on the street a few hours ago."

Mama looked shocked, surprised, and disoriented. "What did you say?"

"Edna Considine. She's dead. It was a hit-and-run driver. And … I don't think it was an accident."

Mama's hands went to her mouth. "Oh my God."

"Who is Edna Considine?" Jillian asked, looking from one to the other.

"She was one of my teachers when I was in high school. She was wonderful."

"And the sheriff called *you* to go there because…?"

"Because Mitch and I saw her in the diner yesterday. I introduced him. He knew I'd want to know."

Mama got her wits about her enough then for some of her anger to flood back. "I'm real sorry about Edna. I really am. But your sister—"

"I have already made another appointment." Rileigh began to pace. "I got there, and Mrs. Considine was lying on the street in a puddle of her own blood."

That was a cheap shot, and Rileigh knew it. She was instantly sorry that she'd said it.

"I didn't mean to … it's just I feel so bad. We started looking at the traffic cams to see what had happened. Watching that car … again and again. I'm sorry I lost track of time. And by the time I realized, it was too late."

Mama and Jillian said nothing. Both of their mouths were set in hard lines, but there really wasn't anything left to say.

"Look, I've already called Dr. Al-Masri's office and talked to her. She's agreed to meet you on Monday after she has seen the last of the day's scheduled patients. At six o'clock."

"I'm not sure I still want to go."

"Don't do this, Jill. If you decide you don't want to go to the shrink because I missed this appointment, it's not hurting me. It's hurting you. Please don't."

Jillian pressed her lips together, and Rileigh thought about what Aaliyah had said, that Jillian was secretly glad Rileigh hadn't shown up. Rileigh supposed she was probably right.

"All right, fine. Monday." But she was still angry and had nowhere to put it. "I was really… I got myself all screwed up to do it, and then … oh, never mind."

Jillian got up and stalked out of the kitchen and up the stairs.

Rileigh put her head in her hands and shook her head. "I'm so, so sorry."

"Well, you best make this next appointment," Mama said. "You don't, and I'm gonna snatch you bald-headed."

That was Mama's favorite meaningless threat, but Rileigh hadn't heard her use it in years.

Jillian didn't come down to supper that night. Rileigh went up to her room, but she wasn't there. She saw a light shining out from under the door in Jillian's studio. She thought about going in and talking to her about apologizing again. But there was no sense in reiterating what she'd already said. She couldn't change the fact that she'd screwed it up, and she was sure Jillian understood that she hadn't meant to do it. But still, the message it sent to Jillian was so wrong. The message was: my job, police work, and anything else I decide to do are more important to me than you are. And that couldn't be further from the truth.

Really? Couldn't be further from the truth?

That voice again. The essential Rileigh. *If you want your sister to believe you care what happens to her, then you're gonna have to do better than you're doing now.*

That was the truth ... in long johns with the butt flap down.

Rileigh got undressed and lay in the dark, staring at the ceiling. What with the turmoil at home, she had managed to keep herself from thinking about the accident this afternoon. But now she couldn't help it. The sight of Edna Considine lying on the wet street ... and that black SUV swerving toward her, not away from her. Somebody ran over her on purpose. Rileigh couldn't prove that but absolutely knew it was the truth.

Who would have done such a thing?

Oh, they'd talked about all the ways it could have been an accident.

Dropped cell phone. Spilled coffee. Sunglasses on the floorboard. The list of reasonable reasons why someone would accidentally jerk the wheel was legion.

Rileigh didn't believe any of them.

Mitch had put out a **BOLO** on a dark SUV — as if there weren't hundreds and hundreds of SUVs just like that driving around in the mountains.

Rileigh closed her eyes and willed herself to go to sleep.

She didn't, just lay there with her eyes squeezed shut, hot tears running out of her eyes, down the sides of her face, and into her ears.

She wasn't even sure who she was crying for. Mrs. Considine? Jillian? Or herself?

Chapter Thirty

JILLIAN STOOD with her paintbrush poised above a canvas of dark blue and green swirling lines. She put the brush to the canvas and smeared it back and forth, pressing hard, like she was trying to push the brush through the canvas and out the other side. Black paint dripped off the brush onto the floor. Then, she found herself using the brush as if she were striking someone with it. She slapped the canvas with black paint, splattering it onto her clothes and face, all over the canvas and the drop cloth on the floor. She dug out a hunk of dark green paint and slapped the canvas with it over and over again. She picked up a bigger brush and smeared all those colors together a quarter of an inch thick. She reached for another brush, her biggest one, and found herself drawing her hand back as if it were a dagger, and she intended to stab it into the canvas.

She froze.

Jillian looked at what she had painted, then at the floor, her clothes, and her shoes. Suddenly, all the air whooshed out at her. She felt deflated — whatever had been driving her to strike the canvas with such force no longer compelled her. But it had not left her so much as simply settled back down deep into her where it lived, down into that darkness. There was such darkness inside Jillian.

She reached up with the brush, scraping the chunks of paint off. She tried to smear around what she had created, to mix the big gobs of color she had splattered there. But it was useless. This would be another canvas consigned to the bonfire in the backyard. She looked around her studio and considered that almost every painting she had created, she had consigned to a burning hell. She looked over to the stack of clean canvases leaned up against the wall and thought to herself, "I'm going to need more canvas."

Then she recalled the line out of that movie about a shark. *Jaws*. She and a bunch of giggling teenage girls had seen it at somebody's house, eating popcorn and drinking the beer they'd sneaked out of somebody's refrigerator a thousand lifetimes ago.

She remembered the giant white shark lifting its head up above the water behind the boat, its mouth open, its ragged teeth bared. So much bigger and more monstrous than the sheriff had imagined. And he'd said, "I think we're going to need a bigger boat."

Jillian needed a bigger boat.

More paint. More canvasses. Because what she was trying to paint was infinitely bigger and more monstrous than she'd been willing to admit to herself.

Jillian picked up the rag she used to clean the paint off the handle of the brushes and tried to clean up the gobs of paint that'd landed on the easel and the floor. She wore a smock that Rileigh had gotten her. A pretty painter's smock that was splattered everywhere with paint now. So were her good running shoes and the bottoms of her jeans. It was oil paint. She didn't think it would come out.

Setting the paintbrush in the container where she kept

used brushes, she gave up on cleaning up the rest of the mess, took off her smock, hung it on the hook on the back of the door, and then padded down the hallway to her bedroom. She stopped and looked down the hall toward Rileigh's bedroom. No light shone out from under the door, so she was asleep. No. She was more likely lying in the darkness, looking at the ceiling.

Jillian almost took a step toward that closed door. But she didn't. She just went to her own bedroom and closed the door behind her. Leaned against it. Felt like crying. But simple tears would not have relieved the bleakness inside her. She was sorry that she had yelled at Rileigh. She shouldn't have done it. But she was so upset. She'd also been relieved, though. She hadn't wanted to go to the therapist. Had been dreading it all day long. And sure, she had screwed herself up to do it. So she was mad that she would have to do that again, get herself into the emotional space again to go there. But she'd been granted a reprieve today. And she was lying to herself if she didn't admit she was glad.

After a quick shower that removed most of the paint from her skin ... most of it ... she slipped into the t-shirt she slept in, climbed into bed, and lay there staring at the ceiling, allowing herself to experience the guilt she felt for having yelled at Rileigh. All Rileigh was doing was trying to help. Where was Jillian when Rileigh needed compassion for what she had been through this afternoon? Seeing that old woman she cared about lying crushed on the street. How much compassion had Jillian shown her sister? Rileigh's was a tough ... Jillian almost thought "job," but it wasn't a job. Rileigh wasn't paid to do that. She had gone out to stand on a rain-slick street and look at the dead body of somebody she cared about just because she wanted to help. And her own sister had not been supportive.

She'd tell Rileigh tomorrow she was sorry. She'd apologize and admit to Rileigh that she hadn't really wanted to go anyway and was already dreading going to the new appointment on Monday. She knew Rileigh would understand.

She let out a long sigh. There was so much between them. They once had been so close, but now the years and the memories stacked up between them sometimes seemed too big and forbidding to climb.

But she'd climb them. She wouldn't give up. All those times when she could have, when so many others did, Jillian had refused to give up. She'd been determined that one day she would *escape*. And now that she was home, now that she had what she wanted, she realized she hadn't escaped at all. She had just changed geography. She had packed all her demons up and brought them home with her. The only way to truly escape was to exorcise the demons. And the only way to do that was to dive down deep into her own soul, grab the demons one by one, and drag them out into the light. She had to look at the ugliness. She had to talk to a therapist. Just as Rileigh had insisted she do. Rileigh, who had supported Jillian no matter what.

Jillian needed to get her nose out of her own navel and return the favor.

Chapter Thirty-One

THE WHITE RHINOCEROS scared the shit out of Rileigh.

Oh, she was expecting it. More or less. Mitch had told her there was a rhinoceros in Gus' waiting room. Still, knowing it would be there was not the same thing as stepping out of the bright sunshine of a summer morning in the mountains into the dim interior of Gus' waiting room and coming face to face with the beady eyes of a white rhinoceros that looked like he got up on the wrong side of the bed today and would dearly love to take his frustration out on you.

She couldn't help gasping.

Gus came into the waiting room from the hallway that led back to the examining rooms and his office and saw her flinch.

"Startled you, did it?" He grinned, revealing his Madonna gap.

"It shouldn't have, but the description somehow did not manage to capture how truly horrifying that creature is."

"You know, I thought the same thing when I saw it.

Only what I saw was live, and all I was armed with was a camera and a twenty-thousand-dollar Canon RF 1200 mm lens. If it charged, I was planning to throw the lens at it." His grin widened. "Come on in. Mitch isn't here yet. Would you like some coffee?"

"No, thanks, I'm good." They went down the hallway to Gus' office, which was itself a Gus masterpiece, a true man cave in every sense of the word. On the walls were the trophies of the kills the caveman had made — elkhorns and moose horns and antelope horns, a stuffed boar, and various other creatures — before the caveman swapped shooting big game with a gun for shooting their pictures with a camera.

"Have a seat," Gus said.

Rileigh plopped down into a chair, facing the small loveseat where Gus sat.

"How you doing?" he asked.

"I'm fine considering."

"Considering …"

"What happened to Mrs. Considine yesterday and the firestorm I walked into at home afterward for missing Jillian's counseling appointment."

"How did that go?"

"It could have been a whole lot worse. It was all my fault. I was an idiot, lost track of time, and forgot what was the single most important appointment Jillian had scheduled in thirty years."

"Are you finished beating yourself up for it yet? I mean, if you're not done, I'd be glad to punch you in the face a couple of times."

Rileigh couldn't help smiling then. "Thanks for the offer."

"What are friends for?"

"I did score a minor victory this morning, though. I got

Mama and Jillian — key words in this sentence are 'and Jillian' — to agree to come with me to lunch today at the Red Eye Gravy Diner."

"How did you convince Jillian?"

"I caught her before she had her first cup of coffee — she was in a weakened state — but it was still a challenge."

"Has she been out anywhere?"

"She's been to the grocery store. Not the big one, just a convenience store. And she went to the hairdresser. But other than that ..."

"How'd you talk her into it?"

"This is just my read on it, and I could be totally wrong, but I got the sense that she felt kind of bad for reaming me out last night, and she saw this as a way to make amends. I don't care why. I'm just glad she's going."

"Who's going where?" Mitch asked as he walked into the office.

"Jillian is going to lunch with me and Mama at the diner today."

"Fist bump," he said and stuck out his fist. "Good for you."

WHEN MITCH CAME IN, he sat in the chair next to Rileigh.

Gus pulled the cigar out of his pocket that he always carried in case he had to examine a "floater," ran it under his nose, smelled of it, and then put it back. It was almost an unconscious gesture now.

Then he said, "I asked you guys to come by today because I have a bit of new information that blows all our theories out of the water."

Rileigh held up her hand.

"Can you hold onto that a little longer?" she asked.

"The first thing I want to know is what the two of you think happened to Edna Considine. I barely slept at all last night thinking about it, watching that SUV swerve in her direction."

"It was only a slight swerve."

"I know, I know. It could have been accidental, for all the reasons we've talked about. The driver sneezed or dropped his cell phone or—"

"We've all jerked the wheel accidentally," Gus said.

"And maybe that's all it was, some stupid tourist who just kept going and is now back home in California, where we'll never find the car to examine it, but—"

"Remember what they taught us at the academy?" Mitch asked.

"I didn't go to the same academy you did."

"They both taught us the same thing."

"I didn't go to either one," Gus said. "What was it?"

"Think horse, not zebra," Mitch said. "The simplest explanation is almost always the correct one. And the simplest explanation is that what happened to Edna Considine yesterday was a tragic accident."

"Alright," Rileigh said reluctantly. "Until we find out different."

"I've got deputies canvassing all those businesses on that street this morning, looking for anybody who might have seen something."

"Right. But if the eyewitnesses were tourists, they could be on their way home to Vermont by now."

Gus steered the conversation in another direction.

"We do have four 'zebras,' though — four murders and three of them make some kind of logical sense. At least they did until I completed the autopsy on Travis Bramley. What killed him wasn't a blow from a hammer or a stab wound from a butcher knife. Travis Bramley died from a gunshot wound under his chin."

Rileigh and Mitch were shocked into silence.

"He was ... *shot,*" she finally sputtered?

"For the bullet to remain inside the skull, we're probably talking about a gun not much larger than a .22. I've seen lots of bullets 9 mm or larger blast all the way through. The .22 tends to penetrate and then kind of rattle around inside there, doing massive amounts of damage."

"We've been hanging our hats on a single murderer because the weapon the killer used was the same all three times," Mitch said.

"And the method — stab and slash for Jody Hatfield and just slash for Clive McCutcheon — were essentially the same. But a gun..." Rileigh said. "There's still the fact that all three of the gang members had their faces removed. Why would three different killers all do that same thing?"

"Removed ... but not the same *way,*" Gus said. "Jody's face was skinned off him, Clive's was dissolved by acid, and Travis's was bashed in with a hammer. Why would a single killer use three different methods?"

"And not to throw a turd into the punchbowl," Mitch said, "but we haven't even mentioned the fourth death — that we're certain was a murder — Derek Jefferson, who was killed in an entirely different fashion from any of the other three."

"I've been thinking about Derek a lot," Gus said. "I know it's a stretch to believe that it's merely coincidental that the murder happened when it did. But merely being in the same timeframe isn't enough reason to believe that the murders are connected. And I can't find connective tissue of any kind. Can you?"

Both Rileigh and Mitch shook their heads.

"At the risk of sounding like Captain Obvious here," Gus continued, "this is what we know. We know that on Saturday night, Jody Hatfield was murdered, and his face was ripped off. Cause of death: the heart was cut open, literally, with a carving knife while it was still in his chest. And that's a neat trick to pull off."

Gus held up a second finger. "On Sunday night, some son of a bitch killed Derek Jefferson using one of his own dental instruments for absolutely no reason anybody can fathom."

He held up a third finger. "Three days after Jody was killed, Clive McCutcheon was murdered on the football field's fifty-yard line, his throat slashed with the same *kind* of knife that killed Jody — no way to determine if it was the same knife. A face full of sulfuric acid later, and he was unrecognizable."

He spread his hand out, displaying all five fingers.

"And yesterday, Travis Bramley was murdered, shot in the head with a .22 pistol, his body dumped in an alley, his face destroyed with a hammer. As far as we can determine, the killer also murdered a homeless woman who was a witness."

"There's a sixth if you count Edna Considine," Rileigh said. "But ... I guess we're not counting her death as a murder."

He paused. "I'm thinking outside the box here, okay? Outside the box that the first box came in. What if the three premeditated murders weren't committed by gang members at all? What if they were targeted hits? The drug cartel wanted both gangs to sell drugs for them. They killed off the leaders of both gangs because they turned down the cartel's offer. That would explain the different murder weapons — different murderers."

"And the rings?"

"Red herrings."

"The faces?"

"Drug cartel brutality. In South America, they cut off hands and legs to send a message about crossing them."

"So why kill Travis Bramley? He was on the cartel's side."

"Travis's murder — a single bullet at close range — is the one murder that looks most like a hitman took him out. Must be Bramley pissed them off somehow, or they just wanted to start out fresh, with nobody leading either gang."

"Soooo ... " Mitch pondered. "A mysterious drug cartel that has kept such a low profile until now that nobody is completely sure they even exist. That drug cartel suddenly steps up, for some reason that's as mysterious as they are, and commits four brutal murders in a week? That's the best you got?"

"Do you have a better scenario that pulls it all together?"

"And Dr. Jefferson and Edna Considine?" Rileigh said.

"Coincidence," Mitch and Gus said the word at the same time.

Rileigh swallowed hard.

Edna Considine, a tragic accident. Rileigh wanted desperately to believe that. But there was that Spidey sense itching in her gut that told her there was something more sinister at work than an inattentive driver who'd dropped their cell phone in the floorboard.

Chapter Thirty-Two

RILEIGH TRIED hard to keep things light and airy after she got back to the house from Gus's office to pick Mama and Jillian up for their lunch date at the Red Eye Gravy Diner. Jillian was quiet the whole trip, her countenance a single high, shrill note.

When Rileigh was a little girl, she climbed onto the piano bench and lifted the lid to look down at the little hammers. It was several months before her mother finally gave up on Rileigh's piano lessons, assuming that there were some kids who just couldn't learn to play the piano, and Rileigh was definitely one of them. But the teacher was a nice lady who explained how the piano worked and how the little hammers fell on the taut wires to make the different keys sound. Rileigh had noticed that the keys for the lower notes were attached to wires that were much longer and thicker than the wires attached to the higher keys. She went down to the end of the piano and looked at the keys attached to the notes as far left as you could go. She hit the farthest key and watched that hammer hit a thin wire strung impossibly tight, producing a high sound that almost sounded like crying. She never forgot that image— the gossamer thin wires pulled so taut they were ready to snap, and somehow, that became a metaphor about people for her. When someone was as tense and frightened as Jillian, she thought about that hammer hitting those taut strings and the crying sound it made. Since Jillian had returned to the mountains, Rileigh often thought that for almost thirty years, her sister's life had been a symphony played only with high notes.

For a brief moment, as Mama and Jillian were getting ready to leave the house, Rileigh was afraid Jillian would bolt. Not just refuse to go, but literally go running out of the room, out the back door, and up into the hills. She had such an awful, sad, scared-rabbit look on her face. But Rileigh saw her grit her teeth, and she didn't run. She went with Mama and Rileigh out to the car, looking for all the world like a woman being led to the guillotine.

Rileigh parked in front of the diner and was gratified to see that there weren't many other cars in the lot — the place wouldn't be crowded. Once inside, Rileigh led them to a table in a back corner.

"It smells so good in here," Mama said. "Don't you think so, Jillian? Don't you think it smells good?"

Jillian nodded her head and draped a smile on her face like hanging a sheet on a clothesline. A Miss Tennessee smile.

"Smells real good, Mama," Jillian said.

"What are you going to have?" Mama plopped the plastic menu down in front of Jillian. "I'm going to have a cheeseburger. That's what Rileigh said was so good. She said that Georgia said she had never had a better cheeseburger than the one she got here."

Mama's pleasant babble formed a barrier between their table and the rest of the diner. For a moment, Rileigh wondered if Mama understood that. Oh, she babbled all the time anyway. But maybe she was doing it right now to keep Jillian's mind occupied. To build a wall of sound around her.

Cookie came to take their order and Rileigh noticed what she had picked up on before, which was that Cookie looked right through you if you were female. The only people on the planet who interested Cookie were those who stood up to go to the bathroom.

"What can I get you ladies?" Cookie asked. Mama turned to look at her then.

"Oh my goodness, you must be that girl Rileigh was telling me about." Rileigh cringed. *Oh please, Mama, no.* "She was just telling me what a sweet, lovely girl you were." Rileigh let out the breath she had sucked in when Mama began to speak. "You got such pretty blue eyes. Oh my, they're pretty."

Mama noticed her eyes; men probably never looked that far up her body.

"I recommend the cheeseburgers. Everybody says they're the best they ever had," Cookie said.

Rileigh finally found her manners and said to Cookie, "Cookie, this is my mother, Lily Bishop. And my sister, Jillian Bishop."

"Good to meet you ladies. Now can you tell me what you'd like to eat, and I'll get your order right in."

"Those blue eyes of yours," Mama said as Jillian pointed to the cheeseburger and told Cookie to hold the onions. "Do you know them blue eyes is something special? You remind me of somebody. I can't place who it is, but somebody I know has got eyes just like yours. Might take me a month of Sundays to figure out who it is, but I'll place you eventually."

Cookie shrugged and said, "It'll be too late then. Today's my last day here."

Rileigh's eyes snapped to her. "You're leaving? You've only been here, what, a few weeks?"

"I got a better job offer, and you got to go where the money is."

Rileigh felt sorry for Big John having gone to the trouble to hire and train a waitress who didn't last a month.

"We'll miss you," she said, lying through her teeth. Personally, she would be grateful to come into the diner and not have to look at Cookie's perfection. But Mama was studying her. Cookie looked uncomfortable under the scrutiny of Mama's gaze. Rileigh figured that was because women didn't fawn over her the way men did. And maybe she didn't know how to relate well to people who didn't respond to her obvious attempts to be the sexiest person in the room.

"What would you ladies like to drink?" Cookie asked.

"I want a vanilla milkshake," Rileigh said.

"Chocolate milkshake for me," Jillian added.

"I'll ... take ..." her mother said, dragging the words out. "This one says peanut butter cup. Is that like a Reese's cup milkshake?"

"It sure is. Just like the cookies and cream milkshake is made out of cookies and cream. And the cheesecake milkshake has cheesecake in it. And the strawberry milkshake has great big strawberries in it. Now, what would you like?"

Mama cocked her head to the side. "You sure you don't remember me from somewhere? 'Cause I'm sure I remember you."

Cookie rolled her eyes and shot a glance at Rileigh, who looked at her sympathetically.

"So about that milkshake, Miss Lily, what flavor would you like?"

Miss Lily. Those words must just go together naturally, because often total strangers called her that and nobody'd ever called Rileigh's aunt 'Miss Daisy.'

"I like strawberries. Have you ever been strawberry picking? You know, one time when I was a little girl, I went picking strawberries on that farm on—"

"Mama?" Rileigh interrupted. "You can tell her about picking strawberries some other time. We need to know what flavor milkshake you would like."

"Why strawberry, dear," she said. "Wasn't you listenin'?"

Cookie beat feet back behind the counter to turn in their order.

"What a sweet young woman she is," Mama said.

Rileigh looked at Jillian, and Jillian had something like a smile on her face.

"I haven't seen a pair of jugs like that since—" Rileigh began.

"Jugs?" Mama said. She looked around. "I don't see no milk. What are you talking about?"

Rileigh and Jillian exchanged a strangled chuckle. "Nothing, Mama. Nothing at all."

"Do you think they're real?" Rileigh asked Jillian after Mama had excused herself to use the restroom.

"Are you kidding me?" Jillian laughed.

"How about that ass?" Rileigh said. "Have you ever seen an ass as perfect as that one?"

Jillian looked back over her shoulder and caught sight of Cookie heading toward another table, this one full of men. And she was strutting her stuff.

"It's too perfect. It has to be fake."

"Mitch said he didn't think there was such a thing as a fake ass."

"Oh, there's such a thing, alright," Jillian said. "If you've got the money, there are doctors who can make ugly women beautiful." She paused. "And keep beautiful women ... *marketable.*"

Rileigh instantly switched topics of conversation as deftly as a figure skater turning in the opposite direction.

"I was thinking about stopping by Walmart on the way home."

Jillian instantly tensed. Walmart was a few more people than Jillian was comfortable being around right now.

"Oh, you can wait in the car if you and Mama want to. I just thought you might like to come in and pick out your own paints. You're getting low on some, aren't you? You're bound to be. You've painted a lot of pictures."

Rileigh kept the conversation light until Mama returned to pick up the burden, hopping from one topic to another like a bird hopping from one branch to the next with absolutely no connection to anything in between.

"Did you know that there's electric cars that can go all the way across the country just by plugging them in?"

Rileigh couldn't resist. "Gonna need a hell of an extension cord."

"I don't think they're quite as advanced as that, Mama," Jillian said. "I believe they can go several hundred miles on a charge, but I'm not sure they can go all the way across the country."

"The guy who makes them makes rocket ships that go all the way to Mars. Surely, he can make a car that'll go from New Jersey to Anaheim."

"Good point, Mama," Rileigh said.

Cookie showed up then, balancing a tray on her hand,

and began depositing plates in front of Mama, Jillian, and Rileigh.

Rileigh would have sworn the burgers were four inches thick.

"There is no possible way the human mouth can open wide enough to take a bite of this hamburger," Jillian said.

"That's what everybody says," Cookie said, depositing a burger equally as large in front of Rileigh and another in front of Mama. Then she started doling out the milkshakes.

"I know who it is," Mama said.

"You know who who is," Rileigh asked.

"I know who it is you remind me of," she said to Cookie. "I had this little girl in Vacation Bible School when I used to teach it." She turned to Rileigh. "She was in the same class as one of George's sisters. I can't remember which one. Maybe it was Claire. No, no, it was Abby. She was in the same class as Abby McGinnis. Had blue eyes and only one dimple — just like you."

Rileigh saw Cookie flinch at the remark.

"Mama, how long ago was it you taught that Vacation Bible School class?"

"Two or three years ago, maybe."

"Abby was in Vacation Bible School two or three years ago? Mama, Abby has children old enough for Vacation Bible School."

"Oh, no, you're right. It's been longer than that." Mama turned her attention back to Cookie. "You sure you wasn't in my Vacation Bible School when you was a little girl? One day, we studied Joseph and the coat of many colors that his father made for him, and the children got to color every square of that coat a different color."

It astonished Rileigh how Mama could pluck a memory so vivid from the Swiss cheese of her mind, but sometimes she came downstairs with her slip on the outside of her dress. Last week, she froze Rileigh's car keys in the ice tray in the freezer.

Cookie picked up Mama's milkshake and pushed it into her hand. "Take a drink of this and tell me what you think."

Mama put the straw in her mouth and sucked as hard as she could. Then she spoke around the straw.

"This thing's so thick it's like trying to suck up concrete." She picked up her spoon, stuck it down deep into her milkshake, dug around until she found a strawberry, and popped it out. "Ain't that a pretty color. That's the color you painted that coat of many colors. You painted the whole thing strawberry pink."

"Can I get you anything else?" Cookie said, obviously anxious to go because several men had come into the diner, and surely she wanted to dangle her very expensive chest in front of them.

"We're fine. Thank you."

Cookie turned and almost bolted for the counter to put the tray down, then hurried to the table of the four men who had just come in. Rileigh was looking at the men when she suddenly recognized one of them.

Oh shit. It was David Hicks.

Chapter Thirty-Three

JILLIAN SAW Rileigh look past her to someone who had come in the door. The look on Rileigh's face was something like shocked disbelief. Jillian cut her eyes to Mama just as Mama looked up and saw whoever it was. Mama's face was transformed by a beautiful, happy smile. So whoever it was Rileigh didn't want to see, Mama did.

Jillian didn't care who it was. If both Mama and Rileigh reacted, whoever it was would be coming to their table. And Jillian was absolutely not okay with that.

Ever since she'd gotten home, Jillian had been hiding in a shell. She'd never had a shell before. She'd never had any protection before. In the past thirty years, she had been nothing but vulnerable, nothing but exposed, totally in danger and at risk every second, unprotected, unsafe. Then she'd thought she was going to die in a dark well with her baby sister. And after she crossed the bridge back into life and was welcomed back into the family she had been snatched away from, she had curled up like a cat in front of a warm fire and didn't ever want to leave.

She had perhaps been in more danger at the end of

her captivity than at any time during it. She had *escaped*. She'd planned it out and pulled it off. And the adrenaline rush of constantly looking over her shoulder, fearing any minute she would be discovered and hauled back—

Even if she'd not come back to the mountains, if she had stuck with the original plan and gone to South America and built a new life, she would have lived that life in constant terror of being found out, of being exposed, of being taken back ... or being killed. Oh, she had willingly traded captivity for freedom, even if that freedom was filled with fear. To be free — that was enough.

If Rileigh hadn't tried to drag her out into the world and a fuller life, Jillian would be content with what she had, grateful for a life of simplicity, unwilling to leave the safety and security of home to venture out into a world full of dragons. This world had different dragons than the other one. This world could, at any moment, confront her with reminders of the life here that she had lost. She didn't want to be reminded.

Mama's broad smile grew even wider as Jillian sensed the person coming up behind her. She turned to look just as Mama greeted him.

"Well, hello, David. So good to see you, son. Seems like I ain't seen you since there was frost on the pumpkin."

Jillian couldn't breathe, couldn't think, couldn't — just *couldn't*. She was frozen in a static state between one breath and the next.

David.

Her eyes were the only part of her body that still moved at her command. And they turned to the man who had now stepped up to their table. He was tall and oh so handsome, with huge, broad shoulders and gigantic, muscled arms. She wouldn't have known him. He had changed so very much — for the better. He'd always been good-looking. Now, with that hair cropped short, some gray at the temples, and that exquisite body, he was an Adonis.

David Hicks.

The man she'd walked out on the night before their wedding twenty-seven years ago.

If she could have made a list of all the people she never wanted to run into in Black Bear Forge, Tennessee, David's name would have been at the top. In bold type, 64-point font. Yet there he was, standing in front of her, looking at her.

Looking at *her*.

Oh, dear God, what he was seeing! The beautiful eighteen-year-old girl who had vanished out of his life didn't exist anymore. She had been used up and ground down until nothing of her beauty remained.

An image flashed in her mind's eye like a comet across a black sky. The image of their senior prom picture. She stood next to him in a formal gown, her long blonde hair flowing down around her shoulders. Her complexion smooth like a doll's. Oh, she had not been the kind of Barbie doll beauty that the waitress with the artificial top and bottom was. Not perfection, but beautiful. She'd known at the time she was beautiful and didn't take pride in it, just accepted it as the way the world was. She knew that David had been attracted to her and loved her, in some part, perhaps in large part, because she was a beautiful girl. But now she was a woman, a forty-five-year-old woman. Ordinary would be the kindest description. And it wouldn't be the one that Jillian would use. She saw her face in the mirror every morning when she brushed her teeth. Sometimes, she'd try to find in that face the girl she'd been when last she'd lived with her family in the Smoky Mountains of East Tennessee. But she could never find that

Jillian. She knew that David was not seeing that girl now either. He was seeing a painful ruin.

If Jillian could have leapt up from the table and run out the door and kept running, she would have run until her heart burst in her chest. But of course, she couldn't run because ... well, she couldn't make that kind of scene. But more to the point, she couldn't move. She simply stared at him and felt so unutterably sorry for him for what he must be experiencing right now.

"Jillian," he said, just her name. The way he had always said her name. Maybe some things never changed. She had, and he had, but that hadn't.

"I heard you were home, and I've been meaning to get in touch with you," he added.

She couldn't speak. She hoped to God somebody else talked besides David, because she certainly wouldn't be holding up her end of the conversation.

"We're glad to see you, David," Rileigh said.

Now Jillian understood the horror she'd seen on Rileigh's face. Rileigh knew how badly Jillian did *not* want to be confronted with a fiancé she'd left at the altar. Rileigh would fear she'd never be able to drag Jillian away from the house again after this disaster.

"Jillian has taken up painting since she got home," Rileigh babbled.

David shot his eyes to Rileigh, but then they came back to Jillian's face. She watched him search her face, looking for who she used to be and not finding her. She ought to say something, anything. But what was there to say?

"You're looking as beautiful as ever," David said. "I'm really glad to see you."

She had to have made that part up. An auditory hallucination. That couldn't have been what he said.

"Oh, David," Mama said, "it's been so long since we've

seen you. Why don't you come to our house for dinner tonight? We're having fried chicken. I'm gonna go out into the chicken yard and pick out the fattest pullet I can find. My mama always called that 'chicken so fresh that, with a little care, it could've lived.' Please come."

She watched David freeze at the invitation and understood how he must feel, how awkward it must be for him to have to say that he had absolutely no desire at all to come spend an evening at Lily Bishop's house.

And she found herself able to speak then, to defend him, to try to get him off the hook.

"Oh, Mama, I'm sure David has all sorts of other plans."

"Well, as a matter of fact, I don't," he said cheerily. "I would love to come and have fried chicken at your house, Lily."

Then he brushed his hand lightly over Jillian's shoulder, barely touching her at all. "I'd love to get caught up, Jillian."

And it occurred to her to wonder if he actually didn't know where she'd been. But then why would he? Who would have told him? Perhaps Rileigh had. Oh, dear God, she hoped Rileigh had.

"Good then, it's a date. We'll see you at seven o'clock," Mama's smile lit her whole face.

There was no way to get out of it now, not right this minute. She'd get Rileigh or Mama to call him later and tell him that something had come up, that the house had burned down or Jillian had dropped dead, something inconvenient that would make it impossible for him to come to dinner. Yes, they'd get out of it that way. She moved her eyes from Mama's face back to David's and couldn't read the look there. It was such a familiar look, but that couldn't be what she was reading. She managed to stammer, "It's good to see you, David. I hope you're well."

"I'm a whole lot better now than I was when I came in here," he said. "Listen, I've got to get back. This is a business lunch. But I'll see you tonight, all of you. I'm looking forward to it."

Then he turned and strode across the room to sit down at the table with the men he had come in with. The men Cookie was falling all over herself to flirt with.

Rileigh reached over and touched Jillian's hand.

"Jillian?"

And Jillian somehow managed to keep from either crying or screaming.

Chapter Thirty-Four

AFTER MITCH HAD LEFT Rileigh and Gus and spent several futile hours looking for Leroy McCutcheon, he pulled into his space behind the courthouse where the Sheriff's Department was located and spotted the Lincoln Town car with the dealership slogan "Nobody WALKS away..." and "Rutherford's Pre-owned Cars and Trucks" stenciled on the door.

His heart sank. He didn't need this today, but then he never needed it. It just got jammed down his throat every now and then. In truth, Mitch had stood up to Mayor J.P. Rutherford on several noteworthy occasions, and Rutherford had backed off his insistence on micromanaging the law enforcement agency in Yarmouth County. Whatever had driven him out of his gopher hole to come put the screws to Mitch today must have been pretty profound.

It had been a while since Mitch had had an encounter with Rutherford. Such encounters were never pleasant because J.P. Rutherford never had anything pleasant to say and because being in the man's presence was an unpleasant experience in and of itself.

Mitch didn't believe he'd ever met anybody quite as un-self-aware as J.P. Rutherford. The man had been elected mayor during COVID when the county's voter turnout was lower than it had ever been in its history. Word had it that he called out the troops, all of them, meaning the huge Rutherford family scattered all over Chicken Gizzard Ridge in northern Yarmouth County, the family J.P. either described as "poor but proud" or as "good people." The family where he had learned to pull himself up by his own bootstraps.

Recently, he'd let it be known that not only was he God's gift to selling used cars — no, not used cars, pre-owned cars — but he was also a politician, and he had aspirations for higher office. No, sir, he wasn't content just to be the mayor of little Yarmouth County, Tennessee.

Unlike in the previous election, he was facing competition in this one. Sundeep Singh, who owned the Quik Stop Convenience Store, had filed to run against him. Sundeep was a friend of Mitch's, a really good man who worked hard and who respected law enforcement, which put him in something of a minority in some circles.

He was also sharp, educated, and had plans to move Yarmouth County forward, plans Mitch agreed with.

J.P. Rutherford was threatened by any competition, but competition as competent as Sundeep Singh obviously scared the shit out of him. He campaigned everywhere he went and never missed an opportunity to shake a hand and ask for a vote. Didn't have any idea how obnoxious he often was.

But apparently, he had either come to some slight degree of self-awareness or had someone in his life who was managing his public image because, in recent months, he had stopped wearing his trademark pastel suits with ties that were too wide and too colorful and shiny black patent leather shoes.

Oh, he still had the big loud voice, the big toothy smile, the glad-handing attitude, and the too-long hair swept back in a style last popular around 1985. But he did seem to be trying to tone down the used car salesman image he projected.

Mitch found Rutherford waiting for him in his office, sitting in his chair behind the desk.

He didn't even leap up in embarrassment at being caught sitting in Mitch's chair, just smiled and stuck out his hand as he always did, the big beefy hand that always grasped his in a too-tight handshake meant to indicate that J.P. was a strong man.

"Hello, Mitch. Good to see you today," Rutherford said.

"Good to see you too, Mr. Mayor." Mitch matched Rutherford lie for lie, then moved around him to sit down in the chair where the seat was warm because Rutherford had been sitting it.

"What can I do for you today, sir?" Mitch asked. His tone was cold, but he was sure Rutherford wasn't sharp enough to pick up on it.

"We need to talk, son." Rutherford stepped to the door and closed it. Then he moved to stand in front of Mitch's desk, probably because somebody had told him that if you stood while the person you were speaking to was seated, you established dominance over them.

"What is it we need to talk about, J.P.?"

"Dr. Jefferson's murder," he said with great gravity.

"There's not much to talk about, sir. We have—"

"I don't think you understand the gravity of this case."

"I understand that a man is dead, that he was murdered in his own office, and there's enough gravity in that to propel an investigation. I'm not sure what else you're talking about."

"Of course you don't. You're not privy to the kind of information I am."

"And that information is?" J.P. leaned over Mitch's desk and spoke as if imparting some great secret. "What you don't know, and I do, is who Derek Jefferson's roommate was at Vanderbilt."

Mitch refused to rise to the bait. He wouldn't ask.

"A man who is a seventh-generation Tennessean—" Mitch wondered if he was talking about Damien Crockett, who claimed to be a descendent of Davie Crockett and was running for governor. He wasn't. He was talking about Crockett's competition. "Governor Bill Lee was Derek Jefferson's roommate, that's who."

Mitch was surprised at that bit of information. Surprised that nobody'd mentioned it, not surprised that it was so. And not surprised that it was of ultimate importance to Mayor Rutherford.

"You also don't know that I got a call yesterday from the governor's office," J.P. continued.

Still refusing to be pressured into dragging the information out of him, Mitch said, "And I'm sure you're going to tell me what that phone call was about."

"It was a polite inquiry about the progress of the investigation. Understated. Bill doesn't want to be seen as putting the screws to Yarmouth County."

Bill?

No way in hell was J.P Rutherford on a first-name basis with the governor, but Mitch swallowed a retort. Mitch got it now. If there was likely to be any political fallout, either way, Rutherford wanted to be on the upside of it. If Mitch was having problems with the investigation, Rutherford could distance himself from the case and cast blame on

Mitch. As soon as Mitch solved the murder and arrested a suspect, Rutherford would swoop in and take credit for the victory.

"Mr. Mayor, I can assure you that my department is doing everything—"

Rutherford held up his hand for Mitch to stop talking.

"You're a lone ranger, Sheriff Webster, out there doing your thing and humbly accepting the applause of your constituents when you solve the crime."

Mitch couldn't think of a single time anybody had applauded his making an arrest in a case. His understanding of the people of Yarmouth County was that they wanted law and order. They wanted to feel safe in their homes. They wanted Mitch to dance along the razor's edge of keeping the riffraff at bay while still welcoming the tourists who represented every spectrum of humanity that existed.

"I got my sources in the governor's office. I know that call was the first, but by no means the last, about Derek Jefferson. That call was polite. The ones after it won't be. The governor is deeply, deeply troubled by the murder of his friend, and he wants answers."

Rutherford leaned forward in his chair. "And I, by god, intend to give him answers! I am hereby issuing an official directive to you. Find out who killed Dr. Derek Jefferson. Find out fast. Arrest that person. That's pretty simple. You will receive the full text of the directive by the end of today. There will be a paper trail demonstrating that the mayor's office has done everything in its power to be helpful."

Before Mitch could respond, the mayor straightened back up.

"I know that Sandeep Singh is a friend of yours. Oh yes. I get around. I have my ear to the ground."

A Friend Like You

You wouldn't have to have your ear to the ground to know that Mitch and Sandeep were friends. It certainly wasn't a relationship either of them had tried to keep a secret. But Mitch didn't say that either.

Rutherford kept going. "I know you'd like nothing more than for that man to take my place in November. But it ain't gonna happen, Sheriff. Mark it down. I'm gonna remain your boss for the next four years. It would be in your best interest to give yourself a little attitude adjustment about me."

It didn't surprise Mitch at all that the mayor hadn't even mentioned the murders of Jody Hatfield and Clive McCutcheon. They were, after all, of a different social level than a local dentist, the former roommate of the governor.

"Let's be clear with one another." Rutherford continued, "I don't like you, and you don't like me. I think you're a showboat, and you think I don't know what I'm doing. Frankly, Sheriff, I could not give a rat's ass whether you like me or not. The only thing that matters is that you respect me and you follow my orders. And I am hereby officially ordering you to drop whatever else you're working on to concentrate your entire force of officers in determining who murdered Derek Jefferson."

"I'm afraid I can't do that, sheriff."

"I figured you'd say that."

"Mr. Mayor, are you aware that there are two *other* outstanding murders that have been committed in the last week?"

"You mean those has-been hotshot football players who run those idiot street gangs?"

"I am currently investigating those two deaths, as well as the death of the dentist."

"Then stop investigating those," the mayor said.

Mitch got to his feet.

"With all *due* respect, Mr. Mayor, how I investigate crimes is none of your business."

Before Mitch could continue, Rutherford interrupted.

"If I don't like it, I can fire you. Is that what you're about to throw in my face?" He didn't wait for an answer. "Then you can appeal the firing to the county council, who will side with you. Let me tell you something, son. Manny Ortega, Greta Oglebay, and Phil Jackson are recent ... business associates of mine." He said the words as if to convey much more than just associates. "It would only take their votes and one other to get your ass fired *by the county council*. There's nowhere to appeal their termination. Oh, I know you're popular with the people. Of course, you are. You put on a good show. But this time, you don't have Melissa Mendoza's televised endorsement blowing hot air up your ass. This time, you're flying solo."

Rutherford reached up and smoothed his hair back before he spoke again. "I have plans that require my reelection as county mayor. Bigger plans. I will need the support of the governor's office to make them happen. This is a golden opportunity for me to endear myself to the governor by handing him on a platter the murderer of his friend. And if I don't have a murderer to hand him on a platter, then I will hand him the head of the county sheriff who couldn't solve the crime! Either way, I win."

Mitch supposed he was right. If J.P. played it right, he could score all kinds of political capital on the back of the murder of a good, decent man.

"I am not bluffing, Sheriff Webster. You drop whatever else it is you think is important, and you concentrate the resources of your office on finding the murderer of Derek Jefferson. Or as God is my witness, I will have your badge."

The man glared at Mitch with a determined set to his jaw Mitch had never seen before. The candidacy of Sundeep Singh had put the fear of God into J.P. Rutherford. He saw his political power and his political future slipping away, and he was scared. A scared man was a dangerous man.

Oh, Mitch had no intention of dropping the search for whoever had killed the three gang members. But he understood that the man wasn't just blowing smoke, that he was scared enough and desperate enough to make good on his threat. If Mitch didn't find the murderer soon, he could be out of a job.

Chapter Thirty-Five

RILEIGH WANTED to kick herself for twisting Jillian's arm into coming to the diner for lunch today. More than wanted to kick herself. Wanted to find at least three or four people who would participate in a gang-whopping.

As soon as David walked away from the table, Jillian sort of imploded. She closed up like she had shutters on the insides of her eyes, and she slammed them shut. Rileigh didn't know what to say. Mama was so clueless that she just kept babbling.

"So nice to have someone at the house. I know what else I'll make. I'll make some lemon meringue pie. Do you think that's a good idea, Jillian?"

Jillian didn't respond.

Cookie came to the table to give them their check. Seemed to be in a hurry to get finished with them. Probably because there were way more interesting human beings in the diner that she could strut her stuff in front of. Cookie hurried away from the table with their money and still Jillian had said nothing.

"Jillian," Rileigh said and put her hand on Jillian's, but Jillian snatched it away. Mama missed the whole thing.

"Are you girls ready to go now? We need to get home and get started on dinner."

What Rileigh needed was to have some time alone with Jillian.

"Yes, let's go," Rileigh said and rose to her feet.

"I gotta pee first," Mama said. "That milkshake went through me so fast I wouldn't be surprised if it didn't even pause inside long enough to change colors."

She hurried across the diner toward the other side, down the hallway that had been occupied only just a week ago by Rileigh and Mitch and Gus and the EMTs waiting for a body to be removed from the storage room.

As soon as Mama was out of earshot, Rileigh took Jillian's hand.

"I'm sorry, I never dreamed... It seems like all I do anymore is apologize to you. I'm sorry I missed your counseling appointment. I'm sorry I talked you into coming here, and you ran into David. I'm sorry, I'm just not doing this very well, and I want to. I'm sorry."

Jillian looked at her. She reached over and patted Rileigh's hand, which was atop her own, but either didn't want to say anything or actually couldn't. Rileigh decided to let it rest. They needed to go home where they could all talk privately about what had happened. She looked up and saw Mama coming back from the bathroom. Then she veered off toward the bar area and made a come-here gesture to Cookie, who reluctantly left the two men. Mama said something to her in her bubbly, cheerful way. Patted her hand, then continued back to the table.

Rileigh hoped she had not told Cookie that she was twitching her ass too much in front of men. Or that she really ought to button up her shirt before her boobs fell out. Or any of half a dozen other inappropriate thing her mother was likely to have said. Rileigh reminded herself it didn't matter since Cookie would be gone tomorrow.

Rileigh, Jillian, and Mama went out to the car, Mama babbling about how good the burger had been. And how disappointing the milkshake had been — too thick to suck up a straw — and her observations on how much Cookie reminded her of her Vacation Bible School student. And didn't David look nice? All in one long stream-of-consciousness monologue.

They got into the car and Rileigh didn't even start the engine. They had some privacy now, and it needed to be said now.

"Mama, that was a terrible thing you just did."

Mama looked stricken. "What was terrible? All I done was tell her I remembered who she reminded me of."

"No, I'm not talking about that. I'm talking about inviting David Hicks to supper tonight."

"Why was that a terrible thing?" Mama asked, bewildered.

And the anger sluiced away. You couldn't stay angry at Mama. It was like being angry at a small child.

"Mama, don't you understand that Jillian does not want to see David Hicks?"

"Why on earth not?" Mama turned to Jillian. "You want to see David, don't you? You like David. You haven't seen him in years."

Jillian said nothing.

"Mama, can't you see how awkward it will be for Jillian to be around him? And right now, Jillian does not need awkward."

Mama looked at Jillian. And for a moment, Rileigh thought she didn't get it at all. But then she surprised Rileigh and Jillian both.

"Oh, I knew it would be awkward. That's why I invited him."

The sisters gaped at their mother.

"Jillian, you remember that swim meet back when you were in junior high school?"

Jillian's eyes snapped to Mama, and Rileigh realized there was a story here she'd not heard.

"Well, do you remember it, or don't you?"

"Of course I remember it, Mama."

Mama turned to Rileigh. "You were too little to go. We left you at home. You see, Jillian had joined the swim team in junior high school. I tried to talk her out of it, but she said it would be wonderful. I tried to tell her that she couldn't swim well enough. But she wouldn't listen, and she joined." Mama left it there.

"What happened?" Rileigh asked.

Mama looked at Jillian, expecting her to continue the story.

Rileigh didn't think she was going to say a word. Until finally, reluctantly, she said, "What happened was, Mama was right. I didn't swim well enough. I couldn't learn all the different strokes. So I wanted to drop out. But Mama wouldn't let me."

"Tell her why not," Mama said.

"She said, 'In this house, if you start something, you finish it.' She said, 'If you start quitting things now because they're hard, you'll be quitting hard things the rest of your life.' She said, 'You signed up for this, and you're going to see it through.'"

"Mama, why are you telling this story right now?" Rileigh asked. "What's the rest of it?"

"The rest of it was that there was a swim meet. And I don't remember the particulars of it, and it don't really matter. What matters is that at the very end of it, the Black

Bear Forge team was ahead by so many points that the coach put in the swimmers who never get to swim just to let them compete. And he put Jillian in the backstroke competition. But Jillian had never learned how to do the backstroke."

"I had been terrified of that very thing," Jillian said quietly. "I told Mama when I was pleading with her to let me drop out that there were strokes I didn't even know how to do — and what if I had to do them? But she wouldn't budge."

Jillian let out a long breath. "Next thing I know, I'm about to dive into the water representing Black Bear Forge Junior High School. I didn't have to win the competition. I could come in last place, and it didn't matter. But what *did* matter was that I had to be able to do the backstroke from one side of the pool to the other and then back. And I couldn't. I tried to fake it. I tried to pretend I knew how, but how can you pretend to know how to do the backstroke? Finally, I just flopped over and swam the breaststroke that I knew how to do."

There was silence in the car then, and Rileigh looked from her mother to her sister.

"And ...? There must be more."

"Our team was the clear winner ... but we were *disqualified*. It was an automatic disqualification if any member of the team didn't do the proper stroke. If you were competing in the breaststroke competition, you had to swim the breaststroke. Or the backstroke. So, we lost because of me."

Then Jillian's eyes cut to her mother. "Why are you telling this story right now?"

"Because of what you learned from it, honey. You told me about it years later. Don't you remember?"

Jillian was quiet for a moment and then sighed out the words, "Yes, I remember."

Jillian looked at Rileigh. "I told her that for months, I had been dreading what would happen if I had to swim a stroke I didn't know how to do. And finally, it happened. The perfect storm. Not only did I have to swim a stroke I couldn't swim, but because I couldn't swim it, the whole team was disqualified in a meet when they had clearly won."

Jillian cut her eyes back to Mama, took a breath, and then continued. "I told Mama that the worst thing I could have imagined actually happened." There was a beat of silence. "And it didn't kill me. It was awful. I got what I deserved for not trying hard enough. It was the most embarrassed I ever was the whole time I was in school. But I survived it."

"She didn't just go survive, you know. She went on to be one of the most popular girls in high school. She went on to be the prom queen." Mama paused for a breath. "She went on stronger than she'd been before because of what happened to her."

Rileigh began to understand why Mama was telling the story.

"I saw David Hicks, and I thought to myself, *this here's the swim meet*," Mama continued. "I know it ain't the same, ain't some simple little embarrassment in school instead of a horrifying life experience. But Sugar, you got through it! If you can get through spending a whole evening with David Hicks — and he'll be nice and kind, and you might even enjoy it — but even if you don't, you'll be stronger on the other side of it."

Rileigh was flabbergasted. She'd had no idea her mother was capable of that kind of higher-order thinking anymore.

Mama reached up into the front seat and put her hand on Jillian's shoulder.

"Sugar, your sister and I are trying everything we can to help you get better. We love you! We'd do anything to help you get your life back. A *real* life. Not some shadowy imitation of a life where you stay hidden in the house all the time."

Mama began to lose steam then, her focus faltered, and you could see she was about to lose her train of thought.

"I just took a chance that maybe this here would help you do that. And if you're mad at me, I understand, and I'm sorry. You know it ain't written in stone or nothing like that. We can call him and tell him we made some kind of mistake or something come up."

She paused, clung to clarity long enough to add. "If you want to *quit*, me and Rileigh will get you out of it."

Then, there was silence in the car. Rileigh didn't know what to say and didn't think she should say anything. The ball was definitely in Jillian's court now.

Jillian let out a long, slow breath. Drew another in. "Okay, Mama, I'll do it. You're right. If I can survive spending the evening with David Hicks, I can ... survive most anything."

Jillian tried for a smile but couldn't pull it off. Rileigh reached across the seat and squeezed her hand.

"I've never been prouder of you than I am right now," Rileigh said.

And this time, the smile on Jillian's face, though small and tentative, was real.

Chapter Thirty-Six

RILEIGH WAS glad Mama hadn't invited David Hicks to come for dinner a week later. If the three of them had had to survive for a week the kind of pressure they were under before he arrived, they'd all flown apart into little pieces.

Rileigh was tied in a knot because she was terrified of what could happen to Jillian. She looked to Mama and saw a strength in Mama she hadn't know was there. Sure, Mama had dementia, and because she did, she said crazy, silly things, so you didn't listen to her, and you didn't believe her. But there was a whole lot more going on in there, Rileigh realized than anybody expected. The strength in her mother had always been there. She'd known it when she was growing up, her mother surviving as a single mom, surviving the suicide of her husband and the disappearance of her daughter. Surviving, period.

Jillian was not completely a basket case, but very, very close. She must have tried on and discarded fifteen different outfits. This one was too dressy. After all, it was just a pleasant impromptu dinner. This outfit was too casual. Looked like she'd shown up to wash a car.

These pants were too tight.

This blouse showed a midriff, and she was too old for that.

This shirt was too low-cut.

This pair of jeans…

These shoes…

Rileigh suffered through every wardrobe change with her, offering opinions that she knew didn't mean anything to Jillian. Jillian wasn't looking for someone else's opinion about how she looked. She was trying desperately to look like the Jillian that David had loved. And that wasn't possible, no matter how many outfits she tried on.

She finally settled on a simple plaid blouse with the sleeves rolled up, tucked into a pair of jeans that were neither too tight nor too loose. And running shoes and, of course, wild, strange socks. Jillian had been famous for wearing strange socks. She had loved finding them in stores and catalogs and trying to find something they went with at least slightly. But the wild plaids and strange designs and bright colors never really went with anything. She found a pair that had stripes in the right color and a design that didn't totally clash with the plaid of her shirt and that made her feel comfortable, wearing wild socks like she used to wear.

They had spent the afternoon trying to figure out what would be the least stressful and most relaxed way to have this dinner party they'd invited David to and had finally settled on a plan.

David would be met at the door by Mama and Rileigh, who would usher him into the kitchen where Jillian would be preparing supper. Mama and Jillian and Rileigh would finish up supper as they chatted amiably with David. Then Mama and Rileigh would go into the dining room and set the table, leaving Jillian and David a little bit of private time. Not too private. Not so private as to be awkward. Mama and Rileigh would be only a few steps away to perform a rescue mission if necessary.

David rang the doorbell as the clock on the mantle in the living room donged 7.30, the two bells singing a duet.

As per the plan, Mama and Rileigh greeted him at the door casually, spoke for a few minutes of totally inane things. Jillian waved and called out hello from the kitchen where she was busy peeling potatoes.

Then Rileigh and Mama led David to the kitchen, seated him at the table, and went back to their stations preparing dinner. Mama kept up a beautiful, light banter of inane conversation sprinkled with just enough craziness to make Jillian and Rileigh feel at home and to let David know that Mama didn't always drag a full string of fish anymore.

"That Travis Kelce was such a nice young man. He was sitting right there in the chair where you are," Mama told David.

His eyes opened wide. "Travis Kelce? You don't mean *the* Travis Kelce,"

"Oh yes, he and Taylor Swift came over after the Super Bowl. I wanted to make taco salad, but we didn't have any tomatoes. So, Jillian went out to the yard and picked some. And I want you to know Taylor Swift went right out there with her. Picked tomatoes just like, just like regular folks."

As Mama proceeded to shoo everybody out of the kitchen to sit at the dining room table, David shot a look at Rileigh, who acknowledged with a slight nod that she knew the Super Bowl Sunday tomato-picking didn't really happen. Then he'd smiled at Jillian. And Jillian had smiled a genuine smile back.

And in that moment, Rileigh knew everything was going to be all right.

She was convinced then that it was possible to ease Jillian back into a space in her life where she could talk to David. Maybe that meant nothing, and maybe it meant something. Rileigh knew David was still in love with Jillian. And she clung to the fierce hope that maybe he would be able to pull her sister up out of the darkness. She clung to that hope right up until Jillian leaned over David to fill his glass with lemonade.

Suddenly, Jillian froze. It was several seconds before Rileigh noticed that her sister had become a statue. Then Jillian dropped the pitcher of lemonade on the table. It was plastic, so it didn't break, but it splattered everywhere, making lemonade wading pools in everyone's plates and adding lemonade as an ingredient to the bowls of mashed potatoes, green beans, and baby carrots.

In the stunned silence that followed, Jillian bolted out of the room and ran through the living room to the coat closet opposite the front door. She flung the door open, dashed inside, and slammed the door behind her.

Rileigh, Mama, and David sat in shock. Rileigh knew what had just happened. It was a worst-case scenario.

"What in the world?" David said, getting to his feet and starting toward the closed closet door. "What's wrong?"

Rileigh grabbed his arm and stopped him. "Do you know anything at all about Post Traumatic Stress Disorder?"

"Hell yeah, I know what PTSD is. Brett Collier, the assistant manager of my gym in Memphis, served two tours in Afghanistan. He had PTSD episodes when he got back."

"You were around him, you saw what he did?"

"I wasn't just around him. I finally talked him into

going to counseling ... and I had to go with him to get him to keep the appointments." She watched it dawn on David's face. "Jillian is having a PTSD reaction? To what?"

"If you know PTSD, you know it doesn't matter what triggers it. What matters is that we help her get back from there to here."

David pushed his chair back and walked purposefully through the living room to the door of the closet. Then he opened it slowly. Rileigh took a step in front of him, but he pushed her gently out of the way.

"I got this," he said. Then he knelt on one knee so he could look Jillian in the eye, and he began to talk to her. She was hunkered in the corner of the closet, cowering away from a reality that only she could see. David told her who he was, who she was, where she was. He told her she was safe, that nothing could hurt her here. He coaxed her into opening her eyes, told her to look around, and asked her to tell him what she saw.

Rileigh and Mama stood back out of the way and watched. Finally, David took Jillian's hand, lifted her to her feet, and led her out of the closet. Jillian looked at Rileigh and Mama, her eyes wild, trying to assimilate reality into whatever horror she'd been living in some other place and some other time.

"Let's go sit out on the porch swing. What do you say, Jillian?" David didn't give her a chance to answer. He just gently piloted her to the front door, out onto the porch, and onto the swing.

Mama and Rileigh stood in the door watching.

"How about you join us?" David said then, as casually as you'd invite somebody to sit down at your table at a party. "Lily, think you could rustle us up some Lemonade?"

And Mama absolutely could rustle us up some lemonade! She scurried off into the kitchen. Rileigh went out onto the porch with David and Jillian and sat down in the rocker as Jillian piloted the swing back and forth in an unconscious motion. The silent swing.

Finally, Jillian spoke. "I'm sorry."

"There's nothing to be sorry about," David said. "We understand. It's all right—"

"No! Thank you for understanding, but it's *not* all right. I'm not alright. And I'm sorry for that."

"You don't have to be alright, Jillian," Rileigh said. "Wherever you've been, you've come back from. And wherever you go, we'll be here for you."

Jillian turned to David and really looked at him then. Not in any hesitant, awkward way. Just looked at him.

"I'm sorry that dinner was such a disaster. I apologize. I'm not ready to talk about this right now."

"You don't have to talk about anything you don't want to talk about," he said.

"And I'm not up to the rest of it." She waved her hand around to indicate everything. "This dinner, I just can't. I'm sorry—"

David got up out of the swing and smiled.

"I'll take a rain check," he said.

Mama arrived then with the lemonade. David took a glass, took a big swig, and set it down on the table. "In fact, I tell you what ... how about you and I go have us a cheeseburger at Red Eye Gravy for lunch tomorrow. How does that sound, Jillian?"

He didn't invite Mama or Rileigh.

His demeanor was casual. And Rileigh knew how really, really hard it was for him right now to appear casual when he couldn't possibly have been anything near it.

Jillian was silent. Rileigh felt like she was sitting on the razor's edge of something.

Then Jillian nodded her head. "Sure, lunch tomorrow. That'd be good."

"I'll pick you up at noon." David didn't try to touch her. He just grasped Mama in a friendly hug, smiled at Rileigh, and then walked down the steps and out through the gate to his car.

Jillian managed to make it until he was out of sight before she started to cry.

Chapter Thirty-Seven

RILEIGH WAS POSITIVELY BEAMING when she slid into the passenger seat of Mitch's cruiser on Saturday morning.

"What?" he asked.

"What, what?" she asked.

"You sound like a parrot. What's with the smile? You keep smiling that wide for very long, and your gums are gonna dry out. What happened?"

"Jillian happened."

"New news?"

Rileigh had called Mitch and told him what happened with David Hicks when he had come to dinner on Friday night. How Jillian had suffered a PTSD episode and wound up hiding in the coat closet. And none of that was anything you'd smile about. But Jillian had agreed to go have lunch with David today. Mitch had figured that was progress.

"Is it about Jillian's date with David for lunch today?"

"No, that's not it."

"Then what?"

"While I was getting dressed and Jillian was still downstairs with Mama, I sneaked a peek into her studio. I heard her up last night, went out into the hall, and saw a light under her studio door. I wanted to see what she'd painted."

"And what did she paint?"

"Oh, nothing exactly. It was just lines and colors. No form of any kind. But I took a picture of it."

"So why does a formless picture of lines and colors put a grin on your face like the Cheshire Cat?"

"Because they weren't black and brown and ugly!"

"What were they?"

"Oh, they weren't pastel pinks and blues or anything like that. Everything she's painted has been formless, an expression of what she was feeling inside. That's why I took pictures of it and showed them to Dr. Al-Masri so she could use them as a window into Jillian's soul. And if that's a window into her soul, her soul is dark indeed. Nothing but swirling, ugly colors and sharp lines."

She paused for effect. "But the one on the easel this morning was *different*."

"Different how, if not pastel colors?"

"I don't think she's progressed that far. But there was color. There was *a lightness* to it. It wasn't ugly black and brown swirls. There was some red and some yellow. Spots of blue. Not a whole lot. But even the dark colors weren't as dark. It was a distinct change from what she's painted before."

"You think that's because David Hicks came to dinner last night, even though he didn't stay?"

"I think it has something to do with David Hicks. That's the only change in her life. And obviously, it's a positive change. I was so thrilled she was willing to go out to lunch with him today. I can't wait to hear what she says when she gets back."

Rileigh smiled. It was a beautiful smile. Not the

glorious smile she'd had on her face about Jillian's painting. But a beautiful smile, nonetheless. And her eyes were so *green* today.

Mitch grabbed hold of his emotions and bit into them as hard as he could. Now was not the time. But he could at least firm up that rain check.

"Speaking of going out to eat. I have a rain check for our big date that wasn't," he said. "And it comes due whenever I call it."

"When would you like to do that?"

"I was thinking sometime next week." Bahama Mama's was out. The restaurant had burned totally to the ground the night they were supposed to be there for dinner. "And we mentioned maybe going to Nashville. I could get us a reservation at Guthrie's Steakhouse."

Guthrie's Steakhouse was legendary.

"Let me check my social calendar," she said and pretended to consider multiple options. "Works for me."

She smiled that beautiful smile again, and her green eyes sparkled.

Mitch stopped his cruiser in front of the gate. Rileigh got out and opened it, then closed it behind them. When they pulled up in front of the McCutcheon house, there was a Ford pickup, all jacked up with big wide tires sitting out front. Mitch had been told Leroy drove a jacked-up truck. So maybe he was home.

They walked up onto the porch, and Mitch knocked on the door. The surly woman who had ushered them into the house on Tuesday greeted them with the same warm welcome.

"What do you want?" She demanded. "We just put Clive in the ground yesterday, and you come sniffin' around here again."

"We're looking for Leroy. We'd like to talk to him."

"He ain't here."

Mitch gestured toward the jacked-up truck sitting out front. "That's his truck, isn't it?"

"No, that ain't his truck. That's my truck."

"Your truck?"

"Hell yeah, it's my truck. Leroy drives it sometimes, but it b'longs to me. And Leroy ain't here."

She didn't exactly slam the door in their face. Just crossed her arms over her chest and stood inside the screen, silent.

"Do you have any idea where we could find him?"

"If I did, I wouldn't tell you."

Mitch nodded.

"Thank you for your time," he said, and he walked across the porch with Rileigh.

"Let's have a look in the windows of that truck," he said under his breath, and on their way back to his cruiser they passed close enough to look through the windows, Rileigh on the passenger side, Mitch on the driver's side.

They both froze at the same time. There was something lying in the tray in front of the cup holders in the console between the seats.

It looked like a ring.

But it was hard to tell because there was a napkin lying over most of it. It could have been something else.

Rileigh surreptitiously tried the door. It was locked.

"I'd sure like to get a look at whatever that is," Mitch said.

The woman was still standing just inside the screen door, tapping her foot.

Mitch called out to her. "I'd like to take a look at what's inside this truck. You got the key?"

"It ain't locked. Leroy don't never ... I mean I don't never lock it."

"Well, it's locked."

"I ain't got the key."

"I thought you said it was your truck."

"It is my truck, but I ain't got the key. And if I did, I wouldn't unlock it for you."

"Fine then," Mitch said. "I'll call and get a search warrant." He doubted this woman understood any more about search warrants than Jody Hatfield's mother did. "You're going to have to put up with Rileigh and me sitting in your front yard for the next two or three hours while we wait for the judge to issue the warrant."

"A search warrant?"

"Yes, and it will allow us to seize anything we find in that truck."

"What do you mean, seize anything you find?"

"How many things can 'anything' mean? Whatever we find, we can take if we believe it's evidence of a crime." Mitch thought for a moment and cast a line out there into the Lake of Deception. "Of course, since you own this truck, that search warrant will give us the right to search your house, too. And seize anything we find in it."

The woman stood ramrod straight, and they could see her mind working.

"What if I just say you can look in that truck?"

"That'd be very nice of you, ma'am."

"If I say you can look in the truck, you can take whatever you find?"

"Only if we believe it is evidence of a crime."

"And you can look in the house?"

"No, ma'am, I cannot. You'd have to give me permission to look in the house."

"Then fine, look in the truck."

Mitch tried the door and looked back at her. "The doors are locked."

"Well, it wasn't locked when it was parked there. Give me a minute." She vanished from in front of the screen door and reappeared a few moments later with a single key, an ignition key. She stepped out onto the porch and threw it at Mitch. Not to him, *at* him. It landed on top of the truck cab and skidded across. If she'd thrown just a little harder, she'd have hit Mitch in the head.

"Here, take the damn key and put it in the mailbox when you're done. But you ain't comin' in my house!"

"Agreed, ma'am. We can't come into your house."

She turned and went into the house, banging the door shut behind her

Mitch fit the key into the lock of the truck and opened the driver's side door. Then he punched the button that automatically unlocked the passenger side door as well. Reaching into his pocket, he pulled out a pen and used the end of it to carefully scoot the napkin away from what was lying in the tray between the consoles.

And lying beneath the napkin was not one ring, but two.

Mitch carefully stuck the ballpoint pen down through one of the rings and lifted it up so he and Rileigh could look at it. It was a Smoked' Em ring. He eased the ring into an evidence bag from his hip pocket and used the pen to pick up the other ring. It was a 35/Zip ring. Mitch enclosed that ring in a second evidence bag, then shoved both bags back into his pocket. They searched the rest of the car and found nothing incriminating.

The two of them then went back to the cruiser and got in, but Mitch didn't start the engine.

"What do you say we take these rings by Gus' office and see if he can positively identify who they belong to?"

Mitch let out a sigh. "Then let's put our heads together *again* because I've got a theory."

Rileigh raised an eyebrow and looked at him, waiting for him to explain. "It's complicated. Let's go see what Gus says about these rings."

Chapter Thirty-Eight

Gus carefully picked up the ring in his gloved hands, holding the sides of it so as not to smudge the ring itself, then put a jeweler's magnifying glass up to his eye and held the ring under a bright light to examine it.

He looked back at Rileigh and Mitch.

"There's no engraving on it, no name or anything like that," Gus said. "But there is a tiny dot near the inside edge with a line above it. It's something you might not even see unless you looked for it."

"What is it?"

"It's the signature of the jeweler who made it. Jewelers who make jewelry, rather than just sell rings and necklaces out of glass cases, are an artistic lot. And it doesn't surprise me that whoever made this ring left a signature on it."

"Does that mean—" Mitch began.

"Yes, it does," Gus said. "The jeweler who put his mark in this ring will be able to look at it and tell us who it belongs to."

Mitch smiled. "But between now and then?"

"Between now and then, I'd hazard a very educated guess that this ring belongs to Travis Bramley."

"And you think so because…"

"I think so because of how big it is. Bramley was the biggest of the three, the widest, had the biggest bone structure. He was the center on the football team. His hands were huge."

Gus put down the ring and picked up the other ring, the 35/Zip ring, that Mitch strongly suspected had belonged to Clive McCutcheon.

Gus performed the same procedure on that ring that he had on the previous one. Then he moved the jeweler's magnifying glass out of his eye and said, "We got lucky this time. There are initials in this ring. C.M."

"So how did Leroy McCutcheon happen to have in his possession the rings of two dead men?" Rileigh asked. She turned to Mitch. "You said you had a theory."

"It's complicated," he said. "But it's the only one I can come up with that explains most, not all, but most of the circumstances."

"Lay it on us," Gus said.

"Have you got a whiteboard?"

"Sure," Gus said. "In that room next to my office that I never have figured out what to do with. I put it up there to help me remember my to-do lists by writing them on it."

Gus showed them to the room. Mitch picked up a marker and wrote "Jody" in the top left corner of the whiteboard and "Clive" in the upper right, followed by "Travis" and "Leroy" in the two bottom corners.

Then he turned to look at Gus and Rileigh.

"Hang in here with me. We've been trying our damnedest to figure out how one person committed all these murders. But I think we've been trying to jam ten pounds of mud in a five-pound sack. I think there's a different explanation."

"Like I said, lay it on us," Gus said.

Mitch pointed to Jody's name in the upper left corner of the whiteboard.

"Jody Hatfield had a Smoked 'Em ring on his finger when he died, and the killer took it. We found Jody's ring jammed on Clive McCutcheon's hand."

"So, let's say Clive killed Jody? He certainly had motive enough. Has had for years. Jody messed with his girlfriend, Lauren Coleman. He'd gone with her all through high school — that's what broke up the trio to begin with. Then they had that altercation when both gangs met with a mysterious *somebody* on the Fourth of July at Smoke Creek Park and came away bloodied from that. We'll call that the inciting incident. That's what set the ball rolling."

Mitch used the marker to draw a line from Clive's name on the right side of the board and made it into an arrow that pointed at Jody's name on the left.

"Clive uses a common butcher knife and stabs Jody in the heart, then rips off his face. He hated Jody for being a 'pretty boy' and said that his good looks had charmed the girl he'd stolen from Clive. Then he takes Jody's ring as a souvenir. That finds us the murderer of Jody Hatfield."

Mitch picked up the marker again and drew a line to form an arrow from Travis's name in the lower left-hand corner to point at Clive in the upper right-hand corner.

"What if, in retaliation for Clive killing Jody, Travis kills Clive? He slits his throat — not the same MO as stabbing in the heart." He turned to Gus. "You said the knife used had a sharp edge — but that doesn't mean it was a butcher knife. It could have been a hunting knife. Didn't you say that?"

"I did," Gus agreed.

Mitch continued. "Then Bramley destroys Clive's face with acid in retaliation for what he believes Clive had done to Jody's face. Clive stole Jody's ring after he killed him, and maybe that's how Bramley finally figured out 'for sure' who the murderer was. That's what he said from the beginning — that he wanted to find out 'for sure' who killed Jody. I think that by 'keeping his ear to the ground,' he found out Clive had Jody's ring. I'm thinking that Travis killed Clive and found Jody's ring on him, then he jammed that ring onto Clive's hand because ... remember what they said about the rings, both Clive and Travis? They said the rings symbolized that *we won*. So, Travis put Jody's ring on Clive's finger to symbolize 'We won!' And then he did to Clive what Clive did to Jody ... he stole Clive's gang ring."

"So that solves the murder of Clive McCutcheon," Rileigh said. "He was killed by Travis Bramley in revenge for Jody Hatfield. Am I getting this right?"

"Yeah, you're following me."

"So, who killed Travis Bramley?" Gus asked.

Mitch nodded to the two rings. "The only way Leroy McCutcheon could have had the rings belonging to Clive and Travis in his car is if he killed Travis."

"I'm not following. Wait a minute," Rileigh said.

"Remember, I said Travis took Clive's ring after he killed him? When Leroy killed Travis, he found his brother's ring and took it back — it had belonged to his brother, after all. And he stole Travis Bramley's ring as a trophy."

"Why'd Leroy smash Travis's face with a hammer?"

"For the same reason Travis poured acid on Clive's face — revenge. But I think it was much more a crime of passion. He didn't lure Travis to some place and kill him. I think he found Travis somewhere and just pulled out a gun and shot him. He wasn't prepared with sulfuric acid, so he used a hammer to get the job done."

"So that solves the third murder."

"That gives us three murderers," Rileigh said.

"Yep," Mitch said. "And two of them have already been executed for their crimes."

"So, you're saying when you arrest Leroy McCutcheon for killing Travis Bramley, you will put an end to the back-and-forth murders?" Gus asked.

"Nobody can guarantee that. The vendettas could go on forever. But I'm hoping when the members of Jody Hatfield's gang find out that Clive died for killing Jody and Leonard's been arrested for killing Travis, they'll call that even. And I'm also hoping—"

"I think I know," Rileigh said. "You're hoping that the members of Clive's gang will be satisfied that Leroy took vengeance for Clive's murder. And they'll call it even."

Gus stepped back and looked at the names and the lines drawn on the whiteboard. "That is one convoluted explanation," he said.

"So, poke holes in it," Mitch said.

"I think it mostly holds water," Gus said. "It answers the major questions with reasonable explanations —the faces, the mystery of three different murder weapons, and how Leroy wound up with the two rings."

Mitch nodded, reading his friend's body language. "But …?"

"But there are still dangly things," Gus said.

That's what Gus called pieces of information that didn't fit into the current theory of what had happened.

"As you so eloquently said before, lay it on me," Mitch said.

"How did these murderers manage to get so up-close-

and-personal with their victims that they could kill them without a struggle?"

"I can't answer that one," Mitch said. "I don't know."

Gus let out a sigh. "But your theory does explain everything else. And somebody famous once said, 'If you wait until you have *all* the information, you will never do anything.'"

"Who said that?" Rileigh asked.

"I have no idea. Maybe nobody. Maybe I just made it up. But it sounds good." Gus turned to Mitch, "I think you've got your killers. And you may never find out the specifics of each murder because the only people who know— the murder-er and the murder-ee — are both dead now."

"So, is it over?" Rileigh asked. "Do you think that once everybody knows who killed who, both gangs will feel like they're even?"

"I hope so because if they don't, bodies are going to keep dropping."

Mitch saw Gus's countenance darken.

"These gangbangers are murdered, and we have half a dozen suspects to sort through. But a fine, decent man like Derek Jefferson is murdered, and a week later, we've still got … *nothing*. No motive. No suspects."

Mitch thought about Mayor Rutherford's tirade in his office yesterday, demanding answers — not because he gave a rat's ass about the suffering of Derek Jefferson's family, but because Mitch solving the case would make him look good.

"We have solid DNA evidence off that syringe," Mitch pointed out.

"To use in court to convict the son-of-bitch — but we have to *catch* him first. And we don't have a single lead."

"How is Tanisha doing?" Rileigh asked.

"Not good. The family's walking around on eggshells. They had his body cremated; that's what he wanted, but they can't do any kind of memorial service because they're afraid the strain of it will send her into early labor. Her mother told me Tanny just sits staring at the jar of his ashes..." Gus didn't finish, couldn't.

Mitch touched his arm. "I'm sorry."

He could tell Rileigh was thinking about her teacher, Edna. They had less than no evidence/no suspects in that case. They weren't even certain she'd been murdered at all. He knew Rileigh was wondering if, somewhere out there, a murderer was walking free and would never be brought to justice for killing her.

Chapter Thirty-Nine

JILLIAN HAD SLEPT MAYBE two hours all night. No, probably not even two hours. She tossed and turned and flipped and flopped. Finally, at about three-thirty in the morning, she decided that the effort was futile, and she might as well get up and do something. She got up quietly so as not to disturb Rileigh and Mama and went into her studio. She did indeed need more canvases and more paint. The thought of that she needed to go buy some surprised her, because she was not immediately horrified at the prospect. She didn't like it. She felt enormously uncomfortable at the thought of going somewhere into a store with a whole lot of people and buying art supplies. But she could see herself doing it, forcing herself, yes. She could still see it happening. Was that because she had been willing to see David?

She had tried to banish thoughts of him from her mind. For the first two or three hours, she lay in bed trying to sleep, that's what she spent her time doing — trying *not* to think about David. But now, as she switched on the lights in her studio, put on her smock, and began mixing paints, she let go and allowed herself to think and feel. She mostly felt overwhelmed. David had looked so good. He looked ten years younger than she did, at least, maybe more than that. He was strong, healthy, thick, tanned, and *gorgeous*.

And Jillian was, well, none of the above.

She wasn't healthy. Of course, she wasn't. She hadn't made any effort to take care of herself. What was the point of that? Her life for the years immediately preceding her escape had been as a house servant. She'd waited hand and foot on the family, suffered the abuses of the arrogant, asshole little boys who were being raised to believe that women were *things,* that they weren't thinking beings, that you owed them no respect of any kind that you needed to keep them covered up, and if it were allowed, cut them up so that they would never enjoy sexual activity just so you could be sure that your piece of property had been used by you alone. Just thinking about it made her nauseous and furious. But she wasn't there anymore. She wasn't some man's thing, some family's slave. She was a free woman. She could do what she wanted, and what she ought to be doing was getting herself together.

She desperately needed to have her hair done. She had to make a decision now about whether or not to color it. That was certainly no decision any Arab woman got to make, but she needed to. If she wanted to have beautiful blonde hair again, she was going to have to create it from the limp, untended, speckled-with-gray hair that now fell, at least in natural curls, to the middle of her back.

She needed skincare.

She needed makeup.

She needed all manner of things she didn't have —

things that'd been ancillary to survival when she was on the run, where staying alive meant making herself invisible, erasing her face so that she couldn't be recognized. Jillian had spent the last thirty years hoping no one would notice her. Because being noticed was not a good thing. But seeing David, just for that short period of time, had been almost transformative. Well, not just seeing him or just being near him, but the emotional battle she had fought to get there.

And the way he had looked at her — had she imagined it? Surely, she had imagined it. She had made eye contact with him for no more than a few seconds here and there the whole time she'd been in his presence. But when she looked at his face, the look on it — she had to have imagined the ... *caring.* She wouldn't, couldn't use the word *love.* It couldn't still be there. Not after ...

He was being kind to her, that's all. David Hicks was a kind man.

Rileigh told Jillian that she told David *the basics* of what had happened the night Jillian vanished. She hadn't elaborated. But you didn't have to be a Rhodes Scholar to figure out that a woman kidnapped into a sex slave ring had lived a life of forced prostitution. He had to know that she had been with ... dear God in heaven, there had been hundreds. Maybe thousands. She'd never counted because that meant that thing that was happening to her body had purchase in her mind, and she wouldn't give it that.

Jillian put paintbrush into a dab of paint on her palette and touched it to the canvas, began to blend it mindlessly with other colors, not concentrating on any form or shape or image.

Light began to puddle in the treetops, indicating that dawn was approaching. When she focused her attention on the painting in front of her, she saw that it was different. It was lighter, brighter, not so dark and sinister as all those that'd come before. Was all of that David?

Breakfast with Mama and Rileigh was awkward, since they wouldn't ask her what had prompted her PTSD episode yesterday and didn't want to jinx her upcoming lunch by saying the wrong thing and possibly triggering another episode. They'd both been grateful to leave the table and go do something else.

Jillian was mildly less obsessive about what to wear to have lunch with David than she'd been the night before, but only mildly less. She tried on and discarded everything in her closet and realized, as she did so, that she desperately needed clothes. She hadn't even thought about it before or realized how many possessions normal women her age took for granted. She set her jaw then. If she wanted ... *things*, then she needed to go out and get them on her own. Like any normal woman would. She certainly had enough money. She smiled about that. Her mother and sister had no idea what she had made off with when she'd left! Jillian Bishop was set up for life. She could certainly afford another couple of pairs of jeans, some good shoes, some attractive shirts, and lots of new underwear and makeup.

But she could have none of those by noon today. So she made do with what she had, put on the blouse with red roses on it that Rileigh had gotten her and a pair of normal, not-skinny jeans.

David arrived to pick her up right on time and did a wonderfully adept job of carrying most of the conversation himself without seeming to dominate it, allowing her plenty of opportunity to talk if she chose. She wondered if he'd literally made a list of appropriate topics because he managed to keep his conversation superficial and focused on the present.

There were no questions that would require uncomfortable answers, no remarks that would be unintentionally awkward. They talked about the mountains and the flowers and summertime, and music, and kept it light.

So, what have you been doing for the last 30 years? That didn't come up.

But her heart sank when they found the parking lot of the diner full. It hadn't been when she came the last time. There would be lots of people in there whom David knew. She prayed there would be no one *she* knew. There was something to be said for having changed so much that nobody recognized you. David spoke to half a dozen people as they walked into the building, and she could see all of them surreptitiously examining her, wondering who she was. Perhaps comparing her to whoever they had seen him with last. She didn't let her mind go there. No. Stay in the here and now. That's all she needed.

They were seated at the table, very near the one she and Mama and Rileigh had sat at the day before, back in a corner, a little private.

Cookie fluttered over to the table like a butterfly and dropped into what was a natural flirt mode that was truly amazing to watch. She leaned too close to David, touched him often, made sure he had a bird's eye view of that cleavage, and even accidentally dropped a napkin so she could lean over and display her two perfect assets.

Watching Cookie bat those black eyelashes and swish her tail, Jillian had a gut-wrenching reality check. This was the kind of woman that a man as good-looking as David should be with. This was the kind of woman people would expect him to have on his arm. Jillian, on the other hand, was like somebody's old aunt, dragged out of the attic and the dust blown off, cleaned up as best anyone could to be suitable for public display.

"So, what are you going to have to eat, Sugar? You want some crinkle fries? I can crinkle them for you," Cookie bubbled.

David took it in stride and placed his order. He seemed to be oblivious to the cleavage Cookie tried to shove his nose into and the two perfect butt cheeks she lifted his way. Jillian saw it, compared herself to it, and came up so abysmally short that it took her breath away.

David instantly sensed the difference in Jillian after Cookie slithered her way back behind the bar.

"That girl is something else," he said.

"She sure is," Jillian said, wanting to somehow become smaller, to just sort of fade into her seat and not be there.

"Don't," David said simply, quietly. He put his hand over hers for a moment, then moved it quickly away.

"Don't what?"

"Don't compare yourself to her."

Jillian was floored at his perceptiveness.

"Every woman in the building compares themselves to her, comes up short, and walks away feeling bad about themselves. It's crazy. Cookie is ... a cartoon." He leaned closer and continued, "Not a real woman like you."

It could have been a common sexy remark if he hadn't said it with such genuine kindness and sincerity.

Was it possible that he saw something in Jillian that she didn't see herself? He must because she certainly saw nothing, not anymore.

"I really feel sorry for that girl," David said.

"What?"

"Don't you? I mean ... she's pitiful." He realized she wasn't tracking and explained. "You think that's not all planned out for a reason? Nobody looks like that by accident. It's like she's wearing a costume — the big jugs, the round butt, the red lips. And the slinky movements. How long did she have to practice to get that sway down?"

Jillian was dumbfounded and just looked at him.

"It's pathetic ... and sad. Something's very broken ... so aching to be noticed that she would go to any lengths, any lengths at all, to be the center of attention. Now, why would a woman do that?"

Jillian had no idea and no response. But David never seemed to expect a response to his questions. He managed to couch them all in rhetorical-question tones so she could answer if she chose to, but there was certainly nothing wrong if she didn't.

"That girl has a story to tell," he said, "and it's a sad one."

Jillian looked at Cookie behind the bar, giggling at a remark some man had made as she handed him his milkshake. Suddenly, she could see it, too, what David had described, the frenetic quality of Cookie's blatant sexuality that wasn't natural for anybody. What had happened to her that made her feel compelled to put on that act?

"The contrast is striking. There's ... *character* so evident in you that somebody like Cookie isn't capable of."

Embarrassed, Jillian said nothing, just stared into his eyes.

Cookie appeared as if magically summoned and set their burgers, fries, and milkshakes on the table.

"Can I get you anything else?"

David paused for a moment, considering.

"I tell you what — how about you bring us boxes for the burgers, cups for the milkshakes. We want it all 'to go.'"

As she swayed her way back to the bar, David reached for Jillian's hand, but stopped short, didn't take it, merely said, "Let's get out of here, Jillian. Let's go somewhere ...

somewhere beautiful. Somewhere we can look at the mountains and the trees and smell the fresh air and just enjoy being alive!"

Jillian found a smile. It felt almost uncomfortable on her face, but uncomfortable in a good way.

"Yes," she said. "Let's have a picnic."

Chapter Forty

MITCH GOT into his cruiser and headed down the winding roads that he had already driven twice today to the home of Clive McCutcheon, where he hoped to find Leroy McCutcheon and arrest him for the murder of Travis Bramley.

He considered his convoluted theory of who killed who and shook his head. It fit together ... like jamming your foot into a shoe that was half a size too small. You could wear it, but it was tight and uncomfortable. His explanation of what had happened still didn't account for why the victims had not struggled. Three burley men, bloodied and bruised in countless barroom brawls — why were they unwilling ... or *unable* to fight for their lives?

But a tight shoe was better than going barefoot, and perhaps they would be able to uncover evidence after the arrest that would make some sense out of the parts that didn't fit.

Mitch genuinely believed that Leroy had killed Travis Bramley, though Mitch had his own private secondary reasons, too. Reasons he wouldn't have said out loud to anybody, but he was self-aware enough to recognize them hanging out in the background, behind the important stuff. Bottom line: Mitch wanted the case to be *over* so that he could go on with his life without the distraction of one-on-top-of-the-other homicide investigations.

Going on with his life involved actually taking Rileigh out on a date to a nice restaurant. Guthrie's Steakhouse, not a noisy, crowded diner. A date where they could enjoy each other's company without discussing anything that involved blood.

And after dinner... well, it was a long drive from Nashville back to Black Bear Forge. Maybe they'd just decide to spend the night in Nashville.

But chasing down the fantasy rabbit hole of *that* thought was way too distracting for now. Mitch would savor it later. He drove his cruiser up the impossibly steep road to the top of the mountain, then down into the secluded hollow on the other side. He pulled off the road at the McCutcheons' mailbox, stopped, and got out of his car to open the gate. He drove across the cattle guard, got out again, closed the gate behind him, and then drove the rest of the way up the gravel driveway to the house.

He was delighted to see that the jacked-up pickup truck he was sure belonged to Leroy McCutcheon was still parked out front. Leroy had been home when he and Rileigh had been here the first time, but now Mitch had probable cause to demand to search the house and flush the kid out.

Mitch parked between the jacked-up pickup and the thick hedge that grew in front of the storage shed beside the house, then got out of his cruiser. He'd only taken a couple of steps when a gunshot rang out, and a bullet flew so close to his head that he felt the air rearrange itself around the bullet after it passed. The round pinged off the top of his cruiser a couple of inches from his head. Dropping instantly to the ground, he pulled his service weapon.

What in the world?

A string of colorful obscenity rang out from inside the house — a man's voice, berating whoever had fired for not waiting until they had a clear shot. Then, the voice addressed him.

"You ain't taking my boy nowhere!"

The voice wasn't coming from the front door. It sounded more like somebody was shouting from one of the upstairs windows. "I done planted one son in the ground and you ain't gonna take my other 'un. He didn't kill nobody, but you'll blame it on my boy just so's you can say you found the killer. But that ain't gonna be the way of it."

Another bullet pinged off the top of the car, but this one came from a different direction. Someone had been hiding in the barn loft when Mitch had driven past. Now, they were firing at him from two directions and had him pinned down. He couldn't go around the front of his cruiser, and he couldn't go around the back.

Taking deep breaths to quiet the hammering of his heart, Mitch felt his mind and body shift into survival mode, where training took over and his responses were automatic.

First up, assess the situation: *deep shit*.

His M4 patrol rifle was clipped to the ceiling rack above the cruiser's steering wheel. It had twenty-eight rounds of ammo. There were a hundred and fifty rounds in the tactical vest in his trunk. But all one hundred seventy-eight rounds were useless because he could reach neither the rifle nor the extra ammo without exposing himself to deadly fire. His service revolver was fully loaded, of course — ten plus one, which meant that he'd loaded the single stack magazine and chambered the first round, then removed the magazine and replaced the round he'd chambered. Still, that was only eleven bullets ... and he was facing three, perhaps more shooters. And he was firing a pistol, while the rounds fired at him were coming from rifles, maybe a 30.06, a deer rifle. The words of his firearms instructor rang in his head. *Never take a knife to a gunfight. And never take a pistol to a rifle fight.* He was not just outmanned, he was outgunned, too.

Definitely time for a bluff.

"Put those weapons down right now," he called out. "I want to have a talk with your son, but you just raised the stakes on that talk—"

"Ain't gonna be no talk, Sheriff," cried a female voice from the barn. "You ain't leaving here alive."

"Do you really think you can kill the sheriff and get away with it?"

"Sheriff? We ain't seen the sheriff," the woman yelled back, "He and that Bishop woman come by here this morning, and we ain't seen him since."

"You and that cruiser are just gonna vanish," the man in the house called out. "With you dead, ain't nobody to say you's ever here. We'll bury your body so deep in the woods, the devil won't even be able to find it to take your soul to hell."

"That car'll be stripped down to the frame before nightfall," called a second male voice from the house, a younger man, maybe the guy who'd fired the first shot and missed. "File off the VIN numbers and sell the pieces for scrap. By this time tomorrow morning, won't be a trace of Sheriff Mitchell Webster to be found anywhere in Yarmouth County."

They'd obviously thought this all through and had been waiting for his return to ambush him, and his current predicament was one hundred percent his own fault. He should have brought backup with him to make the arrest. He keyed the mic on his shoulder in a vain attempt to get anything but static. He and Rileigh had already seen there was no radio coverage in this hollow. He wouldn't be able to call for help.

"When they come asking about you, we'll say we never seen you, and Leroy won't be here, won't be anywhere they can get their hands on him." The woman called from the barn. "He's leaving for Little Rock, where we got family, and there's a job waiting for him. Ain't nothing you can do to stop him."

Leroy was about to make a break for it. Would be long out of the county, on his way to Little Rock, if he got past Mitch, and right now, Mitch was in no position to stop him.

Unless ...

It was a desperate plan. Could go wrong in any number of ways, but right now Mitch was fresh out of other options. Shoving his pistol into his holster, Mitch dropped on his belly, rolled under his cruiser, and crawled toward Leroy's truck.

Chapter Forty-One

Rileigh got into her car parked behind the courthouse. Mitch had dropped her in the parking lot on his way to arrest Leroy McCutcheon. And they hoped — they being Rileigh, Gus, and Mitch — that the arrest would put an end to all the bloodshed.

Rileigh wanted desperately to believe the brutal murders would stop. No more having to carry the news to some poor family that a loved one had been executed.

And once the case was over, she could pick up her life where she had dropped it. She and Mitch could go on that big date that had been put off and put off — and then aborted the night Jody Hatfield was found without a face in the storage room at the Red Eye Gravy Diner.

Her phone dinged with an incoming message. She held it up and read the part where Georgia asked her the perennial question. "Rileigh, if you're in town, would you mind…"

Rileigh didn't have to see the rest of it. She punched off before the *"stopping at the grocery store and picking up some bananas for me?"* part. That family went through bananas faster than a family of orangutans.

When Rileigh pulled up into Georgia's driveway and got out, she was mobbed by the kids who were playing outside. She loved that part of coming to see Georgia. The kids coming to her and hugging her, telling her they loved her. *And then going back out to play.* The parts beyond that, when the kids interacted with each other or with their parents, Rileigh would just as soon skip.

Inside, she hugged Georgia hello and handed her the bananas. Georgia peeled one and shoved it into Mayella's mouth as she invited Rileigh to sit for a cup of coffee.

"Would you like to go with Mama and me to the Celebration of Life service for Mrs. Considine tomorrow?" Rileigh asked. "They're having it in the high school auditorium to accommodate the crowd."

"Sure ... *if* I go. I'll have to let you know." Translate that: Georgia didn't know if Chigger would be around to take care of the kids. Rileigh wouldn't allow herself to get angry at Chigger for always making Georgia carry the lion's share of the burden of caring for their children. She'd reached a truce, of sorts, in her mind after he had stepped up so valiantly when Mason was kidnapped, and Rileigh needed to let that sleeping dog lie.

"So, what have you been doing this morning?" Georgia asked.

And Rileigh told her, watched her eyes get bigger and bigger. When she finally got to the end of the tale, Georgia shook her head.

"I'm so confused. It made sense when you were explaining who killed who and who took whose ring and did what with it. But now my head's spinning."

"All you need to know is that it's over. Or at least we hope it is." Rileigh paused. "And it being over ..."

Georgia lifted an eyebrow, and Rileigh smiled.

"Maybe Mitch and I might find time in our busy schedules to have the big date!"

Georgia squealed and grinned.

"And I'm not the only one of the Bishop girls going out on the town with a man."

Rileigh told Georgia what had happened between Jillian and David and watched the smile on Georgia's face spread so wide that, if the ends met in the back, the whole top of her head would fall off.

"They're having lunch today at Red Eye Gravy."

"Oh, yeah, Red Eye Gravy," Georgia said as if the words had reminded her of something. "Hold on a second."

Georgia hopped up out of her chair and went into the other room, then came back with a shoebox full of loose pictures.

"I was telling you the other day about Abby when she was in high school. Then this morning, when I was cleaning out the hall closet, I found this box of old pictures and decided to look through it and see if I could find a graduation picture of Abby — to show you how slim she was then, in comparison to *now*."

She set the box of pictures on the table.

"I couldn't find that graduation picture, *but* ... I did find *this*." She reached into the box, picked up a picture off the top of the pile, and handed it to Rileigh.

The woman smiling out of the picture was Mama, a much younger version.

"Where'd you get this?"

"It's a picture of Vacation Bible School. Your mama was the teacher, and Abby was in the class. See, Abby's right there." Georgia pointed to her little sister. "I'd forgotten how adorable she was as a kid. No wonder Mama always sided with her in the Sister Wars."

Rileigh held the picture and studied it. The children were standing in front of a banner that read: VBS 2007. "Look at Mama. She looks so different with brown hair."

Georgia beamed. "I knew you'd love seeing your mama so young."

"This settles it. When I start going gray ... L'oreal says I'm worth it."

Then she pointed to the child standing next to Abby in the picture, a chunky little girl with only one dimple.

"That's who Mama was talking about, I bet. Can I take this picture home and show her?"

"Of course, you can take the picture home. I picked it out to give to you." Georgia paused. "But why was your mother talking about that little girl?"

"We were in Red Eye Gravy the other day, and Mama was talking to Miss Swivel Hips and Big Tits, otherwise known as Everybody Loves to Nibble on a Cookie, about the fact that she only has one dimple. Mama told her she reminded her of a little girl from Vacation Bible School years ago — who also only had one dimple. I bet this is the little girl Mama was talking about."

"Abby said that the poor fat girl those guys terrorized was a uni-dimple, too. Remember?"

She poked her finger at the picture of the little girl standing beside Abby. "They're the same age, would have been in the same class. I bet this little girl grew up to be— oh my, she grew up to be the girl they bullied. What's her name?"

Rileigh turned the picture over and read through the names that were handwritten in faded ink on the back and found the name of the little girl standing beside Abby.

"It says here this is Sheila Lane," Rileigh said.

"Lane! That was her last name. I couldn't remember it. That's *her.* That's who Abby said those guys terrorized."

Rileigh and Georgia looked at the little fat girl beside her sister and shook their heads.

"Most people probably don't notice that Cookie is under-endowed in dimple-dom because she's over-endowed everywhere else— they're too busy gawking at other parts of her anatomy."

"Unfortunately, this one-dimpled little girl grew up to be Sheila Lane," Georgia said, "not — what's Cookie's real name?"

Rileigh had to think a moment. Mitch had told her— "Ashlie Neal."

Georgia giggled, batted her eyelashes, and said in an affected, high, squeaky voice, "But they call me Cookie. Everybody *loves* to nibble on a cookie."

Rileigh sat staring at the little girl in the picture with only one dimple, the little girl who had grown up to be the fat girl the football heroes had terrorized for two hellish years.

"Sheila Lane," Rileigh said the name slowly. Then, said the individual words. "Sheila. Lane."

Rileigh suddenly snatched up a crayon off the table, turned a grocery sack over, and wrote out the name. "Sheila Lane." Beneath it, she wrote out Cookie's name, "Ashlie Neal." Then she sat staring at the two names.

"What are you doing?"

Rileigh didn't respond. She just stared at the words. There was *something* about …

Then she saw it. It was one of those things that are so obvious once you see it you can't believe you didn't see it in the beginning.

"Those are anagrams," Rileigh said.

"*What* are anagrams?"

"You know what an anagram is, don't you?"

"Yeah, you take the letters in one word and make it into another word."

"Look at this." Rileigh used the crayon to mark off the individual letters. S/ H/ E/ I/ L/ A. "See, there's the A in Ashlie, there's the S, there's the H, there's—"

"I see it," Georgia said. "The names 'Sheila' and 'Ashlie' are anagrams.

"Lane and Neal are anagrams, too," Rileigh said.

The odds of that being a coincidence were slim to none.

Rileigh would bet on *none*.

Chapter Forty-Two

MITCH HEARD the front door of the house open, followed by footsteps clomping on the porch steps, then the crunch of gravel as Leroy McCutcheon ran toward his jacked-up truck. Mitch saw Leroy's feet as he got to the truck, leapt in behind the wheel, and slammed the door shut. He started the engine of the truck, pulled out of the parking space, turned, and headed down the driveway to the gate ... which Mitch had politely closed behind him when he came through it.

Leroy stopped the truck at the fence, leapt out and ran to the gate. Mitch let go where he was holding onto the undercarriage of the jacked-up truck, dropped down into the dirt, then rolled quickly out from under the truck on the driver's side and got up on his knees on the front side of the door that Leroy had left open. He didn't stand up, remained hidden from the shooters in the house and barn. As soon as Leroy had the gate open, Mitch pointed his weapon and called out.

"Leroy McCutcheon, get your hands out where I can see them."

The young man whirled around, so surprised to see Mitch covered in dirt and kneeling in front of his open truck door that he literally staggered back a step in shock.

"Hands in the air, turn around, and lock your fingers behind your head. Do it, son, do it now."

"You …" he sputtered. "How'd you …?"

He looked back toward the house and barn, where family members still believed they had Mitch pinned down behind his cruiser parked in front of the house, and opened his mouth to shout for help.

"Lock those fingers behind your head right now, or you're a dead man."

"You won't kill me."

"The hell I won't! You think I'm going to stay here and let your family shoot me full of holes and bury my body in an unmarked grave up in the woods? I'm getting out of here *right now* in this truck. You can come with me, or I can run over your dead body on my way out the gate. Your choice. Last chance to turn around and lock your fingers behind your head."

Leroy slowly turned his back toward the house, faced the road, and locked his fingers behind his head.

The people in the house and the loft of the barn could see what was happening down at the road, that Leroy now stood at the open gate in the fence, as if somebody had a gun on him. Though Mitch was out of sight, crouched between the open door and Leroy, it wouldn't take them long to figure out who it was. Mitch was sure they'd quickly check to find his hiding spot behind the cruiser vacant. Even down by the road, he was still well within the range of the rifles they were firing, so he needed to move fast.

Leaping to his feet, Mitch grabbed Leroy from behind, slammed him face down on the hood of the truck, and kicked his feet wide apart to put him off balance. Leaning over Leroy's body on the hood, he jammed the barrel of the gun in the boy's back with one hand and snatched his handcuffs off his belt with the other. Reaching up with an open cuff, he snapped it on Leroy's wrist and dragged the boy's hand down behind his back, brutally shoving it upward until Leroy cried out in pain.

"Give me your other hand — *slow*." He shoved hard on Leroy's pinned arm. "Any sudden movements, and I'll dislocate your arm from your shoulder."

Leroy grunted and whined but did as he was instructed, and Mitch snapped the other cuff shut on his wrist.

Pulling him to his feet in front of him, Mitch growled into his ear.

"Now, we're gonna walk slow to the door of the truck. You're going to get in and crawl over to the passenger side. And if you so much as wiggle an ear, I will take you out and leave you here in the dirt."

As Mitch and Leroy moved slowly in lockstep toward the open truck door, a man and a teenage boy emerged from the house, both carrying rifles, while a rifle-toting woman came out of the barn. Once they established that their pinned-down quarry had escaped, all of them started running toward the road.

"Stop where you are and drop those weapons," Mitch called out to them, "or I'll shoot the boy."

"You wouldn't do that," the man cried. "You're the sheriff. You wouldn't shoot him down in cold blood."

"You mean like you've been trying to do to me? But you got that part right, I wouldn't kill him ... not with the first shot, anyway. I'll take out his right knee with it, then his left, then elbows and wrists. I bet I can empty the whole magazine into him before you cut me down."

"Do it, Mama," Leroy cried. "Do what he says. This son-of-a-bitch is crazy."

The three McCutcheons reluctantly placed their rifles on the ground at their feet — where they could easily grab them back up.

"Walk away toward the creek. Do it now."

The three moved slowly toward the creek.

Mitch moved Leroy closer to the truck.

"Get in slow. Scoot over to the passenger side."

Leroy got into the truck awkwardly, his hands cuffed behind his back. Mitch suddenly shoved him roughly forward, dumping his body half on the passenger seat and half in the floorboard. Mitch leapt in beside him and put the truck in gear, didn't bother to close the door, just lurched out across the cattle guard to the road. He could see the three McCutcheons standing near the creek and they didn't try to interfere.

If he remembered correctly, it was less than a mile to the point where he could use his radio and call for backup.

Chapter Forty-Three

"ANAGRAMS?" Georgia said, confused. "*Both* names are anagrams?"

"Sheila/Ashlie, Lane/Neal," Rileigh said. "First name and last name anagrams — that didn't happen accidentally."

A memory flashed across her mind as bright as a comet.

"Can you tell me a five-letter word where the second letter is Y and it means infant avian? I just love word puzzles, cryptograms, word search, rebuses."

"... and *anagrams*..." Rileigh whispered softly.

"What are you saying?"

"I guess what I'm saying is that this little girl—" Rileigh pointed to the chubby little girl with a single dimple in the photograph "—is Sheila Lane, the same Sheila Lane who was bullied when she got to high school ... and whose name just happens to be an anagram for Ashlie Neal." Rileigh paused to take a breath before she completed the thought. "What if Sheila Lane and Ashlie Neal are the same person?"

"This little girl didn't grow up to be Ashlie Neal," Georgia said. "She couldn't have grown up to be *Cookie!* This kid was already overweight in kindergarten. Sheila Lane was a fat, ugly teenager — so pitifully homely that the guys terrorized her. How could she be Cookie now?"

"She's only got one dimple," Rileigh said, then her eyes unfocused in a thousand-yard stare as she listened to the sudden cacophony in her mind.

"Knock, knock," Georgia said, rapping her knuckles on the table. "Earth to Rileigh, come in, where are you?"

Rileigh's eyes focused again. "What if Sheila Lane changed her name and became Ashlie Neal—"

"She'd have to change more than just her name to pull that off. She'd have to change her whole self."

"Okay, what if she changed her whole self and became Ashlie Neal?"

"What if she did? If that living Barbie Doll is Sheila Lane, why wouldn't she tell anybody? I mean, if you left town a frog and came back home a princess, wouldn't you be blasting it from the rooftops? Take out a full-page ad in the newspaper, rent a billboard, and put up a forty-foot-tall bikini shot. 'Hey, everybody, look at me!'"

"Hard to say what I'd do since I have no desire to look like a Barbie Doll ... well, except for the perfect ass part. I'd take that in a New York minute."

"Well, if *I'd* been transformed like that, I'd sure as shit want to rub some noses in my newfound gorgeousness. I'd go looking for those guys who terrorized me and get some payback."

They both froze. The smile that was starting on Rileigh's face died there as the grin slowly drained off Georgia's face. Neither of them spoke, just sat looking at each other wide-eyed.

"*Payback,*" Rileigh repeated the word, her voice as soft as smoke.

Synapses in both their brains started spitting out new connections.

"All three of the boys who terrorized Sheila Lane are *dead* now," Georgia said, wondering at her own words.

"Not just dead ... *murdered*. And not just murdered ..." Rileigh paused. "All three of the boys who called her ugly had their faces destroyed."

They sat again in wide-eyed silence.

Rileigh felt her way through lumpy, uncomfortable, frightening thoughts.

"The guys in those two gangs have been rivals ever since high school and have hated each other for years. Got into barroom brawls every now and then, but nothing life-threatening ... until Cookie came to town. Then they suddenly started killing each other, all three of them dead within a week."

Struggling to breathe with her chest suddenly tight and restricted, Rileigh simply said, "The dangly thing." Georgia didn't know what she was talking about.

"Gus' dangly thing. When Mitch was explaining how he thought it all went down — who killed who, when, and how — Gus said it all worked out logically and explained all the details of the murders except for one thing, one dangly thing."

"And that was?"

"Why didn't the victims fight back? He said, 'How did a murderer manage to get so up-close-and-personal with their victims, and none of them even struggled.'"

Georgia answered the question: "*Seduction* is about as up close and personal as you can get."

"And if you struck fast — a knife in the heart, a slit

jugular vein, a bullet in the head — there'd be no time for a struggle."

The two women fell silent again, sat at Georgia's kitchen table without speaking. It felt to Rileigh as if the whole world had been wrapped in cotton. Even the sounds of the children's voices seemed distant and ethereal.

"Payback."

Rileigh couldn't breathe for a few seconds after she said the word. Then she reached across the table and took Georgia's hand.

"Sheila Lane came back here with her identity hidden to kill the boys who had terrorized her when she was in high school."

Georgia opened her mouth and shook her head — it couldn't be! — but she didn't say that. No words at all came out.

"Georgia, if Cookie is Sheila Lane — who somehow, by some miracle of diet and exercise and ... I don't know, plastic surgery — if somehow Ashlie Neal is Sheila Lane, then she explains every one of the murders."

Another couple of the puzzle pieces fell out of the sky and hit Rileigh square in the head then. Two names, the words painting portraits of two people in her mind's eye.

"And she did *not* want to get caught in the ruse. She could only pull it off and get away with it if nobody recognized her." Rileigh grabbed a breath before she blurted out the rest. "What if she didn't bite her tongue. What if Cookie cracked a tooth?"

Georgia wasn't tracking. "What? When—?"

"Mitch got a call from Cookie that somebody had vandalized the pictures of the football team on the walls of the diner, and we went there to take a look. Cookie was eating something ... nuts of some kind, I think, and she said, ow."

"And that's significant because…?"

"I thought she'd bitten her tongue, but what if she cracked her tooth? She would've called a dentist to fix it."

"Where are you going with this?"

"What if the dentist looked into her mouth and … saw something, recognized something. What if Derek Jefferson was Sheila's dentist as a child, and he figured out who she was?"

"She would have to keep him from telling anybody, so…" Georgia didn't finish. She didn't have to.

Then Rileigh's mind conjured up and served her a three-dimensional image of Edna Considine, lying dead on the asphalt, her eye sockets filling with rainwater.

"Mrs. Considine. What if she recognized Sheila, saw that miserable, homely teenager in Cookie?"

Georgia's hands flew to her mouth. "Dr. Jefferson and Mrs. Considine."

"Oh, dear God, Georgia, it all fits."

Rileigh would have thought there were no more horrifying thoughts than those she'd just spoken aloud until the worst thought of all landed on her chest with both feet — in army boots.

"Cookie killed both those people because they recognized who she was …*and*…"

"And what?"

Rileigh could barely say the whole word: *"Mama!"*

"What about Mama?"

"Mama recognized her." Rileigh hauled in a ragged breath. "When we went to the diner, Mama told Cookie that she reminded her of a little girl from Vacation Bible School … and Mama was trying to remember the little girl's name."

Rileigh snatched her cell phone out of her pocket, touched favorites with trembling fingers, and hit Mama.

The phone rang and rang and rang. Mama never picked up.

Rileigh was on her feet and moving as she hit the favorites again and touched Mitch's number.

"Where are you going?" Georgia cried.

"Home!"

Racing out to her car, she held the phone to her ear and listened to Mitch's voicemail.

"Dammit," she swore. "Mitch, listen, I'm at Georgia's on my way home to … " She couldn't finish the sentence, couldn't say "to save Mama." So she blurted out the whole story instead, the puzzle she and Georgia had figured out, as she leapt into her car, started the engine, and peeled out, leaving rubber on the road in front of Georgia's house.

Chapter Forty-Four

MITCH PULLED the jacked-up Ford pickup truck off onto the side of the road when he was sure he had gotten into an area where he had radio coverage. He stopped, keyed the mic on his shoulder, and was delighted to hear the dispatcher respond. He said that he had Leroy McCutcheon in custody and instructed her to dispatch Deputies Crawford, Mullins, and Rawlings to the McCutcheon house to disarm and arrest Leroy's mother, father, and brother, who had opened fire on him. The dispatcher replied that Deputy Rawlings was only a couple of miles away from Mitch's present location, so he'd be the first on the scene.

Mitch decided he'd to hand off his prisoner to Rawlings and wait until the other deputies arrived to go with them to make the arrests at the McCutcheon house.

Leroy was still half on the seat and half in the floorboard of the truck, where he'd landed when Mitch shoved him inside. Mitch left him there as he went around to the passenger side, where he would have cover if, for some ridiculous reason, the McCutcheons decided to come after him.

Leroy did nothing but curse for most of the five or ten minutes before Deputy Rawlings arrived. Together, they hauled Leroy out of the jacked-up truck to put him in the back of Rawling's cruiser.

"I didn't have time before, but I have time now," Mitch told him. "Leroy McCutcheon, you are under arrest for the murder of Travis Bramley. You have the right to remain silent…"

Mitch rattled off the rest of the Miranda statement, then began dragging Leroy toward Deputy Rawlings's cruiser, mostly tuning out Leroy's litany of woe.

"I keep telling you I didn't kill nobody," he whined. "I would have if I'd had the chance. But I didn't. I ain't seen Travis Bramley since the Fourth of July."

"Well, Travis Bramley saw you Wednesday night, at least until you put a bullet in the back of his skull."

"Whoa, whoa, whoa, hold on a minute," Leroy said and stopped in his tracks. "Are you telling me Travis Bramley was killed on Wednesday night?"

"You know when he was killed," Mitch said, "given that you were there at the time."

Mitch pulled on Leroy's arm, but the man wouldn't move.

"I was told he got killed on Thursday morning."

"His body was discovered in that alley where you dumped it on Thursday morning, but the coroner ruled that he was killed the night before."

"The night before? As in Wednesday night?"

"Wednesday night is the night before Thursday morning. Yes, that's the order of days in most weeks."

Suddenly, Leroy McCutcheon burst out laughing. He

laughed so hard he could barely stand up, and Mitch had to support him.

"What's so funny?" Mitch asked, but Leroy just kept roaring laughter, tears of mirth streaming down his cheeks. Mitch dragged him toward Deputy Rawlings' cruiser as he laughed until he tripped and fell to his knees. He sat there on his knees, laughing, and Mitch left him to it, patiently waiting until he could control himself. When he had wound down considerably, Mitch asked, "You ready to tell me what's so funny?"

"*You're* what's funny. You got egg all over your face, and you don't even know it."

"How do you figure that?"

"Because I couldn't have killed Travis Bramley on Wednesday night. I have an alibi."

"Right. You were sitting at home with your mother, father, and brother, who are going to be joining you in jail as soon as we can get them there." He reached down, took Leroy's arm, and hauled him to his feet. "The three of you were watching Family Feud together as a family, right?"

"Nope, I wasn't home watching television Wednesday night." He began to laugh again. "My alibi ain't just a bunch of family members swearing where I was. I got an ironclad alibi ... as in iron bars."

"What are you talking about?"

"I wasn't out murdering Travis Bramley Wednesday night ... wasn't 'out,' period. I was 'in,' locked up in jail in Carruthers County on Wednesday night. Didn't get out until first thing Thursday morning."

Mitch had been shoving Travis toward the cruiser, but he stopped then.

"What did you say?"

Leroy was enjoying himself now. "Go ahead, arrest my ass. And I'll sue you for false arrest."

"You were in jail?"

"Call and find out for yourself." Leroy continued to chuckle. "You're gonna have to find somebody else to pin this one on."

Mitch looked at Deputy Rawlings. "Check out his story," Mitch said.

Rawlings stepped aside and called on his cell phone while Mitch loaded Leroy into the back seat of his cruiser.

"It's confirmed," Rawlings said after he hung up. "Burt Williams backed him up." Williams was the Nelson County Jailer. "He said McCutcheon was in his custody, locked in the drunk tank, from eight o'clock on Wednesday night until six o'clock on Thursday morning."

Leroy let out a whoop of triumph then and gestured toward the handcuffs that still bound his hands behind his back.

"Now, take these damned cuffs off me," Leroy said, jeering.

"You're still under arrest, and you're still going to jail."

"You just heard it, I couldn't be the killer. What are you taking me to jail for?"

"We'll start with resisting arrest and work our way forward from there."

Mitch slammed the door of the cruiser and walked away, listening to McCutcheon's laughter.

Deputy Mullins pulled up then, lights flashing, and got out.

Mitch stood beside the cruiser, waiting for the remaining deputies, shaking his head and repeating softly, "He didn't do it. Holy shit. He didn't do it." Mitch sighed. "Right back where we started."

Then he remembered that he'd seen the light flashing on his cell phone, indicating he'd missed a call while he was busy getting shot at.

He pulled the phone out and saw that it was Rileigh. His face registered surprise, disbelief, and shock as he listened to her voicemail.

Cookie?

Then he punched favorites and called Rileigh's number. The phone rang until her voicemail kicked in. No answer. After that, he called Mama's number. Mama's number rang until the voicemail kicked in. Becoming more concerned by the second, he called Georgia.

"No, Rileigh's not here. She flew out of here like a bat out of hell as soon as she figured out that Mama was in danger."

"In danger? Why?"

"Didn't Rileigh tell you in the message? Mama recognized Cookie just like Dr. Jefferson and Mrs. Considine did — and both of them got killed for it."

Her words hit him like a wrecking ball in his chest.

"And Rileigh's at home now?"

Georgia paused. "Yeah, I'm sure she's home by now. She's been gone for long enough to be there."

Mitch disconnected the call and turned to Deputy Mullins. "I'm taking your cruiser."

Leaping behind the wheel, Mitch flew down the road toward Mama's house, keying the mic on his shoulder and redirecting other deputies there. They could go arrest the McCutcheons some other time.

He put his foot down harder on the accelerator and found himself careening around a dangerous corner. If he didn't slow down, he could lose control on one of these curves.

Rileigh was home by now ... so why wasn't she answering her phone? And why wasn't Mama?

Mitch didn't slow down.

Chapter Forty-Five

WITH HER HEART thundering in her chest, Rileigh roared up the driveway to Mama's house so fast her car almost went airborne on the lump at the top, and she had to slam on the brakes to keep from crashing through the fence.

She tried to look at everything at once, so terrified for her mother that she could barely breathe. But nothing was out of place, all looked peaceful. Mama's car was parked out front, as was Jillian's.

And there were no other cars in the driveway. Nobody was here.

It was early evening, and the shadow of the mountain had already crossed over the house, leaving it in the twilight darkness that, in the mountains, grew into the night like the thickening of chocolate pudding. Bright lights shone out Mama's windows. Nothing looked menacing. If anything, the house looked even more welcoming than usual tonight. Relief began to replace the knot of fear that had tied her belly in a knot as she'd raced down the winding roads. And though she leapt out of the car and ran up the sidewalk to the porch, she paused there to grab hold of her emotions so as not to go charging into the house like a mad woman and scare poor Mama and Jillian to death.

As soon as she got to the porch steps, she could hear Mama's voice, basic cheery Mama babble, and full relief washed over her. Mama was fine, prattling to Jillian about something or other that very likely made no sense at all. Rileigh was here now to protect her mother, and she'd keep the woman who had already murdered five people from eliminating the last person in the county who had recognized her.

Five murders. It was mind-boggling. And Cookie had come within a hair's breadth of getting away with it. She'd played the role of air-headed bimbo perfectly and had cast suspicion in every other direction with the swapping of gang rings. Nobody had connected her in any way to the killings. Today had been her last day of work at the Red Eye Gravy Diner. She was free to pack up her things, drive out of Yarmouth County, and never look back. Rileigh was sure she would do just that. She wasn't going after Mama — a crazy old woman remembering a kid she taught in Vacation Bible School decades ago. Nobody'd listen; her secret was safe. Sheila Lane, AKA Ashlie Neal, AKA Everybody Likes to Nibble on a Cookie, could just ... vanish.

And with no other suspects, Leroy McCutcheon might actually have been convicted of killing Travis Bramley, what with the damning evidence of two gang rings just lying out in plain sight in his truck — a truck his mother said he never locked. It'd been locked this morning, though. Cookie had locked it up tight behind her after she planted the evidence in it.

Cookie almost got away with murdering poor Derek Jefferson, whose little girl would grow up now without a father. And Edna Considine, whose accidental death was no accident at all. Rileigh ground her teeth in rage. She would ask Mitch to come along when he went to arrest the little bitch. Let her try to twitch that perfect ass to get out of *that!*

Rileigh opened the screen door, which, of course, squawked in protest. She'd always believed the spring on that door squalled extra loud to make up for the mute porch swing that remained resolutely silent. Mama was still talking, her voice carrying from the kitchen as Rileigh went into the house and through the living room. When she got to the dining room, she could make out the words Mama was saying.

" … and Rileigh will be home directly. And I'm here to tell you she ain't gonna like it one bit that—"

Rileigh burst into the kitchen and interrupted.

"Mama, I damn near ran off the road half a dozen times between here and Georgia's. I was so…"

Rileigh didn't finish the sentence. Couldn't. The words froze on her lips as soon as she saw Mama's face, the look of terror on it. Then, in something like slow motion, she followed Mama's gaze to the other side of the room, where Cookie stood with a gun pointed at Mama's chest.

Rileigh went for her own weapon in the under-the-belt holster at her side, knowing as she reached for it that she couldn't possibly get the gun out in time.

Bang!

The sound of the gunshot from the .22 pistol reverberated like a cannon off the walls of the kitchen. The pain of the slug plowing into Rileigh was like a hot skewer burning into her belly, and she looked down, watching stupidly as the front of her t-shirt turned red before her knees let go, and she crumpled to the floor.

Mama screamed and ran to her, knelt beside her.

A Friend Like You

"Dammit, dammit, *dammit!*"

Rileigh could hear the words, but they seemed to be coming from a long way off, sounding hollow like somebody had yelled them in a cathedral, and she waited for the echo that never came.

"Look what you made me do!" Cookie yelled, but Rileigh didn't recognize her voice — because it was her normal voice, not the high-pitched, squeaky voice she had affected at the diner. "It's all *your* fault, both of you. You think I want to do this? It's all your fault."

Rileigh couldn't feel the floor beneath her, even though she knew she was lying on the floor. Why couldn't she feel it? She felt like she was wrapped in cotton, floating, not touching anything. It sounded like she'd put her fingers in her ears, too, because she couldn't hear. The world was muffled. And a stabbing pain burned like hot coals in her belly. She recognized the pain. She'd been shot before — in the shoulder once, and she'd taken a piece of shrapnel in the leg. But this was worse, exponentially worse. Her whole body was on fire. Then she felt something wet and sticky on her cheek, and she opened her eyes wide and realized that it was blood. The growing puddle of blood beneath her had reached all the way to her face.

And in an analytical, detached way, Rileigh understood that she'd suffered a wound that was *not* survivable. Bleeding this severely, in only a few minutes, she would bleed to death.

Chapter Forty-Six

RILEIGH TRIED to concentrate on Cookie's words, but it was hard to think of anything — the pain in her belly was staggering. She'd always heard that the most painful wound was a gut shot. Now she knew why.

Already, she was beginning to feel lightheaded from blood loss.

"... your fault!" Cookie was screaming. "I don't want to do this! I didn't want to kill Mrs. Considine! You think I wanted to kill Mrs. Considine?"

She began to pace as she ranted.

"Just them. Just those *bastards!* I've spent every waking moment for years planning this, almost a decade. Worked three jobs, and when I still couldn't earn enough money to pay for what I wanted done, I became a hooker. I let strangers paw at me, and that was fine by me. I didn't care so long as they forked over the cash. I charged special rates for special services where they could do whatever they wanted. That ... left marks, but I had the scars removed. I'd have done anything to pay those bastards back for what they did to me! *Anything!*"

She stopped pacing.

"One hundred seventy-nine pounds. That's how much weight I lost, from two hundred eighty-nine to one hundred and ten. Every day, I ate less than a thousand calories and worked out for eight hours — between my day jobs — for two years. Then, I had to pay for 'body contouring' to remove the sagging skin. That took another three years."

She struck a pose. "How do you like it?"

Then she ticked off in rapid succession, "Rhinoplasty." She pointed to her nose. "I didn't like the first one, so I had it redone. Otoplasty." She pointed to her ears. "Got rid of Dumbo, made them smaller, and had them pinned back to my head."

She made a kissing gesture. "I had my lips reshaped. Add enough collagen, and you can make any body part plump and delicious."

Then she jutted out her chest. "Mammoplasty. Breast augmentation. The surgeon tried to talk me out of the size, said they were too big, warned me that I'd 'look like Dolly Parton.'" She barked a grunt of a laugh. "I told him hell yeah, Dolly's exactly what I want to look like. I said they were my tits, and if he wouldn't give me big ones, I'd find somebody who would."

She patted her rump. "And gluteal augmentation for this round ass."

Somewhere deep inside Rileigh's failing thoughts, the words clicked. *Knew it was too perfect to be real.*

"I had my face sanded. It took three times to get all those scars off, and the recovery ..." She shuddered. "It was like healing from third-degree burns. Then, they went over it with a laser to smooth it out. I can never get a tan. My face will only sunburn, and it's permanently about three shades lighter than the rest of me."

She reached for the bandage that covered the burn on her arm and yanked it off.

"This is the first thing I got, this tattoo, to keep me focused on *them*."

Rileigh squinted to make out what was under the bandage. It wasn't a burn —"frozen pork chop, hot grease ... the worst!" — like she'd said. It was the tattoo that had encircled Cookie's arm like a bracelet.

"Three. Little. Pigs," Cookie spat, her voice deep and filled with hate.

She held her arm out and Rileigh could see where she had cut the skin in big X's over each one of the pig tattoos.

"And then there were none," she said.

The whole time Cookie spoke, she never took the pistol off her aim at Mama's chest. Mama hadn't said a word, but she spoke then.

"My baby's bleeding. You got to let me see to her."

"Don't *move!*"

Mama remained still but spoke again, pleading, "Please."

"Let her be. Let her bleed out." Cookie cocked her head to the side. "I hear it's not a bad way to die."

She cast a nasty glance at Rileigh then.

"It pissed you off when I flirted with your boyfriend." She threw her head back and laughed. "I loved every second of it. I love being beautiful."

She moved her hands over her body sensuously. "I love the way men respond to me. I love watching them squirm, trying to act like they're not looking, like they're not aroused."

She let out a grunt of contempt.

"The three little pigs responded. I seduced Jody in that back room, and then I shoved the knife into his heart. I studied how to do it, how to position the knife just right to rip through his heart. I practiced on cardboard boxes — stabbing quick and hard, then slicing sideways."

She smiled in grim satisfaction.

"I saw the surprise in his eyes. The shock. And when I said, '*Piggy, piggy, piggy. Oink, oink, oink.*' maybe he recognized me. I don't know because his eyes unfocused then, and he was dead."

She let the memory go.

"And I felt so relieved. Like I'd been walking around with a boulder on my shoulders, and suddenly, it was lifted off. One down, two to go. I got Clive McCutcheon drunk and promised him we'd screw on the fifty-yard line. And when I slit his throat, he got the same look of shock on his face Jody had." She laughed again merrily. "'Surprise!' I said. '*Piggy, piggy, piggy. Oink, oink, oink.*' And Clive got it. I know he did. He knew who I was before he died. He knew who had *killed* him."

She savored the thought for a moment before she continued.

"Travis was the hardest. Oh, he wasn't hard to seduce. But he was hard to handle. Had his hands all over me, and he was so big and strong. I had planned to take him to the field house where they stored the football equipment and kill him there. But he wouldn't let up, went totally out of control. I killed him in self-defense. He was trying to rape me when I shot him. I don't know if he recognized the words or not, but I said them. '*Piggy, piggy, piggy. Oink, oink, oink.*'"

The girl paused then, a thousand-yard stare in her eyes for a moment. When she came back to herself, she sounded wistful, sad.

"But then I had to kill Dr. Jefferson. I didn't want to do that. Why would I want to do a thing like that? It was just

— I cracked a tooth. And I called the dental practice to get somebody to come in and fix it. I never dreamed it would be Dr. Jefferson. There are six dentists in that office. What were the odds *he* would be the one on call that night— the dentist I went to as a kid? Oh, I played my part, but as soon as he got into my mouth, he saw it. I knew he would. I have an extra ridge on the inside of one of my molars. Apparently, it's an oddity you don't see often. Every dentist I've ever gone to has commented on it. When he saw it, he said he'd only seen it one other time ... and then I could see him connecting the dots in his head."

She sighed. "He didn't say anything outright, but I could tell by the way he looked at me that he knew. I sat there in the chair, trying to figure out how I could get away with killing the other two if Dr. Jefferson knew who I was. He'd have said something eventually, and somebody would have put it together, and ... I couldn't take that chance."

She sighed again. "He left me in the chair while he went to the office to get the paperwork. I looked around and found that icepick thing. When he came back, I told him that something felt funny in the back of my mouth where he'd fixed that tooth. I opened my mouth up wide, and he leaned over ... and I stabbed that thing into his eye. I felt so bad. I didn't want to kill him. But what else could I do?"

The world was beginning to gray out on Rileigh now. She could barely find any voice at all to say the single word. "Edna."

Cookie froze. "Mrs. Considine. She was the only good human being in that entire damned high school. She cared. She would talk to me after school, hold my hand, look deep into my eyes, and promise me life would get better, that after high school things would change.

"She came up to the counter that day, and I was an

idiot. If I just hadn't asked her ... but I knew if anybody would know, Mrs. Considine would, so I asked if she knew a word where the second letter was 'y' and it meant 'infant avian.' And she said immediately, 'cygnet.'"

Cookie was silent for a moment before she continued.

"Mrs. Considine cocked her head to the side and looked into my eyes then like she used to do when I was fifteen years old. And she *knew*, just as fast as she knew cygnet was a baby swan. She said, 'Sheila?' And I managed not to choke. I put my finger to my lips and said, 'Shh, it's a surprise.' But she was quick. She wanted to know 'a surprise for whom?'

"So, I concocted this story, told her I wanted to spend a month or so in town with nobody knowing who I was before I told them. I wanted to enjoy being anonymously beautiful before everybody else got the shock of discovering that the girl they ground under their heels for all those years had turned into a swan, too."

Cookie stood very still, her lip quivering, her eyes squeezed shut, her head shaking head back and forth. If Rileigh could have moved, that was her opportunity. That was the time to jump her. But Rileigh couldn't move at all. The edges of her vision were growing dark, a malevolent blackness closing in from all sides.

"She saw me," Cookie said, her voice quaking. "She recognized me. She knew. She didn't look angry or scared, just ...*hurt.*"

Tears flowed down her cheeks. She reached up and wiped them off.

"But I didn't have any choice." She turned slightly and then focused on Mama. "Just like I don't have any choice with the two of you. Damn it, Mrs. Bishop, why? How could you possibly have figured out I was that little girl in your Vacation Bible School class?"

Mama's voice was terror-clotted. "Please. You got to let me do something to stop that bleeding!"

Cookie's face hardened, then turned back into the plastic mask that she'd been wearing ever since she returned to Yarmouth County.

"I'm sorry, Mrs. Bishop, I can't let you help her. But I can send you away with her."

Cookie took two steps forward, lifted the gun up, and pointed it at Mama's face, and Rileigh wanted to scream. She mouthed the word *No!* but didn't have the air to push the word out into the world.

Then she caught a movement from the doorway, saw red roses there.

Roses?

Jillian had her pistol in a two-hand grip just like Rileigh had shown her. She didn't point the nose of it slightly down to compensate for the kick of the pistol, just squeezed the trigger.

The *bang* was louder than the first shot because Jillian's was a bigger gun. But it was so muffled that Rileigh barely heard.

Cookie flew backward from the impact, slamming into the wall and then sliding down it, leaving a bloody trail in her wake.

Then Jillian's face filled Rileigh's vision.

"You hang on," she cried, and Rileigh felt a sudden pain in her side. Not the burning pain of a hot poker, but pressure pain. She wanted to tell Jillian to stop shoving her, that it hurt. But she couldn't say anything.

Softly, through her stopped-up ears, Rileigh heard Jillian call over her shoulder to David, telling him to "Call 911." Then Jillian's face was all she could see, inches from hers, her eyes a cold, steely blue, her face hard with determination. She was shouting something at Rileigh, and

A Friend Like You

Rileigh could hear the words but didn't know what they meant as the darkness on the edges of her vision rushed forward. What she could see and hear grew smaller, like a camera lens reducing the image to a little circle of light. Then all was dark.

Chapter Forty-Seven

RILEIGH SAT on the porch swing, pushing it silently back and forth with her toe, grateful for this little bit of quiet private time just to smell the glorious perfume of the mountains and feel the fresh air on her face.

She was so unutterably tired of being hovered over.

What do you say? There was no way she could tell Mama and Jillian to bug off that she was fine. Because they had been afraid, not her. She understood that.

She had awakened once when she was in the ICU after the surgery to remove the bullet, and she had seen Jillian's face on one side of the bed and Mama's on the other. It was like they had the same face, wearing the same expression of terrified concern. She'd wanted to tell them, "Hey, I'm good. I'm here. I'm breathing."

But she'd been hooked up with tubes to machines, had them going down her nose and her throat so she could say nothing. By the time they moved her to a private room, she literally had to demand that Mama go home and leave her alone and let her sleep.

Jillian was just as bad.

No, maybe she was a little worse. Mama was more hysterical-upset and Jillian was more stoic-upset, as if so many bad things had happened to her in her life, that's all she expected from it.

You finally escape and come home, and then somebody shoots your sister.

But Rileigh had to admit that she was not the slightest bit tired of Mitch's hovering. And he had hovered, too. She would open her eyes and see his face, and she'd want to smile, but she didn't seem to have control of whatever muscles were in your face that you used to smile. But she smiled at him with her eyes. That was the best she could do before going back to sleep.

Apparently, it had been touch-and-go. She had lost an enormous amount of blood. If Jillian hadn't arrived when she did and used a dish towel as a pressure bandage to staunch the flow, Rileigh would have died. She'd been very close to bleeding out as it was. Of course, if Jillian hadn't shown up, Mama would be dead, too. They both would have been killed by the pathetic young woman who had spent her entire life miserable — bullied because she was ugly, then filled with hatred that ate her soul and left her hollow.

David had brought Jillian home from their day-long picnic, and she had walked into the house to see Cookie holding a gun on Mama. Jillian carried her own gun in her purse wherever she went. She'd said later that David had stared in slack-jawed disbelief when she opened the purse, grabbed it out, and used it. She'd killed Cookie with a single shot.

The squawking screen door cried out its protest as Mama used her butt to push it open so she could carry the tray of glasses and the pitcher of lemonade out onto the porch and set it down on the coffee table.

Mama wouldn't let Rileigh do anything. Even after she'd been released after two weeks in the hospital, Mama was literally at her side every second to do whatever it was Rileigh intended to do for herself. It had been sweet for a little while. Then it got annoying. Now, it was maddening. But there was nothing she could do but smile and go to her physical therapy appointments and work her ass off so that she could get her strength back. That was the only way she'd ever make her mother and sister leave her alone.

She didn't want Mitch to leave her alone, though. No, absolutely not. Jillian had told her that Mitch had arrived before the ambulance and found her lying on the floor with Jillian shoving a pressure bandage onto the wound in her belly. And Jillian had said she'd never seen anybody any more devastated than he was.

"That man is so in love with you it's not just written on his face. Somebody tattooed it there in bright red magic marker."

Rileigh brushed her off. Didn't want to talk about that now … now's not the time…yeah yeah yeah. But she loved hearing it. Oh, how she did love hearing it. The only thing that halfway compared to hearing about Mitch's affection for her was hearing about Jillian's growing relationship with David. Whenever Rileigh thought about that, she smiled so wide it almost hurt her mouth. Jillian and David. All those years by himself, he'd never married. Rileigh was certain that it was because he still loved Jillian. And now that she was back, he appeared to be determined not to let her out of his life again.

As if summoned by her thoughts, Jillian's car turned off Bent Twig Road and into Mama's driveway. She stopped at the mailbox to get the mail, then pulled up in front of the fence. She had been to her appointment with Dr. Al-Masri in Knoxville, and Rileigh would love to know how it had gone — but, of course, she wouldn't ask. She never asked anything. She had made that a rule from the first day Jillian walked back into her life, and that rule was sacred. She'd forced Mama to abide by it, too. When Jillian wanted to talk about what had happened to her, when she wanted to talk about her feelings or her post-traumatic stress disorder episodes or whatever, Jillian would talk about it. But they had no right to ask, no right to dig and pry just because they were curious or even for the loftier motive of "they cared."

Mama set the tray down on the coffee table and saw Jillian getting out of her car.

"Her timing's perfect," Mama said, turning to go back into the house. "Mitch is going to be putting those steaks on the grill any minute now."

Mitch had appeared out of nowhere that afternoon. "Burst full-grown from an oak tree like Tecumseh," he'd joked.

He'd brought with him out of that oak tree a pile of steaks that looked absolutely glorious, and the Bishop family quickly and joyfully abandoned their own dinner plans — spaghetti — in favor of allowing Mitch to work wonders on the grill.

Jillian smiled when she got out of the car, but Rileigh had learned to read her sister's smiles. This one was not phony, but it was forced. Jillian was still suffering the effects of the therapy session that Rileigh knew must have dredged up all kinds of things Jillian would much rather leave buried.

She came through the gate and up the steps and dropped the pile of mail on the table beside the platter with the pitcher and glasses on it.

That's when Rileigh noticed it.

"Your hair!" she cried, and the smile that lit Jillian's face then was genuine. "What did you—"

"Just highlights."

"I need to get me some of those 'just highlights,' too. It's gorgeous!"

Jillian's hair was cut in a long style that left it falling in soft blonde curls around her face. Now, those curls sparkled in the sunlight, the lighter streaks granting depth and texture, the strands of silver among the gold weaving an ever-changing cascade of light. Jillian was wearing makeup purchased on the all-day shopping spree in Nashville that had filled her car with sacks from stores like Macy's, Kohls, and Urban Outfitters that Rileigh knew... and from boutiques like Emerson Grace, Hot Zipper Vintage, Goodbye Girls, and Pauli's Palace that she'd never set foot in. The blouse Jillian wore now above her pair of stylishly tattered jeans had come from a place called The Normal Brand. It was made of some shimmering fabric that looked like dark purple indoors but became violet outside, the pattern deep and mysterious.

"Dr. Al-Masri said to tell you hello."

"How is she?"

"She seems fine. Of course, we generally don't talk about what's going on in *her* life during the sessions."

Jillian's phone dinged with an incoming text, and she smiled when she read it. "It appears that the impromptu cookout set for tonight at the home of Lily Bishop and her lovely daughters will be attended by Mr. David Hicks as well."

"Good. Mitch brought enough meat to feed every blonde man in the Norwegian army."

Jillian sat down in the rocking chair across from Rileigh.

"In today's session, we talked about those first days

right after I left, when I was just eighteen years old," Jillian said, and Rileigh froze in place. Jillian had never offered any information about what was discussed in her sessions with Dr. Al-Masri, only that the psychiatrist had said to her on the day of her first appointment, "You don't have to be okay here." The doctor had told Jillian, "You don't have to put up a front. You can be whatever you are, mad, angry, sad, all of the above, none of the above, numb, but you don't have to pretend. It's okay not to be okay."

Jillian said there were big pillows and comfortable pieces of furniture in the therapist's office where you could plop down, grab a pillow or some big stuffed animal and bury your face in it and cry, if that's what you felt like doing.

Jillian drove to Knoxville three times a week, spilled her guts, opened up her heart, and let it bleed, then drove back to Black Bear Forge. But in all that time, all those weeks, she'd never before volunteered what she and Dr. Al-Masri had talked about. Rileigh didn't quite know what to do with the beautiful gift her sister had given her — this confidence. She didn't know how to respond. So, she blurted out the first thing she thought, which was, "God, that had to be awful."

"Awful on steroids. But I got through it." She laughed a little. "Just like I got through that stupid swim meet when I was in junior high school that Mama brings up every ten minutes."

That wasn't much of an exaggeration. Rileigh had never heard the story until the day David Hicks had invited Jillian to lunch. Now, Mama told it — as if she were imparting some deep family secret — three or four times a week.

"I need a shower. David will be here in a few minutes."

Jillian hopped up out of the chair and passed by

Rileigh on the swing. Rileigh reached out and grabbed her hand.

"Ain't none of my business, sister mine, but I can't help noticing that seems like every time I turn around, I trip over David Hicks. He's underfoot a lot."

"Not any more often than Mitch Webster," Jillian fired back as she went through the squawking screen door and up the stairs.

Rileigh was alone again, pushing the silent swing back and forth slowly, putting together the speech she intended to deliver tonight. She'd decided she had to draw a line in the sand. She'd have everybody together, and she'd tell them all, "Thank you very much for your help, but I'm good now. I've decided to go to Gatlinburg on Monday to have a talk with Wally Hansford." Wally ran Gatlinburg Investigations — the Good GI's. "I'm hoping he's gotten over being pissed at me for becoming a deputy sheriff and that he'll hire me back part-time as an investigator."

She knew that statement would land like a drip of water in hot grease, but she was okay with that — she was tired of sitting around doing nothing. She felt ... *useless*. Jillian had so latched onto painting that it really did occupy an enormous amount of her time, and apparently it was making a big difference in her recovery. She'd only had two PTSD episodes, at least that anybody had told Rileigh about since Rileigh got out of the hospital. But even Jillian was now talking about looking for a part-time job in Black Bear Forge.

The other thing Rileigh was determined to get straight tonight was a definite on-the-calendar date for her and Mitch to go on the big date that they'd aborted when Jody Hatfield turned up dead in the storeroom at the Red Eye Gravy Diner.

Rileigh would have to put on some weight, a few more

pounds, to look as slinky as she had looked in her new green dress that night — the green dress that had somehow convinced Mitch that her eyes were jade green instead of hazel. But she found she had a robust appetite now and had asked Mitch several times to stop by Red Eye Gravy to get her a vanilla milkshake.

Rileigh looked at the pile of mail Jillian had deposited on the table and wondered, as she had wondered a thousand times before, how many beautiful trees had given their lives to make shiny, slick grocery store ads and fast-food coupons that went from the mailbox directly into the trash can. She leaned over and went through the pile, put a few bills on one side, and chucked what she knew was junk mail onto the other side of the table. Then she came to a small padded envelope. She stopped. Froze. It was postmarked Chicago and addressed to her: Rileigh Bishop, 639 Bent Twig Road, Black Bear Forge, Tennessee.

The address label was typed, and she couldn't help but feel a chill going down the back of her neck. She squared her shoulders immediately and shook it off. She couldn't freak out every time she got something in the mail. She'd ordered new gym socks almost a week ago — just one pair to see if she liked it. Now, she could wear them to go running in the morning. Okay, not running. Not yet. More like walking as fast as she could without breaking into a run. But she was sure the doctor would clear her to do that — and everything else other normal human beings got to do — when she saw him for her last appointment next week.

She picked the envelope off the table, tore open the seal, and dumped out the contents onto the table, expecting to see a pair of white gym socks. But what she saw was ... *something* long and slender, smaller than a hot dog, wrapped in a piece of newspaper. A card fell face down on the table out of the envelope. She couldn't move, just sat and stared.

Suddenly, the screen door beside her squawked, and Mitch came out onto the porch, wearing the ridiculous grilling apron Mama had gotten for him with the words "May the Forks Be With You" emblazoned on the front.

"I've finished with the marinade, and I'm getting ready to put the steaks—" He stopped when he saw the look on her face. His eyes shot to what was lying on the top of the pile of mail on the coffee table, and he literally groaned.

Stepping around the table, he sat down beside her on the swing, reached out and picked up the thing that was wrapped in a newspaper. Slowly, he unwrapped it. The previous anonymous box addressed to Rileigh had contained the three bones of a human index finger.

This was not that.

This was the two bones of a human thumb.

The bones clacked out of the piece of newsprint onto the top of the table. Mitch picked up the newspaper and looked at it. He read something there, then looked at Rileigh, who sat absolutely frozen, her eyes fixed on the bones on the table.

"You need to read this." He handed her the newspaper.

Her eyes immediately fell on a brief story that had been circled with a red magic marker. It was about a man who had been murdered. His body had been dumped into Lake Michigan, and when they fished it out, he was missing the thumb on his right hand.

Rileigh didn't will her fingers to open and let the newspaper fall down into her lap. Her fingers just let go. Slowly, almost dreamily, she picked up the card that had fallen out of the envelope with the bones. The previous box had contained a folded piece of paper with a frowny face on one side and the number 5 on the other side.

This was a card that had a picture of a cemetery on the front. Rileigh's name had been written in red ink on the picture, as if it were the name on one of the headstones.

On the back of the card was a frowny face with a number written beside it. Not a number 6 like the card she'd gotten right after Jillian came home. Or a number 5 like the paper inside the box with the finger bone.

Written beside the frowny face on the card she held now in trembling fingers was the number 4.

The End

About The Author

Lauren Street has always loved a mystery. As a kid growing up in bible belt country she devoured every whodunit book she could get her sticky little hands on and secretly investigated all of her (seemingly) normal boring neighbors. Sometimes their pets and farm animals too. All grown up now and living in the UK with her thoroughly unsuspicious (and often unsuspecting) husband, she writes domestic psychological thrillers about families torn apart by secrets and lies. And she sometimes still peers over garden walls to check up on the neighbors.

Also By Lauren Street

The Bishop Smoky Mountain Thrillers

Hide Me Away

Fuel To The Flame

Closer By The Hour

A Gamble Either Way

Calling My Children Home

Too Far Gone

Here You Come Again

A Friend Like You

Replaced with Nolon King

Replaced

In Her Place

Irreplaceable

The Salazar Redwood Forest Thrillers

The Girl Who Couldn't Stop Dying

The Girl Who Couldn't Get Out

The Girl Who Couldn't Be Found

Milton Keynes UK
Ingram Content Group UK Ltd.
UKHW021827260824
447290UK00008B/41

9 781629 553962